The Panopticon Experiment

RACHEL CALDECOTT

Originally published as The Coalition

Current edition The Panopticon Experiment

ISBN: 978-2-9569856-1-7

DEDICATION

Dedicated to my family both living and dead.
Especially:
Chris, Florence and Stanley Thornton
Oliver, Moyra and Stratford Caldecott

ACKNOWLEDGMENTS

With special thanks to Nancy Webber, my best friend and copyeditor; Also to Leonie Caldecott, Sarah Khairedinne, Catherine Briggs, Barbara Murphy Marder, Peter Cox and the Litopians (no, that isn't the name of a band) for their critical input and encouragement, Yan Clauzure, for cheering me on when I got down in the dumps and to Diane Baker, who always had faith in me.

CONTENTS

CHAPTER 1

New Era-London, February

After hearing rumours of 'upcoming civil unrest', Flo went on to the balcony to search the streets below for Lonce. He should have been back from hunting by now. Instead, only a trolley-car lumbered past. It halted for a few minutes to let some passengers off at the corner. On the other side of the street, a tired-looking delivery dog plodded by, large panniers strapped to his back, probably at the end of his shift and keen to get home. Sounds of giggling children drifted upwards. Flo smiled. She recognised most of them from her building, and knew their mothers would be keen to get them in for dinner, bath and bed. The children had other ideas and gathered round the hot chestnut man, shamelessly begging for free nuts.

From the corner of her eye, she glimpsed a quick movement at one of the windows opposite. She looked across, but whatever it was had gone. It was probably someone else looking out for a loved one, or perhaps a trick of the light, or most likely her worry-fuelled imagination running riot. Human supremacist rallies had broken out across Pan-Europe, and Flo supposed it was only a matter of time before the same thing happened here. Odd, though; that particular apartment was normally empty. Anyway, where on earth was Lonce? Just then she caught sight of him, with his distinctive four-legged lope, running towards the building. She lifted her arm to wave.

At that moment an enormous explosion rocked the balcony and she was thrown backwards. Simultaneously, a huge orange and black fireball surged up from street level. The heavy boom of the blast reverberated between the buildings. For a moment it seemed as if the very air boiled in anger, and the world spun out of control. She was vaguely aware of windows shattering, before she landed hard and lay stunned and winded, gasping for breath. A split second later, from the streets below, the screaming started. White dust rained down on her face, mingling with the black smoke, drying her throat and making her cough.

Her breath came stuttering back and she rolled over painfully. Scrambling to her knees, she crawled back to the balustrade, hauled herself gingerly up and peered over. A worrying network of cracks had appeared in the stonework, but she had to risk it. The hot chestnut man lay on the ground, both legs bleeding. His upended brazier had been thrown across the street and now spilled its burning coals on to the pavement opposite. Nearby, a woman sat on the kerb, her arms clutched round her stomach. Was that blood?

The trolley-car had been blown over and the horse lay screaming, still harnessed to its load, while the passengers crawled shocked and bleeding from the wreckage. Flo reeled, feeling the horse's pain and fear directly in her head. Then she glimpsed a young girl staggering through the debris calling for her mother. A fleeting, sharp stab of memory, triggered by the child's cries, stole Flo's breath again.

But where was Lonce? Still hoarse, she leaned out as far as she dared and tried shouting his name. For one brief, horrible moment she thought she saw him, an immobile pile of grey fur, but it was the delivery dog. She spared a quick thought for him and his family. But her friend Lonce, the beautiful snow leopard who shared her life, was still out there somewhere, maybe hurt too. Suddenly, she felt his urgent plea for help. It was needle sharp and made her wince as it arrived in her mind. *Help me. Come!* She was already scrambling across the terrace and into the apartment, her boots protecting her feet from the glass and other blast debris strewn across the floor. *I'm coming, Lonce. I'm coming.*

Another explosion shook the building, and she stumbled slightly. With Lonce's thoughts clear in her head, she threw herself down the stairs, jumping two or three at a time. She skidded round corners, careless of her own safety, and flung open the door to the lobby, assuring him she was on her way. But he no longer responded. She could see him on the other side of the atrium, a matted pile of bloodied fur. He had half fallen through the entrance to the building, and now his body wedged the twisted doors open, his blood pooling beneath them.

Flo raced across the lobby and hurled herself towards him. Frantic, she prayed he didn't have any broken bones before grabbing his forelegs and pulling. The bloody gash on his back leg looked bad, the blood oozing out in a steady flow, but what choice did she have? What if there was another explosion? His head lolled and his huge tongue hung out to one side. His sleek fur caused no friction on the marble floor and she moved him easily. *Don't die, Lonce. I can't lose you too. I need you.* Her eyes pricked with tears. As she tugged him, she felt her panic rising.

She looked out through the shattered windows to the chaotic scene outside.

"Help!" she shouted. As the smoke and dust settled she could make out grey figures picking their way through the rubble, shocked and bloodied. No, they had their own troubles. She was on her own. A trickle of dust dropped from the ceiling above, and a solitary shard of glass fell from the twisted window frame. She hoped the building was safe. She wasn't leaving.

Flo struggled to control her panic. She focused on sending out a telepathic distress call instead. Human neighbours, who had been sheltering shocked, confused and frightened in their apartments, streamed out of the stairway in response and were immediately joined by several of the resident felines. Some of the humans hoisted the unconscious snow leopard into their arms and headed for the stairs. Others rushed on into the chaos outside. The cats, mewling loudly, followed the group carrying Lonce.

The neighbours handled the big cat gently, but struggled with his weight up the stairwell, stopping frequently as he all but slipped from their grasp. The smaller felines wove between them, their eyes wide, tails swishing back and forth as they tried to make sense of the situation. They rubbed their arched bodies against the legs of the human bearers until one man tripped, nearly bringing everyone down, so that Flo had no choice but to ask the cats to leave.

As one, they turned and silently flowed back downstairs.

On her floor, the fourth, Flo pushed open the stairwell door and ran ahead down the corridor to clear the way. The helpers laid the big cat carefully on the living room floor, and someone thrust a medical kit into her hands.

“Thank you. I can manage now.” She said, chivvying them all out, and broke open the seal.

She took some deep breaths and forced herself to concentrate on what she had to do. She wished she’d paid more attention in first aid classes. Wasn’t there something to be done with honey? She found a suture needle but had some difficulty threading it, and his skin was tough and difficult to sew. She did her best, but the results weren’t pretty. Finally, at the bottom of the box she found a small phial of honey, and smeared the antiseptic liberally over the wound, hoping for the best. There was nothing more she could do now except wait. With the immediate crisis over, her body gave in to exhaustion as the adrenalin dissipated. Shivering, she went in search of blanket and pillow, dragged an armchair across the room, and settled down next to him for what remained of the night.

CHAPTER 2

The next morning, George Walton, Flo's legal guardian, and his friend Jack Dyer made their way steadily through the debris towards Flo's building. A lot of clearing work had been done overnight, and now the two men had no difficulty tracing a route between the piles of masonry, glass, splintered wood and metal, while a chain of volunteers tackled the gently steaming wreckage of the communal compost bins. Whatever could be salvaged would be passed on to the Reclamation and Allotment guilds.

The two friends passed half a dozen multi-species teams working together to clear the site, and moved carefully between the Guardia officials who were busy sifting through the rubble, looking for clues to what might have caused the explosion. A junior guard trudged past, head down, talking into his personal recording device.

"Three small bombs placed at different points in the vicinity," he said into the Perd. "The first hit the local reunion hall. The second, damaged the sub-post office, and the third took out the district recycling point and compost bins."

"Any casualties?" George asked as the officer paused in his recording.

"Enough," the guardia said, then spat forcefully. George wasn't sure if he was spitting away dust or the thought of what had happened. "At least two dead, as far as I know. A delivery dog, and the local hot chestnut seller at the corner over there. Maybe a lady from the building across the street," he added. "She didn't look too good, and a snow leopard from here." He indicated Flo's building. "They've taken the leopard inside, though I heard he looked pretty bad. Shame if he goes. Last of his kind, you know."

"Lonce!" George said. "Any news of a girl called Flo? She and the snow leopard are usually together."

"Sorry, I don't know who that is. I can't help you." He turned and walked off slowly down the street, head bent, eyes scanning the ground for more evidence.

George and Jack started running towards the entrance to Flo's building. If Lonce was injured, Flo would be in a terrible state.

Being younger and fitter, Jack arrived first at Flo's door. She opened before he'd finished knocking and leapt into his arms. Then, as a slightly wheezing George stumbled forward, she pulled away from Jack and flung her arms tightly round her guardian's neck. She let out a huge, heartfelt sigh and squeezed harder. He couldn't help feeling thankful that she clearly still needed him. He'd been fulfilling the role of mother, father, adviser and friend for the last ten years, and it wasn't a position he was eager to relinquish.

Together, the two men checked on Lonce while Flo changed the honey poultice. Once finished, they left him to sleep, retreating into the kitchen so as not to disturb him with their conversation, which was wide-ranging and often animated.

Jack, the journalist, focused on facts and evidence.

"We are assuming, for now, that the Human Supremacy League was behind the attack. It seems they are extending themselves beyond the odd demonstration. I'm going to follow up some leads I have. Apart from the three explosions last night, I've heard they are planning other offensives across New Britain. Pan-European authorities are on high alert and the American islands are also anticipating problems. My next article will be looking at the rise of the HSL and their worldwide human-only agenda."

George, the archivist, looked at historical perspectives.

"It has always been so. Since the collapse of planetary systems during the Siklus of the twenty-first century, those people who didn't inherit the communication gene have had some sort of existential crisis. They don't understand their place in the modern world. They don't feel the Coalition government represents them. They are clearly frustrated and venting their rage."

Flo, the teenager, the orphan, the emotive, rolled her eyes at both of them. In her mind, the question of why was far less important than 'How do we stop them?'

Once George and Jack left, she went back to check on Lonce in the living room.

"Don't worry, Lonce," she whispered. "I'll be right by your side until you get better. Just make sure you do." She bent forward and kissed him lightly on the head. *School be damned.*

CHAPTER 3

A few days later, Flo woke from a bad dream to be greeted by the sight of Lonce gazing at her expectantly.

Take these bandages off now. Please. He was finally lucid and his demands arrived clearly in her mind, their telepathic link re-established now his fever had broken. Their way of communicating - part visualisation, part vocalisation - had developed over the past ten years. He now understood her words almost as well as her human friends.

"It looks like you've been trying to do that already. Look at the state of them! How long have you been awake?"

Not long. Hurry. Get them off. He was clearly desperate to clean himself and assess the damage. Flo cut away the stained and slightly chewed dressings, and he immediately set to with his rough tongue.

"Don't pull the stitches out," she warned. "Be careful!" He grunted and carried on fiercely licking every inch he could reach. "So, what happened, Lonce?" she asked after a moment, then waited transfixed as his memories tumbled directly into her mind.

I was hungry. I need big food. First I catch rabbit, but it is not enough. I need more. I find boar. I pounce. I bite neck; a swift - a good - end to life. I eat. After eating, I sleep.

I hear voices. Humans. One leading. Five following. Not far from me. They speak with their hands. I extend my mind in greeting but meet nothing. They are Non-Comms.

They walk in shadows and crouch low. Like me when I hunt. I know humans are not hunters. You choose not to hunt. But these hunter-humans bring trouble with their fire sticks. They do not hunt food.

Lonce turned over awkwardly. Flo noticed that his lighter-coloured belly fur was still matted with blood.

"You missed a bit." She pointed to a ragged clump. Still stiff from his wounds, he couldn't quite reach it. "OK, forget it. Let me do it." She fetched a bowl of warm water and a cloth from the bathroom. "Just keep still while I do this, will you? Watch out! Don't wriggle or you'll spill it."

As she gently washed the blood away, the water in the bowl turned a dull reddish brown.

Confusion, he continued. *Memory coming, memory going. I watched. The older man was angry, he beat a young one, hard, pushing him to ground, kicking him. I never see that before. Then human hunters left forest... I come home. When I near home, blast knocks me to ground. Pain sharp in my leg. Can't move.*

"You'll be all right. It could have been worse."

It hurts, he said morosely, and made a low rumbling growl.

"Well it will, won't it? But you'll be fine." She hugged him. "Lonce, I was so frightened. I thought I was going to lose you." She remembered her part in that dreadful night's dramas as a series of images he could easily interpret, but the memory brought tears to her eyes. Lonce felt her distress and licked her hand.

I am not lost. We will stay together. We are family.

"They were Human Supremacy League, those men in the forest. Both George and Jack think the HSL was behind the attack. Why can't they shut those bastards down? How hard can it be? They must know who the leaders are. They're getting funding from somewhere. They just need to trace the money. How many citizens have to get hurt, or die? Why did my parents have to die?"

She looked down at him, but somehow despite her tirade he'd managed to fall asleep again.

"I need to know, Lonce," she whispered, snuggling back down under the blanket on the armchair. "I'm going to find out why they died and exactly who killed them."

CHAPTER 4

Flo dozed at Lonce's side until a noise woke her. She opened her eyes slowly. The sun was much higher in the sky; morning had already nearly gone. She looked up to see Jack's son, Seb, coming through the door.

She smiled. He made a comical sight, holding his breath and moving as slowly as he could. He wasn't the creeping sort. He was tall, strong, athletic and agile, not a creeper; the sort who made a noise even when he was being quiet.

Flo couldn't remember a time when she didn't know him and his parents, Jack and Laura. When the children were young, the two families spent much of their free time together. Years ago, they'd planned a sailing holiday on Jack's yacht. The plan was to head across Chelsea Sound south to Thornton Heath, round the tiny island of Merton and then back up to the marina at King's Cross. It was quickly aborted when they discovered that six-year-old Flo, normally so brave, absolutely hated being on the water.

She remembered overhearing Seb ask, "Mum, when is Flo going to stop puking?" He'd called her Pukey Flow for years after that.

"You've still got my key, then?"

Seb had been concentrating so hard he hadn't noticed Flo was already awake. He jumped slightly. "I was trying to be quiet," he whispered. "I just came over to see how you were doing. Sorry I couldn't get over before. Dad told me he'd seen you, before he and Mum swanned off again, so I knew you were alive, but that was three days ago and no one's set eyes on you since."

He crouched down next to the sofa and engulfed her in a strong embrace. She let herself give in to it; it was so reassuring to have him close to her. She was in danger of crying and wanted nothing more than to stay wrapped in his arms. She couldn't, though, could she? So she had to do something to prevent the tears which threatened to flow.

"Agh." She pulled back to stroke his face. "Did you lose your razor?"

"Sorry." He rubbed his chin, appearing surprised by the sandpaper stubble. Then he shifted slightly to give Lonce's head a gentle pat before standing up and walking over to the window.

Flo described to Seb what Lonce had seen. She'd already heard what George and Jack had to say; now she wanted to hear Seb's view. He listened quietly.

"You should tell your dad all this," she finished. "When Lonce is better, Jack should interview him. I reckon the men in the woods were HSL. They were certainly Non-Comms and acting suspiciously… probably on their way to plant the bombs. What do you think?"

"There's no way of knowing," he answered. "Just because they're Non-Comms" - he stressed the term and made bunny ears with his fingers - "doesn't mean they're HSL, does it? There are Non-Comms everywhere, but they don't go about causing trouble, and just because they were making hand signals Lonce didn't recognise doesn't really incriminate them. Think about it. It's a bit of a coincidence if he did spot the terrorists. You know, just happened to be at the right place at the right time." Then, to lighten the mood, he added, "They were probably a local club of ramblers on a day out."

"But the beating?"

"Angry ramblers."

"But the hand signals?"

"Deaf and dumb non-comm ramblers." That had the desired effect and she giggled. "So I'll pick you up for school tomorrow, shall I?" He came over and ruffled her hair.

"Talking of school, what have I missed?"

"Not a lot. Miss Pugh went on again about the Siklus being the grand finale." Seb struggled to remember her exact words, switching into a perfect imitation of the teacher's slightly pompous nasal tones. "The inevitable consequence of the Industrial Revolution, I think she said." He paused again. "It was just revision, really. Nothing new. You didn't miss much."

"Sure?"

"She might have mentioned nuclear testing causing tectonic shifts. Maybe something about fracking too."

"Nothing else?" she asked, sarcasm dripping from her voice.

"No," said Seb cheerfully, "I think that's all." He suddenly looked solemn. "Seriously, Flo, get some rest. You look awful. I'll see you tomorrow."

CHAPTER 5

"How can people carry on as if nothing had happened?" Flo asked angrily as she stomped along beside Seb the next day. She was surprised by how quickly life in the area had returned to normal.

"Well, that's not really true, is it?" Seb countered. "Just look around. People are still in shock."

Flo made no attempt to hide her bitterness. The events of the last few days had deeply unsettled her.

"Just because they didn't inherit the gene, the Non-Comms think they're hard done by and turn into a bunch of murdering bastards. What gets me is that no one does anything about them! Not George. Not your dad!" Seb looked shifty. "Look, Seb, don't worry. I don't know what anyone can do, really. And I do know it isn't every Non-Comm who's behind these attacks, only the Human Supremacy bunch. I don't blame all of them. But some definitely sympathise with the HSL a little more than they should. I reckon they must know something, know people involved with the supremacists. You know, like an uncle, or a cousin or someone." She stopped in her tracks and her voice hardened. "The supremacy nutters are out to destroy us, and they should be stopped. Why am I the only one who can see that? It's almost as if someone in the government is on their side."

Seb kept quiet, waiting for her to finish letting off steam. Besides, there was nothing he could really say. He agreed with her.

As the pair entered the school grounds and met their friends, Flo was the centre of attention. Everyone had heard of the bombing in her quarter of the city and, more important, about Lonce's injury.

"He'll be fine," she told each questioner. "It's just a flesh wound. I mean, it bled a heck of a lot, but he'll be all right."

History was the first lesson of the day. It was considered by the authorities to be the single most important subject in the school curriculum. Above the doorway to each history classroom in every school was inscribed the motto Understand the Past to Protect the Future.

Flo was still being passed notes of sympathy when Miss Pugh, the history teacher, burst into the room. As she passed Flo, their eyes met. Miss Pugh's gaze was intense and Flo was suddenly uneasy. Was there something behind that look? Miss Pugh passed on. Suddenly the screen at the front of the classroom was illuminated by horrific scenes of the past, and without any preamble Pugh launched straight into the lesson.

"Let's face it," she began, "our predecessors were, for the most part, a bunch of murderers. There was never a time when people weren't killing each other. Mankind enjoyed killing and loved war. That's why they got so good at it." She glared over her glasses at the class, as if somehow it was their fault, or they'd started to show violent tendencies themselves. Flo and Seb exchanged contented glances.

The hour-long lesson moved along swiftly. The class was riveted, gripped as much by the force of Pugh's personality as by the topics covered.

"Our ancestors were stupid and short-sighted," she said to finish. "They could have had it all, but they failed to understand - or wilfully chose to ignore - the natural order to the world; the order by which everything is connected." She looked around the class. "We tend to think of the Siklus as simply a violent cycle of man-made and natural disasters. But really it was the planet defending itself from Homo sapiens." She shrugged. "And who can blame it? We were the only species to sully our own nest."

In the corridor, the bell rang for the end of the first hour. Miss Pugh stopped speaking so suddenly, it was like a physical blow.

"Now," she said after a moment. Her mouth formed an approximate smile while her eyes remained lit with an angry fire. "For your assignments, I'd like you to pair up and choose one aspect of the Siklus, or of pre-Siklus society, for a report. Decide amongst yourselves who is doing what. I expect at least one pair to tackle the issue of the polluted oceans. And I wouldn't mind seeing a paper on the resurgence of fascism in the twenty-first century. Remember we covered that a couple of days ago."

Flo looked quizzically at Seb. He shrugged.

"Maybe I forgot to mention that," he whispered, apologising.

Pugh continued. "Whatever you decide to do, communicate with each other, and for goodness' sake don't all do global warming. I want your reports to be as specific and as detailed as possible and I want them on my desk by the end of the month." The class stood up and began shuffling out of the room; there was the usual cacophony of chatter, laughter and scraping of chairs.

"Floods," said Seb, turning to Flo excitedly. "We are so doing floods."

Flo was just nodding her agreement when she heard Miss Pugh call her back.

"Flo, dear, wait a moment. I want to talk to you." Flo hung back, curious, while the teacher's eyes followed the stragglers as they left the classroom. Only after the last one had gone did she speak again.

"My dear, you have been through such a lot in your young life," she said. "I was so sorry to hear about Lonce, but thank goodness it wasn't you caught in the blast. That would have been truly dreadful."

Flo frowned, instantly irritated.

"Well, I suppose for me personally it would have been," she retorted, "but it's the same thing… I mean, whether it was me or Lonce, our lives are worth the same, aren't they?"

"Oh, my dear, I haven't expressed myself very well, have I?"

"Miss Pugh, I'm sorry, but I've got another class now. I have to go." As she politely moved to shake her teacher's hand, Miss Pugh pulled her closer.

"If you can't stay now, another time, perhaps?"

"Er, yes, um, all right." She pulled her hand back, turned, and bolted out of the door. Seb was waiting for her.

"Don't ask. Creepy."

CHAPTER 6

By the time Flo returned home from school, she found Lonce ready to go out. He was ravenous. *Hungry. I need food. Rabbit, bird, rabbit. Now.* His need to eat outweighed any residual pain. Whatever energy he had gained from the boar he'd eaten days before had long been used up.

Flo quickly checked his wounds and put on another dressing.

"It might pull a bit, so be careful not to open it up again. But I'm glad you feel like hunting. I wasn't looking forward to doing it for you." Lonce chuffed, a peculiar noise which was the closest he could come to a laugh. He gently placed the image of the rising sun in her mind. "All right, Lonce, I'll see you in the morning."

Once he had gone, she ventured down the corridor and peeked into her parents' old room. Since she had finally moved back into the family apartment after years of being 'looked after' by George, it was the one room she'd never been ready to face. The room itself still carried the memory, and even the scent, of them. At its centre sat a huge pile of cartons; it had been sitting there untouched for years, like some sort of treasure-guarding mythical beast. Her heart sank. Sorting through them would be a colossal task and she really didn't feel up to it yet. She took another look at the pile and sighed. A few more days wouldn't make any difference.

That night her dreams once again turned bad. But there was a different quality to them from usual. She tended to categorise her dreams when she could remember them. There were the obvious ones based on memories and emotions or things which had been worrying her, or she'd seen during the day. There were others designed to teach her a lesson, and finally a few scary ones which seemed to come from some dark place she'd rather not think about. But that night her dream felt like a strange sort of telepathy. It resembled the sensation of mind-sharing.

Virtually falling out of bed the following morning, she launched herself across the room to the bathroom where she coughed and retched into the sink. She looked up slowly, half expecting to see someone else in the mirror, and was relieved to find herself peering back. She smiled grimly. I've got to get better sleep. This is not a good look. "Seb's probably never had a nightmare in his life," she said aloud to her reflection. She emerged from the bathroom and padded barefoot into the kitchen, absentmindedly scratching her behind through her pyjamas as she went.

With the day's first mug of caffeinix clasped firmly in her hand, she went to retrieve the Saturday Gazette from the doormat outside the apartment. The front page was still full of articles relating to the attack. But no matter how personal it might have felt to her, it was simply the latest of many attacks around the New Britain archipelago.

As she quickly flicked through the rest of the paper, her attention was caught by a number of smaller articles concerned with abductions or disappearances. Although she'd noticed these articles before today, they seemed to have a special significance in the light of last night's dream. She read through the articles several times, transfixed and unsettled.

There was nothing for it. She needed to talk. To talk, she needed to go out. There was no point looking in the wardrobe for clothes; everything she owned was strewn across the bedroom floor. It was simply a case of stepping between the piles and picking up whatever she felt like wearing. She found a pair of soft grey hemp-fibre trousers and matching top, before throwing on a slightly crumpled coat, grabbing the scarf which poked out from under her bed, and heading out to George's.

CHAPTER 7

Flo arrived at George's apartment still vaguely uneasy about her dream, but George got straight down to business.

"I need your receipts," he said.

Flo held her hands up in mock surrender. "Strangely, I haven't got them with me. But I did bring milk and cookies."

He looked stern. "I've only got a few months left as your official guardian. As soon as you hit eighteen in, what is it, about six months' time, you'll be responsible for your own household expenses." She sighed and rolled her eyes. He continued. "Bills for the apartment are taken care of automatically from the Finance Guild account I set up for you, but the rest you will have to keep track of. Really, Flo, you must learn to be more responsible."

She managed to look contrite, while secretly wishing he'd just stop preaching. He'd been taking care of her financial affairs since she was seven. As far as she was concerned he could carry on doing it. She let out a huge sigh.

George smiled. "Well, I suppose we can do this another time. Let's put the kettle on."

A few hours later, George suddenly dropped the newspaper on to the table in front of her. "Here," he said. "Have you seen the paper today?"

"I saw, that when the Non-Comms aren't actually blowing things up, they're still holding rallies."

"I didn't mean that. This is far more interesting." He opened the paper to one of the inside pages and pointed to a small article about the continued research into avian/human communication. "Something for you, Flo; right up your street, so to speak. You've always wanted to communicate with birds."

"I've already seen it. It doesn't contain anything new, although the first half contains some interesting technical details." She smiled. "But I will mind-link with a bird one day, just you wait." She flicked through the paper. "But that reminds me. I wanted to show you these. I think they're significant, and I think they have something to do with me." She was pointing to the articles about mammalian disappearances, and was surprised by his reaction. He paled visibly and shook his head.

"Why on earth do you think they have anything to do with you?" He shifted in his chair. "There have always been stories like this. These aren't new. They're sad, of course, but they aren't particularly significant."

"I don't mean I'm involved," said Flo, looking at him closely now. "It's just that I had a weird dream last night. I was inside someone else's head, looking through her eyes." Struggling to explain the experience adequately, she added, "Dream is the wrong word. I experienced being someone else. I was inside them, while at the same time I was at home, asleep in bed."

"Well, thankfully that isn't possible. It's probably nothing but a coincidence," he said shortly. "Dreams are funny old things. Reading articles like these probably triggered it. I doubt if there's anything sinister going on."

Flo was irritated by his dismissal of the idea, and stood up to leave frustrated and sulky. George let her go without argument. As she clattered down his stairs she wondered whether anyone she knew was good at dream interpretation. Coming out of his building she all but bumped into a figure huddled in a corner of the entrance, bundled up tightly against the cold. Whoever it was appeared so startled by her sudden appearance that Flo quickly apologised. The figure, made rotund by layers of woollen clothing, scuttled away without acknowledging her.

CHAPTER 8

At home, Flo found George's talk about her future had put her in the mood for finally tackling her parents' cartons. She stared at the pile for a moment before grabbing the top box and cutting through the twisted twine which kept it closed.

It contained a series of files and loose papers. There were a few scuffed and faded photo-images of the three of them together, and these she pulled out and tucked safely away. Next she pulled out an old-fashioned Perd with a shattered screen. Without thinking, she threw it back in with the other junk, mainly old bills and shopping lists, before dragging the whole carton out to the communal rubbish shoot. She heaved the box up to the lip of the shoot and shoved it in.

It felt good. She dusted off her hands. The Recyclers' Guild would pick it up when they next made their rounds. One down, eleven more to go.

Several boxes later she made an interesting discovery.

"I don't believe it!" She pulled out a notebook filled with her mother's sloping script. It looked like some sort of diary. Flo moved quickly into better light and skimmed through the first few pages. Words and phrases leapt from the paper.

I had the distinct impression I was being carried away....

Fear. Panic. Hopelessness.

I felt I was inside another's head.

Smothered. Unable to breathe.

They looked like research notes rather than a proper diary. She read on. There were detailed descriptions of her mother's dreams. Some were fully narrated, others written in a type of shorthand. The memory of her own experience the previous night made her shiver. The similarities were obvious. Her mother had been having the same sorts of nightmares.

Putting the diary into a pocket, she dragged all the remaining boxes into the living room. Then, box by box, she pulled out all the papers and placed them around her on the floor. She took her time; she didn't want to miss anything. This was her parents' legacy. It was emotional work. Ten years after their death, the pain and guilt were still there, buried just below the surface. She pulled herself together. Negative emotions wouldn't help her now.

The first pile she constructed was made up of her mother's scientific papers referring to genetic research and Professor Guido Lush, the scientist who had first identified the famous communication gene. Lush had concluded that this one mutated gene enabled humans to communicate telepathically with virtually every other mammal species on the planet, apparently by enhancing a part of the human brain. He'd named it HuMaRrItelcom3 and theorised that the mutation had been triggered by environmental pollutants arising from the Siklus.

She read for hours until her eyes were too tired to see properly. Finally, she dragged herself into the bedroom and flung herself, fully clothed, into bed. Within minutes she was caught, a prisoner of yet another disturbing nightmare.

In the dream, she knew her name was Finch. She was grabbed after a long hard night at work on the wards. The first she knew of the attack was a gentle tap on her shoulder. As she turned round, a soft white cloth was shoved roughly into her face, covering her nose and mouth. She recognised the overpowering smell. Chloroform!

Damn. Her legs collapsed and she started falling.

She found herself gagged and bound inside what felt like a small wooden container. The crate was moving and she was bounced, banged and rolled against the rough sides. Instinct told her to kick, so kick she did, but her tightly bound feet hardly made a sound. She was surprised to see paws rather than her own feet. As she watched she saw that her claws barely scratched the surface of the crate, and she felt a terrible sense of helplessness.

Flo woke herself up with a yell. Her pillow was wet. She had been crying in her sleep. She had tangled herself in her blankets and had to kick hard to push them off. She sat up panting, sweating and furious. Mad at George. How dared he dismiss her theories about dreams like that? He was her guardian, her friend. He was supposed to care about her.

She leaned over and grabbed the static phone from the side table and punched in George's number.

"I've been going through Mum's boxes," she said as he picked up the call. "She was documenting the same thing I was talking about. You must have known what she was up to. She made a connection.

But there's something I'm not seeing… the bigger picture. Do you know? There's tons of stuff about animal rights and genetics. What had they got to do with her? What's it all got to do with me and my dreams?"

Silence.

"George. George, answer me. Help me find out what's going on… please. What on Gaia's good earth is happening to me?"

CHAPTER 9

After slamming the phone down from George, Flo flung open her parents' bedroom again and spent an hour thoroughly searching it. She was sure there must be more. There had to be some way to make sense of the notes which were still spread across the living room floor; some key to it all. She opened every drawer and looked in all the obvious places. There were no more notes anywhere. No more papers of any kind which could be of interest.

And then it dawned on her. "You idiot!" She picked up the phone and called Seb. "When can you get here? I need you to come straight away. Meet me downstairs at the entrance to my basement… and bring a torch just in case." She hung up before he could argue. She knew she could trust him not to let her down.

She headed to the basement to wait for Seb there, ready to intercept the Recyclers. They were due any minute, and if she was right she didn't have much time.

Luckily she didn't have long to wait for Seb. He arrived running, an expression of concern plastered across his face.

"What's up? You all right? What on earth are you up to now, Flo?"

"I'm fine, but I need your help to find something I threw away yesterday." He stood there unmoving, an expression of disbelief, or outrage, on his face. "Please?" she added. "Remember how we used to sneak down here to play explorers when we were little. I thought you might enjoy it."

"Right. Now I know you've lost it. I've better things to do than rummage through your garbage!" He turned to go.

"Look, it's important." She grabbed his arm. "I'll explain everything later. I just need to find Mum's old Perd. I think it holds the key to everything that's been going on."

"I have no idea what you're talking about."

"You know. The bombing the other day, the increased HSL activity, the abductions."

"What abductions?" he asked, horrified.

"Don't you ever read the papers? Mammal-citizens have been disappearing from the city, and I've been dreaming about them. Oh, Seb, stop looking at me like that! Let's get on with it. I'll explain more later, I promise."

Every apartment had access to a communal chute system which took certain types of rubbish efficiently into the basement. Her pile was located somewhere on the far side. They wove their way through the discarded detritus of her neighbours, silently thanking the Guild of City Planners for collecting organic waste in communal compost bins outside. Nevertheless, the shadow-filled expanse smelt vaguely of rodent urine and other less easily identifiable substances.

"Tell me again why we're here," said Seb, pushing past her. "I'm struggling to see the point. So let's just get it over with."

"Look, Seb. I'm sure my stuff is just over there." Flo pointed. As she took her eyes off the floor she missed her step and slipped on something oozing from a box. He turned back in time to see her falling backwards, legs shooting out in front of her, and landing heavily on a nearby pile. He bent down to help her up. "I can manage." She slapped his hand away. "Just go and find Mum's Perd. I'm fine." With a shrug, he carried on. Although only a few feet separated them, she lost sight of him occasionally as he disappeared behind a particularly big heap of rubbish.

"Can you see it?" she called. He didn't immediately answer, but she could hear him scuffling about and occasionally swearing. Impatient for results, she called out to him again. "Well, have you found it?" She let out a whoop of joy as Seb retrieved the Perd from a carton and held it victoriously over his head.

"You owe me," he repeated a minute later, after placing it in her hand. "Big time!"

Back in the apartment, Flo watched with impatience as Seb fiddled with the Perd. After several minutes, and a change of saltwater batteries, he'd got it to turn on, but the display screen was still shattered and useless. He handed the recorder to Flo who held her breath as she tried switching it to vocal playback.

Her mother's voice suddenly filled the room. "The earliest references to animal experimentation date from ancient Greece." Flo jumped and dropped the Perd. Seb hastily picked it up and gently laid it on the table between them. He reached over and squeezed Flo's hand. Claire's disembodied voice continued. "Both the philosopher Aristotle and the anatomist-physician Erasistratus performed experiments on living animals. Later, a doctor called Galen in second-century Rome became known as the 'father of vivisection'. In seventeenth-century Britain, a physician called William Harvey studied the circulation and properties of blood by also experimenting on animals."

Flo's stomach turned as she listened to gross descriptions of animal testing. Even Seb was looking nauseous and miserable.

According to Claire, by the late nineteenth century animal testing and experimentation were the norm. By the twenty-first, so was genetic modification.

"At first these experiments served a genuine scientific or medical need, but by the time of the Siklus the quest for knowledge had given way to the thirst for entertainment. Some scientists no longer considered whether they *should* do something, but simply whether they could. So they created goats with spider genes, and crossbred big cats, and created myriad other hybrid species."

"How could you have done this stuff?" Seb shouted at the Perd.

"However," continued the recording, "the twenty-first century was a time of contradictions. On one hand, discoveries were being made every day about the intelligence of other species. New legislations were brought in to protect them. On the other, new drugs still had to be tested on at least two different species of live mammal." Flo lost her battle over nausea, and she ran retching to the bathroom. When she returned to the living room, Seb looked at her sympathetically.

"Ready for more?" he asked gently. "I think we're nearly at the end."

"Ready as I'll ever be."

But something was going wrong with the Perd. Seb checked the batteries, but they were fine. Somehow, the original material must have been corrupted or damaged in some way and they struggled to make out the words.

Some references to the HSL were just about audible amongst brief spurts of white noise.

Flo jumped. "Did you hear that? Was that something to do with non-comm legal rights?"

"I didn't catch it all. Sorry."

"Hang on. What was that bit? It sounded like Mum said 'laboratory' and then a moment later 'Lush's gene' or something." But I couldn't make out anything after that."

At last the recorder stopped working altogether and they sat in silence thinking about what they'd learned. Flo's rage broke the silence.

"Typical! We sat through hours of horror stories about the past and then, just when we get to the important bit, the Perd packs up! Seriously, you couldn't make it up!" She was furious. "Animal rights, HSL rights, Guido Lush, abductions, experimentation. What does that combination mean?"

"It's probably something really, really obvious," said Seb.

"This is useless! What has it got to do with the dreams? Hers or mine? This is just sick, pointless stuff. It isn't going to help me find out what's going on!" She stood up and walked around the room, as if changing perspective would make her see connections.

Then she understood. It was obvious now. There were two distinct threads to her mother's research. Entwined and inseparable.

"I know what they're doing."

Leaving Seb to lock up, Flo rushed off to confront George.

CHAPTER 10

Flo stood on the doorstep glaring at her guardian. With a sigh, he moved aside and let her in.

"I've figured it out, George. No thanks to you. I've looked at all the notes my mother took, listened to her Perd, and I agree with her. At least, I understand part of it. Those HSL bastards were behind the mammal disappearances then, and they're behind them now. I think they're experimenting on animals to figure out how telepathy works." She paused to see if he had anything to say. When he didn't, she continued. "You know how jealous the Non-Comms are of the rest of us? They're trying to find a way to be just like us, like by altering a gene or two, or something." He fidgeted around. What was up with the man? "George, why didn't you tell me the truth?"

"Flo, I couldn't tell you before. How could I? There was no point; you were too young."

"And the dreams? What do you know about them?"

"Just like you, your mother had been having nightmares and noticed they seemed to coincide with reported disappearances. So, as I told you before, she needed to investigate the disappearances – the abductions - but never had any definite proof of anything. Along the way she came up with an interesting theory." Flo resisted the temptation to interrupt him, and George continued, "that's all it ever was. A theory. You know how we have to make a conscious decision to mind-share with mammals, even for an alarm call?" Flo nodded. "Well, your mother believed, given the right circumstances, telepathy didn't have to be conscious. She was looking into the idea of a next evolutionary step. She believed these dreams were evidence of communicating through the subconscious, and that more changes were coming. We haven't stopped evolving."

"So," Flo sat down slowly, "the dreams I've been getting are like alarm calls into my subconscious?" She stared at him. "I'm the latest evolutionary step, you think?" She didn't wait for him to answer. "All right, it's fair enough to conclude telepathy can evolve, that we can evolve. I agree. Evolution is the least of my worries. We're all the product of evolution. But," her voice took on an edge, "it doesn't really explain what the HSL is doing grabbing mammals in the first place, and why I'm involved in it all, does it? Is my theory at least right? Are they trying to be like us?"

"Not exactly," he said with a sigh. "Your mother was convinced they were trying to eliminate the gene altogether. Or at least suppress it."

She gasped. "But that would take us back to pre-Siklus times!" George held his hand up.

"Let me finish," he said. "The thing is, your mother and I - and others, like Seb's parents - believe Lush was wrong. There is probably no single gene responsible for telepathy. Of course, it was understandable that Lush drew that conclusion, but we're sure he was mistaken. Whatever it is that enables communication between species, has got to be more complex than just one extra gene."

"So are you saying you were all in on it - you, Jack and Laura? And you all think, thought, think that no matter how much the HSL tries to eliminate the Lush gene, it won't make any difference?"

As if relieved that the information floodgate was open at last, George talked quickly. "Yes, I am. The gene may well help communication, but it isn't the whole story. We think it's likely it works in conjunction with all the other genes… a knock-on effect, I suppose you'd call it. Lush's gene interacting with the others we have in common with other species. You've noticed some creatures are easier to talk to than others, haven't you?"

"Of course. Everyone knows that," she replied, slightly irritated. "It's easy to mind-share with Lonce."

"That's because you and he share about ninety per cent of your DNA and the genes seem to play off each other. Pigs and chimps are even easier, because we're all about ninety-eight per cent the same. In other words," George continued, "just removing Lush's one gene isn't enough. It'll never be enough. In order to stop communication they'd have to unravel everything… all the genetic code… and that can't be done."

Watching him closely, Flo could see some sort of inner turmoil playing out across his face, but he must have come to a decision, because he turned and hurried to the room he used as an office, returning a moment later holding a piece of paper.

"Look," he said as he unfolded it. "I got this note a few days after she died. She was definitely on to something. But she didn't tell me what."

Flo held out her hand. "*Rosendale has the key*," she read. "What the -. Who's Rosendale?"

"Not 'who', 'where'. It's a little outlying island on the north-east side of the archipelago. For some reason she suspected animals were being taken there."

"And then she and Dad were killed. What a coincidence."

"Flo, you know I've always believed your parents' death was a case of being in the wrong place at the wrong time. I never suspected a deliberate assassination. And I still don't," he added quickly. "We have no proof of foul play."

"You may not, but I do. I know who killed my parents, and I'm going to make them pay, even if I have to go to Rosendale!" She stood up abruptly to leave, but George grabbed her arm.

"Flo, there is no proof of anything, and I meant what I said. I still don't believe your parents were targeted, but if they were," he paused, "then there is even more reason for you to stay away from all of this." She pulled away from him. "Flo, I'm serious. It could be dangerous."

"Let go of me! You're not my dad. I'm nearly eighteen and I can do what I want and you can't stop me. I have a right to follow up Mum's notes. If you won't help, Jack will!"

She fled. She was desperate to talk to Seb, and to push her face into Lonce's comforting, warm, living fur. She needed to confront Jack too, and Seb would know how to get hold of him. She ran all the way back to her apartment, hoping Seb was still at her place.

But the first thing she needed to do when she got home was to beg Lonce's forgiveness for the past sins of her species.

CHAPTER 11

Seb had gone by the time she got home. While Flo stood fumbling with her keys, Lonce appeared, back from hunting again. He looked up at her, sensing her anguish, and they entered the apartment together in silence. Flo flopped on to the floor next to him and leaned back on the sofa. Her mother's files were still spread across the carpet. She rested one hand on Lonce and he licked it with his powerful and rasping tongue. With her other hand she absentmindedly picked off the strands of his fur which clung to her clothes.

What's wrong? he asked silently. She shared with him some of the disturbing information she'd found out during the day.

"I've been digging around, and I've found out all sorts of stuff about my mother's research. A side I'd never heard about before." She sighed. "I don't know what to think any more." Lonce sat still, listening. He was good at that. "Humans bred dogs until they developed awful genetic faults. They created entirely new species of animals just for the fun of it. They tortured them, they experimented on them…" Tears fell as she told him all she had discovered. She was ashamed and embarrassed to be human. How could he ever forgive her?

She searched her pockets for a handkerchief. Finding nothing, she resorted to her sleeve. Pain gripped her heart.

"I'd always been told my parents died by mistake. George always said they'd just been at the wrong place at the wrong time. But I was sure it had been my fault; I caused it. That last day with them had been so happy. Like it was happier than usual, you know? Mum found something in an antiquary shop and wanted to show us all. I begged and begged her to let me see it before she showed Daddy and Uncle George. She was so excited, but it turned out it was only papers. I remember being really disappointed. I couldn't believe she was getting so excited over papers. But that was Mum all over. I can see her now, laying them out on the table at George's house. I never understood the fuss. But for her it seemed like a big deal, and to celebrate she said Daddy would buy me hot chestnuts on the way home."

Lonce sat up fully now. He watched her face closely, reading her emotions as they flickered across her brow. "I ran on ahead. I knew the way home. I could have done it blindfolded. I heard Daddy asking Mum for some change for the hot chestnut man. The three of them were standing there next to the brazier. Dad was chatting and the man was laughing." Lonce watched her tears fall. "And then, boom, it was all over."

Lonce remembered that day too. He had watched the family pass by and was struck by the energy which seemed to pour out of them. He'd seen the small one run ahead laughing, her eyes shining with happiness. He'd watched the two adults stop and chat to the old hot chestnut seller. He heard the explosion and he'd witnessed the aftermath. Boom, it all began.

She squeezed Lonce tightly and begged forgiveness.

I cannot forgive you. You do nothing wrong. All this happened a long time ago. Humans nearly destroyed us all. Humans paid the price." His steady warm, damp breath caressed her face as his thoughts reassured her. "They not see us as equals. But now humans learn. You accept, we are different from you. Different, but equal.

"But you don't understand, Lonce. They are doing it again!"

CHAPTER 12

After locking up Flo's place earlier, Seb had returned home. Today's revelations, whatever they meant, had left him feeling deeply disturbed. He could only imagine what Flo was going through. His parents were away somewhere, but at least he had some. Until now he'd often envied Flo her independent lifestyle. But today was different.

He decided to do her a favour and start Pugh's project, maybe even do it all, just to give her a break. It helped him forget the things he'd heard on the Perd too, and he was grateful for that. He worked for hours, frequently nipping into his parents' study to raid their shelves. By early evening he'd finished, exhausted. At least he'd been interested in the topic.

He stood in his parents' study one last time, checking he hadn't missed anything useful among the books, papers, and artefacts acquired on their frequent voyages around the world. His eye fell on a box labelled *Seb* sitting on the bottom shelf of one of the bookcases. He smiled. His mother couldn't help herself; she had to save all his childhood junk. Thinking he might find something to amuse Flo with, he pulled it out and put it on the desk. In it he found an old diary, the only one he'd ever kept, which he'd forgotten all about. Opening a page at random he started reading.

He cringed at the atrocious spelling and the constant references to Flo. Oh no. Mum, you kept this?

10 Jan. by Sebastian aged 7 and a harf and three days!

George brorte Flo over to our house yestaday. They shut me out of the living room when she arived. I don't no why, becos Flo is my best frend. Flo brorte a snow lepard with her. I tryed to listen at the door. His name is Lonce. Flo woodent let go of him. Flo woodent talk. Flo is going to stay at our house for a while mum said. That is ok. I like Flo and Lonce is cool. But I dont think im her best friend any more. Lonce is her best friend now. Flo is talking today. She told me to go away. Mum says I must be payshunt with her. Her mum and dad are dead now. She needs time mum said.

Seb wandered, still giggling to himself, into to the kitchen to get some more tea, taking the battered diary with him. His early life summed up in a few pages. He smiled to himself as he flicked through the pages of badly written, boyish script.

And then the phone started ringing.

"Come back, Seb. Please. I need you."

CHAPTER 13

New Era-London, Guardia Station, Interrogation Room 5
Witness Statement 1.1 of Melissa Gryfe née Harcourt
Species: Human
Sex: Female
Affair: Rosendale
Deposition signed in the presence of K9 Officer Dante. Monday, 1 August

Having explained to Melissa Gryfe her rights, Officer Dante signalled for the bureau's Perd to be turned on. They were recording her statement, noting carefully that she was cooperating with the authorities under her own volition.

Dante was a larger than average dog of indeterminate ancestry who had been with the K9 unit for the last three years. He was accompanied - as all the K9s were - by a human counterpart. It was more a question of practicality than hierarchy. This sort of division of labour made the force extremely efficient. Turning on Perds, for example, was easier with hands rather than paws, while dogs were unbeatable when it came to detection and investigation. Dante was popular within the force. He was good at dealing with people, and tried to make his human counterpart feel he was not merely there just to open doors, turn on equipment and type reports. As an excellent judge of character he managed to tease out skills from his assistant which complemented his own. Many other officers had followed his example, and built similar collaborative relationships within the force.

But on this occasion, the human stayed in the background. Dante, as superior officer, was the one to coax information out of his witness, Melissa Gryfe. Her answers to his well-practised telepathic questioning, recorded onto the official records.

Melissa, when you are ready, please tell me when you first heard about the HSL?

"I've been hearing about the HSL all my life." Melissa sounded bitter. Dante glanced down and checked the recording levels of the Perd. This was going to be important testimony and he didn't want to risk getting it wrong.

She continued, "Father insisted the Coalition was an oppressive dictatorship which was ruining our lives. He complained constantly about everything, especially veganism. He said it was an infringement of our human rights, because as humans we are omnivores and we can, and should, eat everything."

Dante nodded. As a carnivore, his experience was different. Amongst humans, he knew, veganism or vegetarianism was the norm. There was no need to enforce it. Most people found themselves uncomfortable eating creatures they could have a conversation with.

Society functioned very well by respecting life in all its forms. The nature of creatures was respected too. Carnivores remained carnivores and herbivores remained herbivores because they had no choice in the matter. Between carnivores and their prey there was balance and understanding. As with everything in nature, life and death danced for eternity. But omnivores had choice. Humans chose to be vegetarian because they could. It felt right.

"People like my parents resented being forced to eat meat in secret."

Dante interrupted quickly. *I'm curious. How did they obtain meat?*

"We imported it, as far as I know, from countries with lax rules. I never went into the details. If I needed meat I used one of the suppliers my mother had used, but where he got it from I didn't know. I never asked."

Dante made a mental note to check this information out further. His human counterpart nodded, already planning moves to crack down on the illegal meat trade.

"But it wasn't only that that Daddy hated," Melissa continued. "He moaned about the recycling laws, talking about our human ability to create, not just mimic or reuse." It was not Dante's job to pass judgement or comment. Just record and observe. Melissa had now retreated into the past. Her memories were coming thick and fast, in surprising detail. The K9 officer's mind wandered for a moment while he speculated on a future career as a psy-therapist once he got too old for Guardia work.

"He would often say how we have the duty to create new things," Melissa was saying, snapping the dog's attention back to the present. "For him, recycling ancient technologies was a waste of our talents. He often said humans are superior to all other species, that we are as good as it gets: the top of the evolutionary tree."

How did those comments make you feel? asked Dante, curious.

“Well, the line about evolution made me laugh as I got older. He didn’t actually believe in evolution, he just referred to it when it suited him.”

Melissa, how long had your father been involved with the HSL? Do you know?

“I’m pretty sure he’d been a member since before he married Mother. I know he met her at one of their secret fundraising meat dinners. The HSL has been around for a long time, longer than the Coalition, longer than any of the guilds even. Ever since the Siklus nearly destroyed the planet, there have been people who’ve wanted to rebuild society as it was before.”

It must have been very confusing for you as a child growing up in a family run by a father with illegal HSL values. Dante was feeling a wave of sympathy for this human woman.

“It was hard. I was always pretending to be something I wasn’t. I was constantly worried I’d risk some sort of punishment from the state… or from my parents. You have no idea what it was like, living with them in a world which condemns the values of the HSL and constantly tells us it is immoral to put humans first.”

But as children of the Human Supremacy League you were told something different, weren’t you?

“Yes, but-” She stopped and looked anxiously at the dog. “My parents honestly believed there was nothing wrong with the old ways. They were not bad people.”

But surely you must have heard about the atrocities the HSL were responsible for?

“I never believed it. My parents were not monsters and did not condone violence in any form.”

Don’t worry; your parents are not on trial. Now, if you don’t mind I’d like you to tell me about your husband, Marcus Gryfe.

“His full name is Marcus Anthony Gryfe. My parents introduced us. I’d never given Marcus a second thought. He was just one of the people my parents nurtured. Whenever they found someone who could be useful to them, they fawned all over them. Dinners, parties, gifts and invitations were all offered to the favourite of the day. I couldn’t quite understand their fondness for most of them, but I didn’t really consider it any of my business. My parents sent me off to boarding school in the New Bristol Hills when I was about ten years old. I hated it there.

“They resented me for being born a girl. Try as they might they never managed to conceive the precious boy they’d dreamed of; the boy who was going to give the family name to future generations. The best they could hope for with me was a good marriage and a hyphenated surname.”

Dante wondered how he could get her back on track. But she turned to him and added, “You have to understand what my life was like, officer. During the seven or so years I stayed at the school, I was groomed and trimmed into the perfect wife-material Mother had always wanted, and Marcus was ambitious enough to be willing to marry into our family. By the age of eighteen I had, apparently, blossomed and caught his eye. Mother started saying things like, Marcus Gryfe was ‘sweet on me’, and it would be an honour if he proposed. I hardly knew him, but at eighteen I was still too scared of her to say anything."

So when did he propose? said Dante. *You say you hadn't known him long.* He was finding it hard to comprehend the behaviour of Melissa's mother. Why give her daughter away to someone she barely knew?

"He did it during one of my parents' dinner parties, just after the main course plates had been cleared. I was at the far end of the table, sandwiched between Mother and a strange little scientist called Ulrich. Ulrich made my flesh crawl and I spent most of the evening wishing I was somewhere else. I remember how the room hushed when Marcus stood up. First, he thanked my parents for the food. The mixed grill had impressed him. Then he thanked everyone present for their support and so on. Then suddenly he announced that I'd agreed to be his wife. The cheek! He'd never even asked me! It turned out that while I had been upstairs with Mother, getting dressed, he'd been coming to an arrangement with my father.

"Everyone toasted us. He called me over to join him. As I stood up, Mother whispered in my ear, and I'll never forget what she said." Melissa's eyes were looking back to the scene as it replayed in her mind. Dante waited. Silent. Transfixed. Melissa took a deep breath. "She said I was to remember that women of our class do not make scenes. I was to accept him, and that was that."

Dante looked steadily at her. *But surely you could have said no?*

Melissa laughed a bitter laugh. "Not really. My prospects were so limited, it didn't take me long to realise sooner or later they would marry me off to one or other of their cronies. By refusing Marcus I'd merely be postponing the inevitable. I could do worse, I thought. Marcus would be successful and we would have money. With that sort of power behind me, I could recreate my life the way I wanted it. So what if I didn't love him?"

A single tear trickled down her cheek and Dante signalled for the Perd to be stopped. He had heard enough for the day.

CHAPTER 14

Early February

Flo had pulled herself together by the time Seb arrived. She'd dried her tears and calmed right down, but was still snuggled with Lonce on the floor as Seb walked through the door.

"There," he said. "Prepare to thank me. No less than five kowtows please. I'm your knight in shining armour who has single-handedly relieved you of the burden of Miss Pugh's project." He grinned at her. "There's enough stuff here for a fairly dramatic beginning, although I did wonder whether man-made earthquakes might have been better for a school project. Like Old Italy splitting right down the middle. That would have been cool to do. I bet Pugh would have liked that." He looked around trying to find an inch of free space for his papers, but the carpet was still covered with Flo's own piles. "You still haven't put this all away?" he said, stating the obvious. Without waiting for an answer he went back into the kitchen and dumped his work on the table. She followed him in silence, annoyed that he seemed to have forgotten she had asked him to come over because she needed to talk. Seb, meanwhile, was determined to cheer her up and distract her from the horrors of their earlier discoveries.

"I've been working on this on and off all day. Take a look at the figures. They're incredible." He started to pass Flo the first page, but snatched it back, preferring to read it out loud himself. "I wrote it as if we'd done the research together; I didn't think you'd mind. Anyway, just listen to this. I won't read you all of it, just the best bits." He cleared his throat grandly before starting to read.

"Any studies of the history of flooding will ultimately reveal a pattern. There have always been devastating floods, but from the late twentieth-century onwards we see the numbers of floods dramatically increase." He glanced at Flo, checking she was paying attention. "Instead of one big flood every hundred years or so, within a relatively short time there were multiple flood disasters every few years." He started listing dates and numbers until he ran out of breath, then looked at her expectantly. "All right, I can see you're not impressed. What are you thinking?"

"It seems like an awful lot of numbers. Are you sure you've shoved enough facts and figures in there?"

"OK, maybe I was a bit heavy in that bit, but there is some great stuff here we could work on."

"Seb, I-"

"Look!" He flapped the papers at her. "Here I talk about the diseases spread by the floods. It was like the medieval Black Death thing all over again. There was even a municipal truck which would go round each morning to collect the dead. But then the collectors got ill themselves."

Flo cleared her throat. Seb continued, trying to ignore her. "Or this bit? With the human population dying, there was no one to maintain and operate the Old London flood barrier, until a surge of water poured in and all the low-lying areas of the city were submerged."

Flo wasn't sure what to say. He'd worked so hard, and now she was going to tell him he'd wasted his time. "Seb, that's brilliant. I can't believe how much work you've done already. But I," She struggled to find the words.

"But what, Flo? But what? What's wrong? I can tell you don't like it. What's not to like? It's a brilliant topic. Can you imagine what it would've been like? Right here, survivors would have been killing each other over the last canned food supplies. They'd have taken shelter from the floods in any tall buildings that were left. Sooner or later they'd have starved to death anyway. The old skyscrapers would have been like vertical cemeteries, until the water ate away at their foundations and they crashed down." Again he paused, hoping he had finally impressed her. She still looked unconvinced and he misread her. "What, Flo? Did you want us to do the work together? Or did you want to do the whole thing yourself? I mean, honestly, Flo, but what?"

"Wait, Seb. What is wrong with you? You know what I've been through today, or have you forgotten? Why are you so mad?"

"Oh, I don't know." He rubbed his eyes and shook his head. "I didn't sleep too well last night either. I had the weirdest dreams; nightmares, really." He sighed again. "And all the stuff we listened to on your mum's Perd was disgusting. Sorry, if I'm out of order. I overreacted. I'm tired."

"That's all right. You're forgiven." She smiled, suddenly pleased by the way the conversation was going. "Don't you understand how important this is? How special? Why didn't you mention you'd been having nightmares too? Didn't it occur to you it might have been relevant earlier, when we were listening to all that stuff? What were they like?" She shook her head, wondering how he could be so obtuse sometimes.

"Hardly important, Flo. Anyway, they've all faded a bit now, so I'm not sure how to describe them." His voice took on the dislocated monotone people use when they are recounting their dreams, but for once she was riveted, not bored. "I saw lots of trucks filled with mammals… they were being unloaded into a huge round building near the sea. It was raining… there was a storm at sea. I saw rows and rows of cages… there were cries and screams. First I was in one of the cages, then outside it."

"Then what?"

"I don't know… it was weird."

"For Gaia's sake, Seb! It all ties in! You've seen the piles of papers, Mum's dream diary. And I even told you I'd dreamed the same sort of thing. Maybe not the trucks, but I was the central character, I mean it was me being taken somewhere. I felt something bad was going to happen. Why didn't you mention all this earlier? Apparently it might be some sort of evolutionary step."

He shrugged, but she could tell he was thinking about it, because he had a little frown. Then she started to tell him about shouting at George, about her determination to finish her mother's work, about asking his parents for help.

"One, we know my mother had special dreams too." She counted the points out on her fingers. "Two, we know she was working with your father on something connected to them, and to the abductions that were happening at the time." She took a deep breath and a huge leap in reasoning. “Look, you know my mother did tons of research. You’ve seen and heard it. And so three, we could use her notes for our project. It’ll give us a legitimate reason to investigate what my mum was up to. Why she was killed. Jack and George will have to help us, it’s for school.” She gave him her most winning smile. The one he could never resist.

“You’re mad! You have no idea what you’re getting yourself into. My parents aren’t going to help you. I won’t let them. There is no way I’m going to let them risk their lives for your crazy project. Your parents are dead, Flo. Dead and buried. You’re obsessed. As for the importance of those dreams, Just forget it!”

“You don’t know what it’s like! You have parents! You haven’t seen them die and blamed yourself for it all your life! I have! I was convinced it was my fault. But now I think they were murdered. If that’s true, it means I’m not guilty. Someone else is, and I want to know who. And it means I share something special with my mother. Is that so hard to understand?”

He stood and headed towards the door. “Seriously, dreams are just dreams. They don’t mean a thing!” His hand was on the doorknob. Flo looked at him, astonished.

“Please, Seb. What’s got into you? I need you to help me with this. I can’t do it without you. Please!” But he was out of the door already.

Lonce had continued sitting on the floor during their fight, for the moment forgotten by his two friends. The aggressive interaction between them shocked him.

Many times in his life humans had puzzled him. But until his recent encounter with the Non-Comms in the forest, he had never really felt threatened by them. The differences between their species had never bothered him before. Now, as he listened to Seb and Flo argue, he became aware of the complexities of human nature and the vast differences between their species and all the others.

Flo talked of evil. She asked forgiveness.

But this world is better now. The Coalition is good. Most humans are good too. Flo and Seb are my friends. Blood is in past. But my friends are angry now. My friends shout and cry. The dark times come again. Men in the forest, the Non-Comms, bring it.

I love Flo, Seb, George, but I not love all humans. I am last of my kind now. Humans did this. Zoos. Flo tells me. My ancestors spent their whole life and death as captives. That is hard to forgive. Hard to understand. Flo tells me, before Siklus, before zoos, we lived in high, rocky places. Far, far from here. The air was different there: cold, crisp, clean and thin. N'Era-London air no good. Flat land air. Thick town air. I want taste mountain air before I die. I have skill. I am good hunter. I find high, rocky place. A place to live before I die. What I know dies with me. I am last of my kind.

I love Flo, I trust her. She says not all humans bad. More good than bad. If true, why is evil still here?

CHAPTER 15

Flo stayed at home with Lonce for the next few days, barely venturing out. She didn't want to see anybody, especially not Seb or George. Lonce's leg had healed and he no longer needed her help, but she was still cross with the others, so stayed stubbornly at home. Her nightmares were getting worse. Every night was filled with ghastly images of caged mammals. Sometimes she seemed imprisoned too, her arms pinned down and a terrible weight on her chest. Each time she woke in a panic only to find the bedclothes had wrapped tightly around her as she tossed and turned. She could barely move. In the middle of the night the sense of being alone and powerless was almost unbearable. She contemplated contacting Miss Pugh, but quickly thought better of it. There was something a little off about the teacher's efforts to enter her private life. Nightmares or not, Flo didn't think she was quite desperate enough for Miss Pugh.

Seb won't be able to stay away. He'll be back. Just give him time. She hoped she was right. She couldn't stop herself from brooding over their last conversation. He'd been cruel. The one person she'd counted on had turned on her.

She was right. He turned up a few days later wearing his warmest outdoor gear and carrying an enormous backpack.

"I'm sorry, Flo. I feel terrible for the things I said."

"Seb, I knew you'd understand."

"I haven't changed my mind, we're still doing floods, but I'm not here to discuss school. Get ready," he said, squeezing past her into the apartment. "We're going camping."

"Don't be stupid, Seb. Spring hasn't properly arrived yet. I may be depressed but I'm not suicidal! Anyway, I'm still not talking to you." He ignored her.

"It's the beginning of March. Winter has nearly finished, but you've been too busy moping to notice. Do you know Helyn, Jonathan's girlfriend? Her parents have a holiday cabin on the far side of Regent's Forest, overlooking the bay near Kensington Isle. A bunch of us from class are going indoor camping. We might even get around to studying. You never know." A cheesy grin lit up his face. "Apparently it only has an open fire for heating, which is why I've brought extra sleeping bags. It'll be warm in front of the fire but the rest of the house will be freezing. They only use the place in the summer, so there won't be any fresh food, so…" he opened his backpack and revealed a vast assortment of delicious foods, "I brought all your favourites."

"Is that your version of 'Sorry, Flo, I was totally out of line and an utter moron'?" He shrugged. "Look, Seb, I forgive you. You can't help being a complete idiot and a heartless bastard. But I've got a lot to think about. That stuff Mum was writing about is still going on, I know it. I hate the HSL so much it's like a solid lump inside me and I've had more dreams. You think this is just me obsessing about Mum and Dad. but it isn't.

Something bad is going on. The dreams are messages."

"Stop!" he said. "I told you, I don't want to get involved. I'm just trying to do something nice! So for goodness' sake shut up!"

"But-"

"Listen, Flo. If we find out anyone else has been having nightmares as well, then we'll talk about it. If not, end of discussion and you'd better apologise to me."

"I swear, Seb, if you tell me to shut up or interrupt me again, I'll floor you."

Reluctantly she threw her camping gear into a pack, making sure to include a functioning can opener and ample toilet paper. Seb was brilliant in many ways, he was practical about fixing or making things, but you could bet money he hadn't brought toilet paper.

As the three friends left the building Flo spotted someone standing in the hot chestnut seller's spot. He or she was stamping their feet against the cold as if they'd been there for a while. Flo called out, "He doesn't work here any more, so there's no point waiting." The figure waved, and headed off in the opposite direction.

CHAPTER 16

The walk through the woods to the cabin was fun. They met up with their friends from class and joined the happy, rowdy group. As soon as they entered the forest, Lonce loped off on his own to hunt. The rest of the crowd walked together, heading northwest towards the head of Paddington Bay.

"You know, Seb," Flo said quietly, "I don't know much about Helyn's family. What do her parents do? How come they have this place in the woods?"

"As far as I know they're boat builders. We've got one of theirs. The family has been managing these woods for generations. They might even own them, for all I know. In any case, they have the right to use the trees for their business, with the usual proviso they replant two trees for every one they cut," Seb murmured. "I heard they're stinking rich, so I bet the cabin will be quite luxurious." They both jumped as Helyn silently materialised at their sides and joined in their conversation.

"Don't expect too much luxury, Seb. We only ever use this place in the summer so it'll be damp and chilly now." Seb and Flo looked at each other, embarrassed. Helyn moved off with a smile.

"That was awkward. Do you think she heard anything?"

"Probably, but Helyn won't mind. She's very level-headed. Anyway, it's not like we were saying anything negative. It's just a fact. Her parents are stinking rich, yours are dead and mine are always travelling. That's just the way it is."

The path suddenly opened out into a clearing and the group found themselves looking at a huge wooden house. In front of it, a dead tree trunk had been carved into a spectacular totem pole. Figures of many species – humans, non-humans and plants - merged and entwined joyfully in the protective embrace of Mother Earth and the Green Man. A small plaque at the bottom indicated it had been a 'gift from the people of Grand Columbus'. If the word 'gift' could hardly do justice to the huge totem, then the word 'cabin' wasn't adequate on any level for the house rising up before them.

As on all post-Siklus buildings, the roof tiles were high efficiency solar panels which clipped simply into the structure of the roof and fed directly into the battery array kept in the attic. Each tile could be unplugged and replaced without compromising the whole system. This made changing damaged tiles easy and inexpensive, not that it looked as if Helyn's family had to count the pennies.

"Hey, Helyn, are you sure there's room for us all?" Stan, the class joker, called out as soon as he saw the house.

"No. You boys will have to sleep outside," she teased. "Come on, it's not that special. Let's go in and get sorted. We've got a lot to organise if we're going to be comfortable." She opened the door and led them straight into an enormous living room with a huge open fireplace at one end. The hearth was so clean it clearly had never been used.

"Let's divvy up the jobs," suggested Lora. "Where's your wood pile?"

"Out back, I'll take you. Then I'll show you what beds are available and how the kitchen works."

For the next few minutes the group worked in teams to organise the cabin. Stan and Lora ferried in dry branches and logs from a pristine woodpile, while Jonathan and Helyn attempted to light the fire. A few moments later there were angry complaints about stinging eyes.

"Quick, open all the windows and doors." Jonathan shouted. Thick smoke curled up over the mantelpiece before dispersing higher up under the ceiling, but before long, the fire was hot enough to drag the smoke up the chimney and the room soon cleared.

Once they got settled in, with the fire burning steadily and the beds allocated, most people joined in preparing a range of dishes for dinner. Ellen produced a guitar from somewhere and started quietly singing.

"Why don't you sit down and relax, Flo?" suggested Lora who had noticed how aggressively her friend was chopping and slicing the vegetables for roasting.

"No, it's fine. I'm enjoying myself." Flo made a conscious effort to chop more slowly. The others, meanwhile, got on with laying the table. Flo was still fundamentally too disturbed by everything that had been happening to be easy company. That wasn't going to change in a hurry, but perhaps amongst this group of friends she could begin to ease up.

"Hey, everyone, come and get it!" Seb called when at last Helyn and Lora pulled the dishes from the oven. "There's something for everyone. We've got roast veggies and beans - with or without cheese - steamed kale, sweet potatoes and three pulse stew." They crammed round the kitchen table. After a couple of initial burns to their fingertips they happily munched their way through all the platters of food. Occasionally a light-hearted fight broke out over a crispy sliver of potato or bell pepper which had stuck to the dish, but there was no ill feeling and no one went hungry.

Several conversations were going on simultaneously and Flo struggled to hear what was being said at the far end of the table. Helyn and Stan seemed to be arguing about Miss Pugh.

"All I'm saying," said Helyn, "is last week she was extolling the virtues of the twentieth century. She did a whole lesson on animal testing for human health, and the advantages of plastic packaging for food storage. Don't you remember? And now she's swung round again."

"Look, I don't think she was extolling anything of the sort. She was just telling us what went on," Stan protested. "You know what she's like." Before Flo could get up and join them, the platters had been cleared and a huge fruit crumble placed on the table in their stead. Conversations lapsed again as the friends helped themselves to the steaming pudding, the only sounds now those of appreciation.

"Don't worry, Flo," said Lora a few minutes later as Flo got ready to stand. "There's no need to wash dishes too. You helped prepare; it's someone else's turn. Besides, you've been through a lot recently, so it's just good to see you out and about again."

"Yeah, thanks. You too. It's been a while." Just then Flo heard a familiar scratching sound. "That sounds like Lonce." She got up to open the window behind them, and watched as Lonce bounded effortlessly over the windowsill into the room. Tired from hunting, he flopped down on the floor in front of the fire and started grooming. The two girls went to join him.

"So what is going on between you and Seb?" asked Lora suddenly. "I mean, are you two ever going to get together properly? I know you both want to."

"What? No! I mean seriously, what? There's nothing between us. He's like Lonce. They're my brothers." The big cat looked up at her and blinked. "All right, Seb is more like my brother than Lonce, obviously, but ugh. No. No way!"

"Sure. Sure he is. He's more than a brother. I have a brother; trust me I know about brothers." Lora grinned and nudged Flo in the ribs. "So what cha gonna do?"

"What? Aren't you listening? There is nothing between us. and even if even if I liked him, he sees me as an annoying sister."

"Ah ha!" said Lora triumphantly. "I'm so good at this. I bet Helyn I'd get you to admit you liked him, and I have."

"You did what?" Flo didn't know whether to be cross or embarrassed. "Well, you lost the bet. There is nothing between us, there never was and there never will be. You're both deluded!"

Lonce chuffed in amusement. Flo kicked him gently.

"I'm the girl he used to call 'Pukey Flow', just because I was sick every time I was dragged on to his parents' boat when I was little. Lora cracked up. "I'm telling you, he doesn't like me that way."

"All I know is the way he looks at you. He likes you. He's not looking at you like a sister."

Flo took no notice. "All right, maybe I do like him, but I don't want to like him. I don't want things to change between us. I've got him, I've got his parents, I've got Lonce and I've got George. That's it. I don't have anyone else." She couldn't disguise the edge of desperation in her voice now.

"I'm sorry. I shouldn't have said anything."

One by one, the others settled around the fire to relax and chat. Because there were so many of them, there was more light-hearted scuffling over seats, but soon everyone was comfortable. Most conversations seemed to be related to school and the various projects they'd chosen to work on.

Suddenly Seb stood up. He looked embarrassed and a little unsure of himself. Flo watched, curious, as he coughed to gain the attention of the whole group. What was he doing?

"I don't quite know how to bring this up," he began, "but I promised Flo I would ask. So here goes. Have any of you had any strange nightmares recently?"

A couple of the boys sniggered. "Yo, Seb, are you going to wake us up with your screams in the night?"

"Only if I dream of you, Stan!" Seb countered. Everyone laughed. "Seriously, Flo and I have both had some really weird nightmares lately and they seem to be getting more frequent."

"I've had a few strange things happen. Not dreams so much; more like hearing cries and whimpers at night, but while I'm awake," said a girl called Marine. "I haven't told anyone because I thought I was imagining it."

"Me too," said Helyn quietly.

"And me," said Stan, suddenly serious. His classmates were surprised. Stan's natural tendency was to clown around. "My whole family's been having nightmares every night for about a week now," he added, grinning, "but we put it down to the dodgy-looking mushrooms Mum used in her terrine." There were giggles in the room, either at the idea of dodgy mushrooms, or at Stan's mother's cooking abilities.

Gradually more and more of them admitted to having had strange dreams, or sight and sound disturbances. Only the group's two token Non-Comms seemed to be unbothered by nightmares. Feeling a little awkward by the turn in the conversation, they hastily volunteered to make caffeinix for everyone. One, a girl called Sarah, caught Flo's eye as she left. Flo smiled at her. After all, her genetic makeup wasn't her fault. Sarah smiled back and Flo was touched by the genuine warmth she saw in her expression.

The evening passed comparing notes and Flo became increasingly convinced she was right: something was going on and the Comms were being asked to help. All the dreamers reported stormy seas and some sort of large ring-shaped building. And cages… cages and cells, full of desperate-looking animals.

CHAPTER 17

Flo and Seb soon found themselves the only ones awake, the others having sloped off to the bedrooms or their improvised beds on the floor. They sat together quietly in front of the fire, Flo thinking about everything they'd heard that evening, Seb's arm a reassuring weight around her shoulder.

Apparently he didn't want to spoil the mood any more than she did, and seemed to enjoy sitting quietly with her, his head resting on hers. Suddenly she couldn't imagine life without him, and was still wondering where that thought came from when he got up unexpectedly and started rummaging around in his bag. He came back to the fireside and placed a small packet in front of her. It wasn't her birthday and it certainly wasn't any sort of public holiday, so Flo had a fleeting but horrible suspicion he was going to spoil everything between them by doing something stupid.

"Go on, open it," he said. She hesitated, not knowing quite what to say. She was nervous. Seb had been her best friend for ever. How could he do this to her? All sorts of wild thoughts were flying through her brain. Lora was right. How was she going to deal with some sort of romantic, soppy gift like a ring or something?

"Go on, Flo, it isn't going to bite you." He stood looking at her with a stupid grin on his face. Her hands shook slightly as she broke open the seal on the packaging. But she could see now she hadn't been thinking straight because the colourful cloth pouch which appeared was far too big and heavy to contain a ring. Trying to ignore the tiny hint of disappointment, she carefully opened the pouch to reveal what was hidden within its folds.

It was the smallest, sharpest and absolutely the most beautiful knife she'd ever seen, and fitted neatly across the palm of her hand. The handle was silky-smooth polished cherrywood. A small, semi-circular niche, the exact size of her index finger, had been smoothed out in the handle just below the blade. The blade itself looked otherworldly. A pattern spun and whirled its way across the metal, like the grain of some exotic wood, or the glisten of oil on water. She found herself holding her breath as she ran her thumb across the blade to test it. This was a miniature lethal weapon. She was speechless. She sat there turning it over and over, testing the weight and the balance of it. It was perfect in every way.

"I hope you like it," said Seb casually. "It's the best I've ever made."

"You made this? Seb, I had no idea you'd got this good! Wow! Those extra classes are paying off. It's lovely. Thank you." She wasn't sure what to do. If she'd been standing she might have hugged him. But she was still on the sofa and he was standing in front of her. It just seemed too weird now to stand up and give him a hug, so she sat there grinning like an idiot. He sat down and grinned too.

"How did you get all these patterns?" she asked quickly, breaking the spell of shared embarrassment.

"Well, I could give you the quick, simplified answer, the detailed one, or the super-fast one. Take your pick."

"Start with the super-fast and we'll take it from there."

“Well, you see, it’s magic, and if I tell you how it’s done I’d have to kill you. No, seriously, it takes ages to get it right and I’m no master yet, but if you’re really interested I’ve got some books you can look at.”

“Thanks but no thanks, Seb. I think I’ll pass. But what you’ve made is truly lovely.”

“Thank you,” he said modestly, and beamed at her. “Yes, I’m quite happy with it.”

She looked closely at the result of his labours. So much work had gone into it. He had always played down his skill, but quite apart from the hours it must have taken, making this little knife had required all the knowledge and craftsmanship he possessed and now he had given it to her. It meant more than any ring.

In the early hours of the following morning Flo was woken by the worst nightmares so far. Seb was snoring erratically next to her, and she eased herself out from under his outstretched and extremely heavy arm, taking care not to disturb him. A frown occasionally flickered across his brow. She stared down at him in the half-light, and decided against waking him. She suddenly just wanted to get home. It hadn’t been a good idea to come. She wasn’t ready for socialising, although the tales of her schoolmates’ nightmares had been interesting. Helyn seemed to be dreaming and occasionally let out a little cry, and Flo heard some of the others tossing and turning as well.

In the kitchen she hastily scribbled a note of explanation and thanks to the rest and drank a cup of cold water before quietly opening the cabin door and easing out into the cold, dark forest. She headed back home, her holiday over and any benefit she might have received replaced by her growing sense of unease. The dream-warnings were real. Evolutionary step or not, they meant something.

CHAPTER 18

Flo kept up a brisk pace. There were already quite a few people on the streets. Market traders were setting up their stalls for the morning, calling greetings to each other and to the early-rising gardeners who supplied the local greengrocers. The licensed waste collectors, who gathered up the organic material left by horses and other creatures, were also out in force, their thankless task to distribute the aromatic mix to the local Allotment guilds.

She walked quickly. The wind coming off the water beside her was bone-chillingly cold at this hour. How snug she'd been at the cabin, curled up with Seb. She longed for the summer. New Era-London, home to around 90,000 assorted citizens, the largest city in the world, was great in the summer, but damn cold now. Flo looked out over the grey, choppy water. In the distance were the medicine plantations, run by the Apothecary Guild, but it was still too dark to make them out. The gently undulating open land, given over to witch-hazel, poppy and hemp cultivation, was still in near darkness. The more delicate medicinal plants were housed in giant geodesic domes. Before her eyes the early dawn light was just beginning to play across the higher planes of their roofs, making them glint pink.

Where she walked now, along the waterfront, the grass between the road and the water's edge was trim and pristine; kept so by the Association of Grazing Mammals. Willows had been planted at regular intervals along the water's edge.

As she walked along Flo remembered a distant conversation with her parents.

"The Regional Coalition Government planted these willow trees the year you were born," her mother had said. "Now look at them."

Flo remembered the juvenile trees which, even all those years ago, were big enough to enrapture a child and to provide shade or shelter to the scores of picnickers who came in the summer. Now the trees were tall, wistfully drooping giants. Flo pushed aside a cascade of bare branches and stepped inside to stand quietly within the embrace of the tree, waiting for dawn. She looked around her and sighed. How the cityscape must have changed since the Siklus. Unrecognisable, she supposed, to someone from the past. Signs of the egalitarian society which had replaced the old one were everywhere. Suddenly she had the strong feeling the HSL would never succeed in undermining the status quo. The various species had too much to lose. When push came to shove they would fight to protect it. Wouldn't they?

She looked up into the willow tree again, remembering she had to pick up more willow bark and poppy painkillers. She'd been told willow bark and clove oil had soothed her gums as a tiny baby and George claimed that not only did willow help his heart, but its tea settled his stomach. Treating Lonce had cleared out her stock at home. In her state of semi-permanent tension she'd probably need to resort to willow for her own stomach.

But it was too cold to loiter; she needed to move. Flo stepped out from the wintry arbour and started walking briskly on.

Reaching her building she clumped morosely up the stairs. What is wrong with me? I could have stayed and waited for everyone to wake up. Seb will be furious when he wakes up. She shivered. The higher she climbed and the closer she got to her own apartment, the greater grew her sense of disquiet.

She crept along her corridor, feeling very silly. She could see her front door up ahead. It was slightly ajar.

All sorts of scenarios crossed her mind. Burglars? The neighbours must have heard something, surely? Why didn't they call the Guardia? If only I hadn't let Seb take me away. It's going to screw things up... I'll have to spend hours talking to the Guardia about it. She could feel herself getting hot with anger and fear.

With a yell she kicked the door hard, and as it flew open she leapt inside. Her front door led straight on to the living room. She stopped short, and reached round for the light switch. The living room was empty of life but it had been ravaged; completely taken apart. The hearth was still glowing and she could see the corners of burned scraps of paper amongst the ashes.

"Oh, no! The bastards! The bloody bastards!" Flo shouted. Nothing had been left untouched. Paintings had been pulled off the walls and some of them had been slashed. Every cushion had been hacked and the stuffing pulled out. All the piles of her mother's notes and the dream diary had gone into the fire. Books and ornaments littered the floor. The drawers in her mother's old wooden desk had been wrenched right out. The family shrine, with pictures and mementoes of her parents, was destroyed.

As she moved around the room her feelings of curiosity, tinged with a sense of violation, grew.

They wanted Mum's work destroyed, that she understood, but why slash Dad's paintings? Why break Mum's antiques? Or the personal little shrine? She turned to the corridor leading to the bedrooms and bathroom. She paused. The door to her parents' old room was slightly ajar. She knew she'd left it shut. She crept hesitantly along the corridor. Too many things were wrong here. The door to her room was closed and so was the one to the bathroom; she never shut those doors. Living alone, there was never the need. But her parents' door? Her mind started playing tricks. They're back? No, don't be silly. Not them, but someone else. She couldn't hear a thing. Not a creak. Not a breath. Not a heartbeat other than her own. She turned back to her bedroom door, too frightened by what she might find to venture further towards the room at the gloomy end of the corridor. She hesitated, fear suddenly making her unable to move. Her hand rested on the doorknob.

Suddenly the door behind her opened and a cord or something was flung round her throat. She was dragged backwards into the bathroom. Her feet slipped on the tiles, but her soft-soled shoes made no real sound, just a quiet squeak and scuffle. She couldn't breathe, couldn't call for help. At first she flailed around, trying to hit her attacker, or get her fingers into his eyes. She struggled vainly to turn around. She couldn't. She was completely helpless. But the need for air was overpowering. She clawed at the cord round her throat. She scratched deep gashes in her own skin while trying to breathe. She heard him grunt with the strain of trying to kill her. Her vision tunneled and she could feel a pulse inside her eyeballs. Her chest burned. Her muscles went into spasm and she must have kicked out with her left leg and hit some bottles on the side of the bath. She tried to focus her mind to call for help, but couldn't think. She had no control… Then her panic took an almost physical form and she could feel it burst through her head as a mind-yell stronger even than her call for help with Lonce after the attack. Stronger than anything she'd ever experienced before.

Help me! I can't breathe! I can't breathe! It was a silent scream of such intensity she was surprised it didn't knock her attacker down. She understood the power of a life-or-death mind-call. It was not something to do lightly. *I don't want to die!* More intrusive than any bell, bugle note, or regular distress call, it would have the power to cut through sleep-states and compel the receiver to answer it. Neighbours' dreams turned violent and frightening; they were roused from their sleep, confused and panicked, and had to respond. They tumbled out of bed unsure what to do.

Seemingly from nowhere Lonce launched himself into the bathroom and Flo's assailant loosened his grip enough for her to sink down, gasping. Lonce leapt over her, teeth bared, claws out, going for the throat. The man grabbed a bottle and flung it towards Lonce, and used that second of distraction to push past them both and out through the door and into the corridor. Lonce's claws made contact with his shoulder and Flo heard the fabric of the man's shirt rip and his sudden gasp of pain. She heard him running, and then recognised Seb's shout of alarm as the man barreled into him. She heard more cries as the intruder pushed through the gathering crowd of concerned residents outside.

Seb started to follow him, but Lonce called him back. *Flo needs you. Call medicos.* The snow leopard was sniffing her, assessing her injuries through his sense of smell. He nudged her head and gently licked her scratches.

"Sorry, sorry," said Seb, running into the bathroom a minute later. "They always ask really stupid questions before they'll dispatch anyone. Go after him, Lonce. I'll look after her. They'll be here soon." Lonce turned and bounded out of the apartment. He could still smell Flo's attacker. *Sweat, fear, pain. His shoulder hurts. That pleases me.*

She could hear her friends in her mind, but her head was spinning and she was experiencing the most excruciating pain of her life. Her head was going to explode. The pain in her eyes, throat and chest was calming down, but not in her head. It hurt so much; her eyes watered but it was too painful to cry. Looking at Flo's injuries made Seb gasp out loud. He knelt beside her. Bruises had started to come up, and where she'd scratched herself she was still bleeding. He held her in his arms and kissed her face and hair, but knew even as he murmured her name that she didn't even know he was there.

CHAPTER 19

The man known as Grey made it to the street without being stopped. He was furious. The watcher had told him the girl and the snow leopard would be gone for several days. He'd have to reconsider her employment. A blunder like this could have had serious consequences. What were they doing back? His only consolation was that civilians are slow. His years of training and personal fitness were paying off now. But that damn cat had caught him on the shoulder. He glanced down to assess the damage. He could feel the scratch begin to sting and throb. Funny, how pain only starts once you look.

Grey carried on running; there was no time to tend to the wound. He'd left his hydroride round the corner.

As he rounded the corner he was horrified to see a group of the market traders huddled around the hydroride, examining it admiringly. No one in the crowd could afford such a ride; they made do with horse-drawn carriages. Indeed, hardly anybody in the city ever bothered with private vehicles; there was no need. Public transport was efficient, comfortable and cheap. Besides, few people ever felt the need to rush anywhere.

He ran forward shouting at them to step away, the authority in his voice causing them to fall back without question, but one elderly man was too slow and Grey shoved him roughly aside. The man stumbled and fell forward, and the other bystanders immediately bent to his aid.

Grey leapt astride the saddle, the palm print recognition technology in the handlebars instantly recognising him. The engine started immediately. Before anyone could stop him he was already gone. The hydroride cornered well on the cobbled road and he sped off, zigzagging round pedestrians and carts.

Lonce ran after him, following the smell and the energy trace of his prey, relying on intuition to interpret the information he was receiving from his senses.

My prey leaves few tracks. No footprints. Smells disguised. The road, between tall buildings, gives no clear sight. My body pulled by ghostly trail; I am connected to the man I hunt. I follow, but never fast enough. I run without pause. I run until I can run no more. My wounds pull and ache; blood seeping, stitches pulling apart. Breathing hard now. I fail. My prey rides something I not recognise. He is too fast for me.

CHAPTER 20

"What were you thinking?" Seb whispered to his unconscious friend as he carried her gently to her bedroom. "Why did you leave us there? You could have woken me; I wouldn't have minded. I woke up and you'd gone. Lonce was fast asleep, you didn't even wake him. Oh, Flo, what's going on?" As he laid her on the bed he kissed her head again and covered her with a blanket, then went back to the living room to call George. The door to the apartment was open and a number of concerned neighbours kept popping in to see what all the commotion was about. It was all Seb could do to keep them from bustling into Flo's room to check on her themselves.

He was still waiting anxiously for George or the Guardia to turn up when a medico arrived. Seb was still cross with Flo for leaving the cabin without telling him and filled with intense hatred for whoever had done this to her, so he greeted the medico rudely.

The young doctor took one long look at Flo and ordered Seb into the kitchen.

"Get some hot water going, and if she has any cabbage, shred some and put it on to boil."

"Why?" demanded Seb, angry at being excluded from her bedside. "What are you going to do, have dinner with her?"

"Just get on with it. I don't have all day," snapped the medico before leaning over Flo and rousing her gently. He opened his bag of emergency rescue remedies. “Don’t worry, my dear,” he said, using his professional voice. “You’re safe. I’m just disinfecting your scratches, so it might sting a bit. That’s perfectly normal.” He started to work on the worst of the injuries and Flo winced.

A few minutes later Seb peered round the bedroom door, concern for his friend written all over his face.

“What shall I do with the cabbage? It’s pretty soft now.”

“Nothing. Keep it for supper. I just wanted you out of the way while I assessed her.” The medico grinned at Seb. Seb glared back at him. Turning back to Flo, the medico said, “There. That made you smile. You’ll be all right, my dear. No permanent damage done. You might feel a little discomfort while I put a poultice on your neck for the bruising.” She flinched. The medico spoke into his Perd, describing her condition and listing his treatment. He spoke in such a quiet monotone that Flo drifted off to sleep again. “Patient’s eyes bloodshot – treated with rosewater eyewash. Recommend repeated applications, every four hours. Self-inflicted lacerations and scratches on throat disinfected with mild solution of tea-tree. Severe bruising caused by near strangulation of patient by an unknown assailant – bruising on neck and upper torso treated with arnica. Green clay poultice on throat.”

Turning once more to Seb, he said, “Try to get her to use her Perd.” Seb looked puzzled. “It’ll help with the psychological trauma. She should talk into it about what’s happened and how she feels and so on. Describing the events will give her some distance, which I believe will be beneficial. Call me any time if you need me again. Do reassure her she's a very lucky girl and she'll be fine."

Sometime later, when she awoke, Flo could hear people talking and moving quietly about the apartment.

"Make sure you take a couple of swabs from the leopard's claws," someone said. "I hear he got a good swipe at the burglar."

"One of my men is doing it now."

It all seemed a long, long way away. Flo drifted off again. When she finally woke it was late afternoon and she found George and Lonce sitting at her side. George was smiling, but he couldn't hide the anxiety in his eyes.

"The Guardia were very thorough," he said. "They spent at least two hours photo-imaging things, fingerprinting everywhere and interviewing all your neighbours." Flo croaked feebly. He patted her hand. "Shh. Don't try to talk. The medico says you need to rest your throat. Lonce did his best to follow the intruder, but the bastard had a hydroride and was too fast for poor Lonce. He still isn't back up to form after his injuries, so I think you need to reassure him a bit. He's feeling very cross with himself." Lonce refused to catch her eye, but sat next to her, head bowed. She reached out a hand to stroke his neck.

"There's a film of black fingerprint dust over practically every surface," George went on. "Not that you'd notice, of course, given that you are congenitally untidy." More seriously, he added, "I thought you'd like to know that all your neighbours tried their best to be helpful, but most of them were too slow. Seb and Lonce beat them to it." He helped Flo sit up in bed and gently placed a shawl around her shoulders. "When I got here the neighbours were all standing around in their pyjamas, eager to answer the Guardia's questions. The only one who actually tried to do anything at all was the woman next door." George laughed. "Apparently she made a valiant attempt to stop him by throwing something at him as he ran past. Luckily for her she missed or he might have rounded on her too." Flo made a mental note to thank the woman as soon as possible. "You'll never believe what she said to the Guardia. She said she'd been worried about being bored once she'd retired. But apparently it's the most excitement she's had for years! Can you believe it?" Still smiling, George turned and beckoned to Seb, who had been hanging around anxiously waiting for her to awake. "Seb, come here. She can't talk yet, so you'll have to wait for her explanation for leaving you and Lonce in the woods."

"That's all right, George. She doesn't need to explain. She was just being her old annoying self."

CHAPTER 21

Flo was safe, but she wasn't at peace. Far from it. Apart from a few scraps here and there, virtually all her mother's research had been utterly destroyed, along with her Perd. Some blackened curls of paper in the fireplace were all that remained of the written notes, while everything else in the living room had simply been trashed. To Flo this implied it wasn't a simple burglary. She stayed in bed and felt sorry for herself. Her throat ached, and the scratches stung.

George, Seb and Lonce took it in turns to check up on her while quietly tidying up the apartment. No one mentioned the loss of her mother's work. She could hear the comforting noises as they shifted things around, sweeping up broken glass and talking in low voices, but she didn't want to leave her bed to join them. She didn't even want to mind-share. She gulped down the sleeping draught which the medico had left at her bedside and drifted immediately into a dreamless sleep.

"How are you feeling?" George asked, when she emerged from her bedroom two days later.

"Fine. Don't need this." Her voice was barely recognisable and she tugged at the poultice the medic had strapped on.

"No, sorry, you're stuck with that for another day or so," George said. "I don't envy you – I don't know what was in it but it smells as though something wrapped itself around your neck and died there a month ago."

"It did."

She padded round the apartment in her slippers. She had to hand it to George and Seb: they'd done a fantastic job of tidying up. They'd found other cushions for the sofa and chairs somewhere, and thrown a colourful cloth over the sofa to disguise the mismatched patterns. All the broken objects had been removed, and her father's paintings, at least the undamaged ones, were back on the walls. She gently took them down again.

"Don't you want your father's paintings?" George asked. "I've sent the others off to a restorer I know. If anyone can save them, he can."

"Time for a change." Speech was still painful for her and she was quickly getting into the habit of placing a hand protectively across her throat. "Put them in storage."

He nodded, patting her arm. "By the way," he said, "a couple of things happened while you were asleep. First, I had a chance to talk to an old friend of mine in the Guardia who, it turns out, is in charge of this case. Given that only things directly connected to your mother's research were totally destroyed, Dante agrees it seems likely this was no ordinary burglary." She rolled her eyes. "I know, Flo, I know. Everyone is taking it very seriously and they will be checking up on the fingerprints and genetic samples as fast as possible. I don't know about these things, and I couldn't tell if my friend Dante was optimistic or not. You know how unreadable these Guardia chaps are. He did say they don't have many prints or DNA details on file. After all, there isn't really that much crime around. A lot depends on whether your intruder's got a criminal record or not. He said they'd let us know tomorrow." Flo nodded, and then held up two fingers.

"Ah yes, thanks for reminding me. Your history teacher, Miss Pugh, called a couple of times. She seems very concerned. My teachers were never so worried about me when I was a boy. She's remarkably persistent in some ways. She's clearly very fond of you. It was all I could do to prevent her rushing over to see you."

Flo groaned. Miss Pugh's persistence was getting too much.

CHAPTER 22

As any sensible person could have predicted, the Guardia came back with the test results several days later, not by their promised 'following day'. K9 Officer Dante explained that there had been no prints left by the attacker, but the DNA material taken from Lonce's claws matched a man who had been arrested, and rapidly released, some years before.

His name's Harold Grey. He was picked up in connection with a terrorist attack ten years ago, said Dante through a clear and precise mind transfer. *However, we have a problem, George. My assistant and I have looked through all the records we have in connection with Grey, and I admit I'm a bit puzzled. It looks as if the evidence is definitely pointing to him, but word has come down to us from above to let it drop. Someone in the human branch of the hierarchy is busy pulling my tail, and I'm beginning to suspect some funny business was going on at the time of the original arrest too.* He shook his head with exasperation. *Between you and me, it smells rotten, but my paws are tied. My entire team has received word to let this one slide.* Although mind-sharing, he nevertheless leaned closer to George in an irrelevant gesture towards privacy. *To my mind, it suggests HSL interference. The force has been compromised from within.*

"Surely not?" George said. "I don't believe it. That's only your opinion."

Not believing me isn't going to make it any less true, said Dante patiently. *I've done as much digging as I can without setting off departmental alarm bells. My colleagues, humans I've known for years and trust completely, have been helping. As long as he stays out of trouble, or at least doesn't get caught, we can't touch Grey and he can go about his business as usual.*

"And what exactly is his business?" asked George quietly.

After Dante took his leave, George stood up slowly and made his way back into Flo's bedroom. He had a lot to think about, and as he looked down at Flo's sleeping form he was grateful she had missed the K9 officer's visit. Behind him, in the living room, Lonce emerged from his favourite snooze spot underneath a cloth-covered side table and padded silently away in search of Seb.

CHAPTER 23

"The key is Rosendale." Flo's voice still croaked slightly.

"Where is Rosendale, anyway?" Seb asked. They were poring over the information provided by Lonce's inadvertent eavesdropping the day before.

"Don't know exactly. George said it was an outlying island in the north-east." She grabbed a battered map of the New British Archipelago.

"Ah, we're screwed. Look where it is," said Seb, looking over her shoulder. "It'll take at least a day to get there."

"I don't care how far it is. We're going. If you imagine I'm going to miss a chance to get even with my parents' killers, you've got another think coming!"

"Okay, okay, I know. Calm down. This talk of killers and revenge is getting a bit much, you know." He looked away, and muttered under his breath, "You're also assuming they killed your parents."

"Don't tell me to calm down," she snapped. "You still owe me an apology."

"What for?"

"For not taking the dreams seriously."

"I'm sorry, then. But how about you apologise to me?"

"What do I have to apologise for?"

"For sneaking off and coming back here alone."

"Fair enough. I apologise. Now what do we do?"

They both stared at the map, willing it to yield a solution. Flo had assumed this would be a New Era-London-based investigation, but now, whether she liked it or not, a trip to Rosendale was needed. As they stood there, momentarily at a loss, Seb put his arm around her shoulders and gave her a friendly squeeze.

"Maybe we need to rethink this before we charge off around the archipelago. Talk to George, get him and the authorities involved."

"Didn't you understand what Lonce overheard? We're on our own. We can't trust anyone." She turned to him with a confident smile. "But don't worry, I'll think of something."

A few days later, Flo was back at school. She found Seb staring at a piece of paper he'd just picked up off the floor. All of a sudden he laughed out loud.

"You're not going to believe this," he said. "Talk about synchronicity."

Flo tried to read over his shoulder. "What? Where did that come from?"

"Don't know. I found it on the floor. It's one hell of a coincidence. I was about to throw it in the recycling bin. Someone must have dropped it."

The flyer proudly announced the chance to win a holiday by entering a competition. *Want a Holiday Filled with Action, Excitement and Adventure? Camp Rosendale offers a huge range of adventure and learning activities, team sports, climbing, orienteering and swimming. It is the perfect place for young men to forge new friendships and enjoy new experiences in a safe, controlled environment. Call: 67.04.69.8 for your application form.*

"So this is what Lonce overheard the K9 officer tell George about. Now it makes sense. It's a holiday camp."

"Yup, it is. Look. And it certainly goes a long way to solving the logistical problems of investigating Rosendale. Well, for you at least. I'll have to make my own way there." She found it hard to hide the resentment in her voice. He looked sharply at her.

"What do you mean?"

"Read the small print, numbnut. It says 'Due to limited facilities, the competition is only open to male humans.' See? They are holding a series of tournaments all over the archipelago. Winners from each location get a free place. It's all right though. We don't need to travel up together. Lonce and I can come up and join you later."

"But," he said slowly, "I might not win."

"Of course you'll win. Why wouldn't you? You're the fittest boy in the school. You do all those races, swimming competitions and things." Her enthusiasm was almost catching.

"Yes, but…" She could see him thinking it through and getting more excited by the minute.

"You've got all those medals and cups at home, remember? You didn't win them for staying at home knitting, did you?"

"I suppose I might have a chance." He smiled hesitantly. "It's got to be worth a shot, I suppose."

"Only thing is though, Seb, you can't enter the competition as you. Your parents are too well known."

"You're right. That's that then."

"Don't be silly. We just have to make you into someone else."

"How?"

CHAPTER 24

New Era-London, Guardia Station, Interrogation Room 5
Witness Statement 1.2 of Melissa Gryfe née Harcourt
Species: Human
Sex: Female
Affair: Rosendale
Signed in the presence of K9 Officer Dante.
Tuesday 2 August

Are you ready, Melissa? asked Dante. He was still treading carefully. She'd been through a lot already.

"I'm fine. Let's get on with it." Melissa sounded more in control than she had at their last session. She nodded to the junior human officer to indicate she was ready to be recorded, and started speaking immediately. "I no longer knew exactly what my husband thought or what he did, and I suspected he was keeping things from me. He'd always been wonderfully predictable, and he still spent Friday evenings drinking with my father in his den. But something must have subtly changed, because I noticed him more. You know how you can live with the same picture on the wall for years, and barely notice it until it hangs crooked."

Dante gave a non-committal grunt. *Melissa, you've told me already you were aware of what people were saying about the HSL being a terrorist organisation.*

"As I told you," she snapped, "as far as I was concerned it was all nonsense. The HSL was just a bunch of people with too much time on their hands. They were certainly no threat to society. They weren't even recognised as a real political party. It was simply that the Coalition had no opposition to blame, so they used the HSL as a scapegoat for their problems. Marcus would come home on Fridays full of rabble-rousing talk. Between him and my father, they'd come up with various ideas to change the world, ranging from staging theatrical protests and rallies to kidnapping strategic Coalition members."

Really? Dante was once more on alert.

"Of course, I didn't take anything he said too seriously. It was all testosterone and alcohol-fuelled big cigar talk and I didn't think either he or my father would really get involved with anything illegal or violent. They were manipulators, both of them, not action men."

But we now know there was some action going on, don't we, Melissa? What can you tell me about that?

"Marcus came up with the idea of summer camps on Rosendale. These soon became very popular, and were ideal for fundraising too. Supporters paid astronomical fees for the privilege of sending their children to camp to experience Spartan conditions."

Anything else?

"Practical lessons in survival and outdoor pursuits, I was told. I had no reason to think otherwise. Several of our friends sent their sons there and it seemed overall to be beneficial to the boys."

Were the camps only open to HSL supporters? Surely there aren't enough non-comm boys of the right age to make the camp viable?

"It offered alternative dates for Comms and Non-Comms, so it was always busy. It even gave free places to boys of particular physical ability, who couldn't afford to go otherwise."

I see. Now, apart from Marcus and your father, who was involved?

"I never met any of them in person. But one night Marcus asked me to bring some more brandy into the den and then he more or less ordered me to bed. He had friends arriving. But I loitered on the landing in order to get a glimpse of these so-called friends. Two men I'd never seen before arrived, so I hid in the shadows and watched. They were obviously military types, all taut, uptight and anal by the look of it. They saluted him. I nearly gave myself away by choking. Why would they salute him? How ridiculous. Marcus looked as though he'd burst with excitement. Then they all went to join my father in the study. I heard my father's voice welcome them. He called them Black and Blue, or some other silly made-up names."

They were Captain Grey and Sergeant Blue. We know all about them. Did you have contact with anyone else?

"One day we were due to entertain a group of elderly supporters as well as a controversial HSL figure. I spent the day receiving deliveries of contraband meat, cooking, and generally making sure everything was ready for the evening. Throughout the morning, Marcus prepared his notes for the manifesto which he wanted to present that evening. It was about raising the HSL from a group of simple Non-Comms who grumbled in secret to being a real contender for power; a political party to rival the Coalition.

Who was the controversial figure, you mentioned?

"Lewis Greenback, one of the leading lights in the HSL movement."

Ah, Greenback. Dante knew the name. Greenback had been hauled up in front of a Coalition board of inquiry for famously claiming there was a persistent gap between non-human and human intelligence. It was a well-known case, but Dante had always been puzzled why he'd been treated so leniently by the authorities.

Melissa was still talking. "The dinner seemed to go well but I couldn't really relax and enjoy it. We never hired waiters for HSL dinners, as you couldn't count on their discretion, so I was constantly leaving my seat to serve or clear courses. Occasionally I heard Greenback making some remark. He liked the sound of his own voice and laughed at his own jokes. I hated his laugh. 'Fhwarh, fhwarh, fhwarh.'

What sort of things was he saying?

"That no other mammals are as smart as we are and so on," she muttered, clearly embarrassed by saying this to a senior canine officer. Dante was impassive. "He also said the HSL had no quarrel with mammals as long as they didn't interfere in government or try to influence national affairs."

Hmm, is that so? What about the rest of the evening? Is there anything else which sticks in your mind?

"Greenback didn't give my husband a chance to present his manifesto publicly. That upset Marcus a lot. I think he was worried Greenback was going to claim credit for his ideas later."

What was in your husband's notes? What was this manifesto?

"I'd never seen it before. He gave it to me before going up to bed. I clutched the papers so tightly I scrunched them a bit on one side, so I put them on the table and started to smooth them out with my hands, glancing through them as I went. There didn't appear to be anything new; it was the same old stuff I'd been hearing about for years."

Like?

"Marcus wanted to change the language we use. He wanted to reintroduce the terms human beings and animals. He was proposing a new Bill of Rights which limited civil liberties to human beings only. He proposed that human-only culture, history and traditions be taught at schools…"

Dante couldn't help himself. He barked.

"But there was more," Melissa went on. "Horrible stuff. As I turned the page I read something which made me realise I no longer knew the man I was married to. In his last paragraph he had linked us all to something so terrible it made my blood run cold."

CHAPTER 25

Early April

"What are you up to? You should be out training!" Flo was indignant. She'd barged into Seb's bedroom expecting him to be doing press-ups or something.

"Hmmm, remind me to put a lock on my door," he replied. "Funny how weeks can go past when nothing much happens, then all of a sudden everything is full on. We were so caught up in our plans to get me to Rosendale, I nearly forgot to hand in my application for the Crafts Academy."

"I'm sorry, Seb, that was rude of me. I didn't think."

"Stop being sarcastic. I love you, Flo, but,"

"You love me? Now who's being sarcastic?"

"Stop being stupid," he snapped. He was getting cross.

"If you insist. Anyway, you'll be fine. I heard your metalwork teacher has promised to sponsor your application."

"Maybe if you'd leave me alone, I could finish it before I do the damn challenge thing next week and go running round the archipelago like a spy."

"Sorry, Seb." She put her hands up in surrender and backed out of the room, already planning how to persuade him to agree to her idea their next move. It involved identity theft, and she suspected it would take them a while to agree how this should be achieved.

When Flo knocked on George's door the next day her guardian seemed delighted to see her. She hadn't seen him for a while and she suspected he'd been deliberately keeping a low profile during her latest bad mood. She hoped an offering from their favourite bakery would make up for it.

"Ha-ha. Do you really think you can win me over so easily? After your recent behaviour I deserve at least an entire cake," he said, stepping back to let her through. As she passed him she leaned forward and planted a kiss on his cheek.

"Out of my way, old man. I've come to apologise to you, but I need something to drink first." She preceded him into the kitchen; her plan was to keep him in there rather than in the living room, where the corridor to the office was clearly visible.

"What are you doing tonight?" he asked her, as he filled the kettle. "I have to take some colleagues from the New Americas to the theatre… you know the sort of thing, dinner and a show. I wondered whether you'd like to tag along." He carried on chatting as he pottered about the kitchen preparing their drinks and finding a suitable platter for the cookies.

The beginning of a new plan started to form in her mind.

"No thanks, George. Seb and I are doing something. So what are you going to see? Are you having dinner before or after the show? And who are these New Americans anyway?"

"Oh, they're a lively bunch who work in the National Archives at Bluefield on Grand Columbus Island. I hope to introduce you to them sometime. In fact, while we're talking about it, I was considering going out there next year to see how they get things done, but, given they are closer to your age than mine, perhaps you should go in my place. What do you think? Next year, once you've graduated school?"

"I'm not sure what I'm planning to do yet. I know you'd like me to work with you, like mum did, but I don't know..."

"Don't worry about it now," George said quickly, cutting her off. "I was thinking out loud really. Anyway, I still have to get through this evening. I expect they'll have boundless energy. You know what New Americans are like. Big, expansive personalities, you know the sort. It'll exhaust me, although it'll also be fascinating to meet them at last. I've been corresponding for a couple of years with the head of the archives. She's got some interesting thoughts about the damage wreaked on the entire New American psyche by the Siklus."

"What do you mean?"

"Well, self-blame seems to have had a devastating effect on the national identity. I get the impression that prior to the Siklus they had all been a bit too proud of themselves and their achievements; a bit too reliant on technology and industry; too many vested interests to bother with the state of the environment. I'm sure they still teach you that in school.

"Yeah, we've studied the old Americas quite a bit, particularly last year."

"Anyway, the Siklus put paid to dependence on technology. But the collective guilt trip lasted for decades, despite a small movement to blame everything on Old China." He paused long enough to arrange the cookies on the platter. "But you can't keep people like that down for long. They went on to embrace the new world order like no one else. They've managed to transition quite smoothly. It really is impressive. Honestly, what they've done in the last hundred or so years is unbelievable. Their history of inter-species cooperation is phenomenal. Most of their cities were destroyed, entire states disappeared." He paused again and then changed the subject. "Anyway, I thought a show followed by a late dinner. The show is something or other, I don't really know. It had good reviews in the *Gazette.*"

"You just don't want them to know you are an old fuddy-duddy. So what time do you think you'll dump them and come back here to bed?"

"It isn't a question of dumping them, you know. But I think I could reasonably bow out at about one a.m. be in bed by half past."

"Talk about living dangerously, George. So what time does the show start?" With any luck she'd have hours to search his files.

"Well," he said, thinking out loud, "I have a few things to do before the show. I guess I'll leave here at about six-thirty and do what I have to do before meeting them at their hotel. Show starts at eight… should be a jolly nice evening."

The water was boiling and the cookies looked enticing. The revised plan was clear in her mind, and now she was ready to talk about some of the other stuff which had been bothering her. There was no point in alerting him to the fact that she was still angry about her mother's research. It was better all round if he believed she'd dropped the whole subject.

She sat down opposite him and rested her chin on her hand, elbow firmly on the table.

"I'm so sorry if I've been weird, George. I guess I was having what you used to call 'anger issues'. The burglary really threw me for a while. But I feel better now."

"It has been a strange time for us both, I think."

"I miss my parents so much. Do you think they know what I'm doing now? How I've turned out? Do we stay connected after death?" She didn't give him the chance to respond. "I feel connected to my mum. Especially now, with these dreams…" She stood up and moved restlessly around the kitchen before sitting down again. George sat there in silence, watching her.

"Why do you think Grey broke into my apartment that day?" she said suddenly. George raised his eyebrows. "I mean, we're all agreed it looks like he was targeting my mother's work and he'd been involved in her death, aren't we?"

"Maybe," he said slowly. "Go on." She could see him struggling to look non-committal. She recognised the symptoms - the shuffling in his seat and the refusal to meet her eyes - as signs he was trying to hide something.

"So why now? Why me? Why after all this time? Was the bombardment the other day something to do with me, Lonce, my mum's work, or what?"

"Who knows what goes on in the tiny, warped minds of people like that of terrorists? They have no logic or humanity. We'll never understand the motivation or the timing. Have you spoken to anyone about anything we've discussed?"

"No, just you and Seb. I might have said something to Miss Pugh some time before the burglary, but she's a teacher, she doesn't really count. Of course, the other night at the cabin with my friends from school we all discussed our nightmares, but the attack at my apartment happened the following morning. No one had the chance to pass on information about me, if that's what you're implying."

"You're right. Perhaps it is just all coincidence."

"But you know as well as I do there is no such thing, George."

They both jumped at the sound of the doorbell, but it was George who went to answer it. Seb stood shivering on the doorstep, looking slightly sheepish with his new haircut. It took George a moment to recognise him, and he'd been so caught up in the conversation with Flo that he forgot his manners.

"Good grief, Seb, what on earth have you done to yourself? I wonder what your parents will think of it."

"Hi, George. I had it done this morning. Actually, I was looking for Flo. Is she here? May I come in?"

"Sure, sure. Sorry. Come in. Flo's in the kitchen."

When she heard Seb's voice, Flo relaxed.

"Oh my goodness, you look amazing!" She rushed over to rub his head. "I've never seen you with such short hair! Oh, wow! I can't get over it. George, George, doesn't he look amazing!"

“He’s certainly unrecognisable,” said George hesitantly. “His own mother would have difficulty.”

“Come on then, Seb. You can walk me home.”

To his credit, Seb took the change to their agreed script in his stride. “Well, that was the plan, wasn’t it, Flo?” He smiled at her sweetly.

“So, when were you going to tell me you’d changed the plan?” Seb asked, once they’d got outside. She clapped her hands enthusiastically.

“Let me tell you my new idea.”

CHAPTER 26

Flo, Seb and Lonce stood outside George's building. They were all feeling uncomfortable about what they were about to do.

"You said this was going to be fun," Seb said. Lonce looked from one to the other. The renewed tension between his two friends made the big cat uncomfortable, so he feigned sudden interest in the general state of his claws.

"Well, in a manner of speaking, it is. Sort of," she answered. "Besides, what alternative do we have?"

"For a start, we could have told George everything about our plans and asked him to help us."

Flo gave him one of her most withering looks. "How would that have gone down, do you think?" Seb opened his mouth to speak, but she held up her hand to stop him. "Seb, this is stupid. Let's not fight. I'm sorry. But this is a much better way, you'll see. This is the best way. Come on, don't be a numbnut. You just don't like it because I changed the plan without consulting you. I thought you'd be pleased. This is what you wanted." She pulled out a set of keys from her pocket. "I can't do this without you. Will you please help me?"

Seb continued to look stern until his good nature overcame his anger. He shrugged and his mouth broke into a broad grin. "Come on then, let's get on with it. It's getting cold and we're wasting time. We've only got until one." He turned to Lonce. "Are you ready, Lonce? Get into lookout position." Lonce turned and bounded off. Within seconds he had completely disappeared from view.

As soon as Lonce had gone, Flo and Seb headed into the building and up the stairs to George's floor.

"Are you sure he's out?" Seb whispered.

"He should have left by now." Flo tried listening at George's door. "I can't hear anything, so I guess he's gone."

"There's only one way to be sure." Seb pressed hard and long on George's doorbell. No answer. Flo opened the door and turned on the lights, calling out George's name. They couldn't take any chances. The apartment entrance opened straight into his large, comfortable living room, with the kitchen and both bedrooms leading off it. But the office itself was housed in what had once been three other bedrooms, and was separated from the heart of the apartment by a long book-lined corridor. They shut the door behind them and stepped in.

"I don't know about you," said Seb, "but I think this is weird."

"Yeah, I know what you mean. I've known this place all my life, so I don't really see it any more. Now I'm a burglar, it looks quite different." She headed straight to the kitchen. "Normally he keeps his office keys in this pot." She picked up a simple pre-Siklus white bowl. The potter's name was embossed on the bottom: IKEA. "I always tell him to use something less valuable for his keys, but he never listens." She replaced the bowl gently on the counter and they headed together down the corridor to the office.

Once in they turned on the lights and went straight to the cabinets which contained the paper records. The majority of George's files were kept with the rest of the archives in the basement; he only kept the data he was still working on in this room. 'Politics', 'Business', 'Technology', 'Development' and 'People' each had its own section, and they quickly found the drawers containing details of the characters George came across during his broader research of pre-Siklus life.

As they flicked quickly through the files they found themselves drawn into the stories of these long dead individuals, preserved for posterity in George's meticulously ordered archive. Every few minutes one of them would stop their search in order to read more, until Flo caught sight of the clock on George's desk.

"Look, it's already half past ten. We need to get a move on. At this rate we'll be here to welcome George back from his night on the town. Just grab anything suitable. We can alter the details from home, rather than waste time here. You won't be able to use the card anyway without making a few changes."

"We only need to find a youngish man, then," said Seb. "If we're going to do all the real changes from home we can pick anyone."

"You're right. I was hoping for a perfect match. We'll take the next file which comes out male under the age of twenty. Agreed?"

"Race you," he answered as he grabbed one. "Look, this one was way under twenty. Oh," Seb put the file back hastily. "He was just a little kid when he died."

Flo could feel she was getting irritated again so quickly took a deep breath and pulled out another file. This was the one, the mother lode. Timothy Richard Watts had been nineteen years old when he died. He'd had two sisters called Merissa and Carolyn and his parents were Paula and Terry. Like Seb, he'd been a keen swimmer, and both boys had the musculature of people who spent a lot of time in the water. There were assorted newspaper articles about his brief swimming career. He had short light brown hair and a wide smile, not unlike Seb at all. Finding this card was serendipitous.

"Seb, prepare to be amazed. No need to alter any details apart from the date of birth."

They stood together reading the papers. Seb shivered. "He even looks like me."

Suddenly they both caught Lonce's mind-call, from his position outside in the street.

He returning. He will open door soon.

"Which door, Lonce?" Flo and Seb asked simultaneously. "The one on the street or the one to the flat?" They stuffed files hastily back and slammed the drawers shut. Clutching only Timothy's file, they fled the room. Seb hit the light switch and Flo quickly locked the door. "Which door, Lonce? Answer us!"

In street, in street. He returning with other people. He going in now. I see them. Waiting for elevation box.

"Quick, Flo, he's coming up. Put the keys back and let's get out of here!"

As Flo dropped the bunch of keys into the bowl she heard an ominous clink as the metal keys struck the porcelain and chipped it. A sliver of glaze lay on the table. She spat on her finger, dropped a little saliva on to the broken edge of the rim, and tried to balance the missing part back in place. It fell off.

"Flo, I can hear the lift!" called Seb. She tried again. "Flo, hurry up! What are you doing?" Her hands were shaking; the urgency in Seb's voice was throwing off her concentration.

"I'm coming. Hang on." She tried one last time. The chip of glaze stayed on the rim, held temporarily by her improvised glue, and she hoped it would balance there until George next touched it. Then perhaps when it fell off again he'd blame himself. Then she turned and followed Seb out of the apartment, switching the lights off as she left. The door was self-locking so they ran directly to the stairwell. The door had just shut behind them when they heard the lift doors open and the sound of cheerful voices.

Flo and Seb tumbled, giggling, out of George's building and looked round for Lonce. At the corner they glimpsed movement, but it seemed to be just someone returning home from a night out. A second later Lonce bounded up and licked Flo's hand, before roughly nudging Seb in the thigh.

"Phew!" said Seb. "I'm glad that's over. We could have done with a bit more warning though, Lonce. What happened?"

Distracted by someone in street. Sorry. Gone now.

"Listen, George and his friends might come out again, so let's head home," said Flo. "Seb, I'll see you tomorrow. Come on, Lonce. That's enough excitement for one night." She turned to go, then stopped and turned to Seb. “Thanks, Seb. I couldn’t have done it without you. Night.”

“Night, Flo. Sleep well – if you can.”

CHAPTER 27

Rosendale, April

Walking around the laboratory, Professor Ulrich Feldman was feeling particularly positive. He had a plan. His many years of preparation were soon going to pay off. He would assume the ancient scientific throne once occupied by such heroes as Fulton, Moniz, Freeman and Watt. He smiled. His mother would have been so proud.

Before arriving on the island, he'd read up on the location of the new lab. *His* new lab, he thought happily. The building itself was so ancient it gave the whole enterprise cachet, and he was delighted to have been chosen to head the team of scientists and genetic engineers. Jeremy Bentham himself would have been proud too. To know that the prison he'd designed back in pre-Siklus times was still in use today. Ulrich chuckled. The telepaths liked recycling and upgrading things, didn't they? What could be better than this, turning an ancient prison into a centre of learning and science?

The layout of the Panopticon was perfect. Bentham certainly knew his stuff. Every cell in the doughnut-shaped building was overlooked twenty-four hours a day by observers in the central tower. Ulrich could monitor the behavior of his test subjects. He could wake them when they nodded off, check what and when they ate, and note when they defecated. He'd know if they tried to communicate with each other, physically or mentally. He could punish them. Mammals could be sneaky and he wouldn't put it past them to fake certain behavior in a naïve attempt to stop the experiments. A slow mirthless smile spread across his face and he shrugged. Sooner or later they'd forget he could see them and they'd show their true natures.

Of course, until he could get his hands on better, he'd have to make do with archaic equipment. That was one of his main frustrations. It was making his work far trickier than necessary. While not as old as the building itself He supposed the scientists at the government facilities had state of the art apparatus, while he had to make do. Without decent results, Gryfe wouldn't open the HSL coffers. Above all, Ulrich had set his heart on an expensive new scanner. Still, he wasn't going to let it drag him down. He had a large enough supply of specimens for the procedure. Some of them were bound to give him decent result. It was just a matter of working through them methodically.

The latest subjects were primed and ready. Earlier experiments on rabbits, cats, dogs, and most recently a couple of rhesus monkeys, had been promising and the odds were getting better each day. But if he were honest, the size of their skulls made accuracy a little hit and miss. He laughed to himself. He'd have to remember that when making his presentation to Gryfe. How often does a man get to make jokes about an ice pick, an eye socket and a mallet?

That's why he was looking forward to working on the chimp. She was bigger all round than the other primates. Size would count. Getting the pick through the thin bone that separated the eyes from the frontal lobe was easy enough, but wiggling it around to sever connections in the brain was a little trickier.

But the chimp was a troublemaker. That morning she'd bitten several of the technician's fingers clean off. A shame, really; the lad had been a good worker. Perhaps he'd go light on the anesthetic just to teach the chimp a lesson. No, even he couldn't bring himself to be quite that heartless. She had almost human eyes. It would be very disconcerting.

he was nervous, particularly when his winner's voucher actually arrived. It turned out he had to state whether he was a Non-Comm or a telepath. A sub-clause explained that because of the nature of some activities, segregation was inevitable. Different dates were available to each group of boys.

Under Flo's watchful eyes Seb marked himself down as a Non-Comm.

"I bet they secretly support the HSL. For all we know they're building an army," he grumbled. Flo was feeling unaccountably cheerful and tried teasing to lighten his mood.

"Have you heard the rumours?" she said in an overly theatrical whisper. "It's going round school that the boys come back changed."

"Do they come back with three nipples?" Seb whispered back, clutching his chest and pretending to be worried.

Flo laughed. "Well, that would certainly take a bit of explaining in the changing rooms."

"Hmm," Seb said, suddenly serious. "As I said, maybe they are building an army."

"Well, if they are, we'll stop them!"

CHAPTER 29

The day of departure arrived. Seb had been adamant that he didn't want Flo coming to the station with him, so they said their farewells the night before. Even in a city with a population of over ninety thousand, there was bound to be someone who recognised Flo, and anyone knowing Flo would be aware of her long-term friendship with Seb, so they couldn't afford to be seen together.

Seb was still feeling apprehensive as he made his way to the station. His naturally optimistic nature had taken some hits recently. He'd been practising his own form of mind control on himself ever since Flo had finished the ID card, and repeated his new details to himself several times a day. "My name is Timothy Richard Watts. My parents are Paula and Terry Watts and I have two sisters, Merissa and Carolyn." He plodded through the bustling concourse towards his platform, wondering for the tenth time how he'd let himself get involved. The new security protocols had made the simple act of catching a train extremely time consuming and for once he was pleased that he'd arrived with nearly an hour to spare.

He could see hastily erected barriers at the entrance to each platform and queues of people already waiting to go through them. Most had papers at the ready and these were being checked and double-checked by human and dog officers. At the sight of the dogs, Seb's palms began to sweat. Was it his imagination or were they taking particular care with the passengers in the line ahead of him? A couple of people were roughly hauled out of the queue and marched off towards a waiting carriage, their hands bound behind them. To Seb's eyes their treatment looked excessively rough, and he found himself speculating about what they'd done and what was going to happen to them now. Coalition authorities were not usually known for their aggression, so this new behaviour made him feel uncomfortable. The line moved slowly forward and he shuffled along nervously with it.

It was crazy. He'd never seen anything like this. As if answering his thoughts, a man behind him said suddenly and rather huffily, "I mean, seriously, I doubt very much this is going to do any good. No terrorist is going to get caught this way. What a waste of public money."

There were only a few people in front of Seb now. He pulled his papers out of his pocket and checked them again. It was a perfectly good ID for someone called Timothy Richard Watts, and certainly looked authentic enough. He checked his other pocket, but as he pulled out the ticket, the ID slipped from his fingers and fluttered to the floor. The man behind him bent down quickly and picked it up with slightly trembling hands.

"Not a good day to lose this, lad. You'll need to show it in a minute. The authorities are being a little too zealous if you ask me; carting anyone off they don't like the look of." Seb swallowed and silently cursed Flo and her hare-brained schemes. This really wasn't going to work. "Come on, lad, stop dreaming. Move along. The train will go without us." The man nudged Seb forward a little too roughly.

He felt sick. The dogs would smell more than fear at this rate. In any case, they'd read his mind. Seb looked up into the stern face of the officer. He gulped, silently repeating the mantra of his new name. But the guard wasn't interested in him. He was focused on something else. Seb turned his head and followed the guard's line of vision. For some reason, the man behind Seb, who had been so keen to board the train, had pushed other passengers out of his way and broken into a run. He only managed a few paces before the dogs brought him down and subdued him. Another human guard joined them to take the man away.

"Papers, please, sir," said the guard at the queue, but he was distracted by the scene taking place a few feet away and barely looked at Seb's ID. "Thank you, sir. Move right along the platform now, please, sir."

And with that, to his surprise, Seb was through.

Flo had decided to follow Seb. She wanted to make sure he got off all right and found herself feeling a little apprehensive about their whole scheme.

There was all the usual noise, smell and bustle of a busy station, which served both goods and passenger trains. Carts and hydrotrucks wove through the throngs of passengers. Flo found herself a comfortable spot on a raised viewing gallery from where she could see most of the activity. Almost directly below her she could make out Seb in front of the entrance to his platform. His coat collar was turned up high, and his shoulders were hunched as he shuffled forward in the queue. She frowned. Even at this distance she could tell he looked guilty of something. She wanted to tell him to relax. He was supposed to be a Non-Comm, so he'd have to start acting like one. She could only watch from afar and will him to look less suspicious, and was actually holding her breath when the man in the queue behind Seb suddenly broke away and bolted.

Thankfully, she saw Seb being waved through the barrier and lost sight of him briefly, but moments later she spotted him heading towards one of the doors of the train which had just pulled up to the platform. People were flowing off it, while others waited impatiently to get on. There was a fair amount of confusion as the porters struggled to keep up with their temporary employers, equine hooves clattering on the concrete of the platform as their owners jostled with the humans to help passengers and their luggage on and off the train. Before she knew it, Seb had boarded.

From where she stood she could see the loading bays at the side of the station, where crates were being hoisted on to freight cars at the front of Seb's train. The human passengers probably didn't even know they were there.

With nothing more to do, Flo was turning away when she was suddenly hit by a wave of fear and nausea. Her head reeled, and she staggered before finding support against a wall. A couple of people reached out to steady her, but she shrugged them off, bile making her mouth taste bitter. *So frightened. Help me. So cold. Oh no, no, no. I'm going to be sick. Help! My head hurts. It's so bad! What's happening?*

She was receiving some sort of telepathic transfer. She struggled to regain her composure and started running along the walkway towards the stairs which led down to the loading bays. As she drew closer the feelings of confusion and fear got stronger. She could see the crates being roughly lowered on to the cars and with each sharp bump of a cage she felt a simultaneous jolt of pain. She had no doubt now that animals were being loaded on to the train cars against their will.

Around her, the people on the viewing walkway and on the main concourse below carried on as normal. How was it possible that no one else had heard it? Even if the majority of the travellers that day were by coincidence Non-Comms, surely there were enough telepaths to sense what was happening. There were so many Guardia about now, how could they be unaware of this mental anguish? As she watched, a few people stopped in their tracks and appeared to be listening, but then they shook their heads and carried on as before. An elderly man stuck his little finger in his ear and wiggled it as if to stop an attack of tinnitus. He looked puzzled for a while and then got on to his train. Could it mean that a psy-block was in place? She'd heard rumours about psy-blocks; who hadn't? The most popular urban myth was that the HSL used them prior to their attacks. She'd never believed it. But now she wasn't so sure. What other explanation was there?

She was at the top of the stairs and could see the train doors, both passenger and freight, being slammed shut. It was too late for Seb to help her.

Standing at the top of the steps she did the only thing she could do. She screamed. She screamed at the top of her lungs to get attention. Heads spun round, people searching for the source of the scream, and she raised her arm to point towards the loading bays.

"Stop them!" she yelled, just before she felt a firm shove from behind and went tumbling down the metal stairs.

CHAPTER 30

Seb felt the train arrive before he saw it. A wave of purposeful movement made its way down the platform as the feeling of anticipation spread from passenger to passenger like a yawn. There was a hissing, grinding and shrieking of metal as the train pulled up to the platform, and when the carriage doors were flung open the sound of whinnying and shouting obliterated any official announcements coming over the tannoy system.

Just a few seconds before boarding, Seb had glanced up and spotted Flo on the raised viewing gallery above the platform entrance. The sight of her trying to look inconspicuous was funny. He smiled to himself as he watched her affectionately. She was an integral part of his life. He hated leaving her behind as he headed into the unknown, but at least she'd be joining him soon. He shivered with anticipation of what was to come as he hoisted himself up on to the train.

Seb was surprised by how many passengers he recognised from school, at least half a dozen. Logically, this meant - if they were heading to Rosendale as he was – they were all Non-Comms. How come he'd never noticed how many Non-Comms there were? But then again, except in emergencies telepathy only happened when humans and other mammals chose to communicate, so there was no real way of telling from the outside who was a telepath or not. Nevertheless, he was well known at school, and if anyone recognised him questions would be raised. He concentrated hard on blocking his mind. Flo would have enjoyed assuring him that that wasn't a particularly hard task for him. He hoped a short haircut and an empty mind would be a good enough disguise.

The route north fascinated him and he spent most of the time gazing out at the unfamiliar landscape. The line curved gently round the New Era Glassblowing Works. Heat exchangers harvested the hot air from the furnaces, so the works not only provided the citizens with glass, but produced hot water and electricity too. A few minutes later the train picked up speed as it left the narrow 'industrial' belt behind and passed the methane mines which supplied energy to the city, and not long after that he had left the metropolis behind and was being carried through the countryside.

To his untrained eye it seemed well organised. The woodlands certainly looked well managed. Neatly stacked wood piles at the sides of the lanes gave free firewood to anyone wishing to help themselves. Land which wasn't forested was turned over to cultivation in the form of vegetable allotments, orchards or larger crop fields run by the guilds, all bordered by miles of hedgerows which were home to myriad other species. Of course, centuries ago these had been designed as barriers and boundaries, to separate properties and imprison animals. But now any creatures found in the countryside were there through choice. The ancient hedgerows, now thickened beyond recognition, continued to serve a purpose: to protect the land from erosion and provide comfortable habitats and safe highways for smaller species.

There were signs of spring everywhere. Wild flowers decorated the expanses of green grasses, while pale pink and white blossoms peeped out from between impossibly bright leaf buds. He'd heard that before the Siklus much of the land had been used for the rearing of livestock for meat production, while virtually everything else had to be imported from abroad. His mind boggled at the stupidity of it. In the distance, on the higher ground, he could make out windmills churning away, a line of carts in front of each. Bakers waited patiently to collect heavy hessian sacks full of last season's grains, now milled into flour.

Down in the valleys, he caught sight of the occasional watermill paired with a foundry or forge. He was briefly reminded of his application to the metalworking academy, and was sending out a fervent prayer to be accepted, when he was startled out of his contemplation by someone talking. It was one of the other five passengers in his compartment; the only woman. She was introducing herself to the rather stuffy-looking man sitting opposite her, and looked at Seb to include him in the conversation.

"Hello. I'm Mary, and this is my husband Charlie," she said, indicating the man in the seat next to her. "We've just got married and we're going to Harrogate for our honeymoon."

"Mary, love, you don't have to tell everyone, you know," said Charlie. "I'm sure no one's interested."

The pompous-looking man shook hands with both of them and wished them all the best. "Roger

Donahue. On my way to Rosendale on business," he said, before turning to Seb and shaking his hand too.

"Um, Tim Watts," said Seb.

On either side of Mr Donahue sat two restless boys about Seb's age. They were also apparently heading to Rosendale.

"Look here," Mr Donahue said as the lads leant over him again to pass something across. "Perhaps it would be easier if I swapped seats with one of you so you can sit together."

"Nah, it's all right. You're not bothering us," replied the bigger of the two while his friend snickered. "Stay where you are, mate."

They carried on as before until they got bored. Then they started moving around the compartment, shouting out to their friends in the corridor, opening the windows to look out, fiddling with the fold-down tables and jostling the other occupants in the process. The businessman used the first opportunity to move to the corner seat, but the boys soon noticed.

"Oi. We told you, you weren't bothering us. You can go back to your place."

"No, um, well, no. It's quite all right. You know, I sort of prefer it here, if you don't mind. It'll be better all round."

"Get back in your al–lo–cated seat."

Mr Donahue stayed where he was and looked defiantly at the boys. The tension suddenly got worse when Charlie the honeymooner decided to be a hero.

"Look here, chaps," he said. "Show some respect. You're not the only ones in this compartment." His bride clutched his arm, silently urging him to keep his mouth shut.

"How about you show us a bit of respect?" replied the bigger of the two, while his friend sniggered again.

"If you don't settle down, we'll have to ask the conductor to have you removed."

"Go ahead, lover boy! My uncle is the conductor on this line. You'll make his day."

Suddenly Mr Donahue harrumphed, and snapped his paper taut before folding it and placing it carefully on the seat next to him.

"As I said," he started, slowly and deliberately, "I'm off to Rosendale on business. My job is chief buyer of medical supplies for the N'Era-London Hospital. I go to Helmsley to buy chloroform."

"So, what's your point?" said the big bully, but Seb could see he wasn't quite as confident as before. Clearly this confrontation wasn't going the way he'd planned.

"My point is, I go to Rosendale several times a year and have many friends on the island. Including," he paused and surveyed them over his glasses, "including Mr Grey, who runs the vacation camp up there. Any more lip from either of you and I'll have a quiet word with him. He'll make you wish you'd never been born."

Grey… Grey… Rosendale *is* the key.

The bullies conveniently developed a keen interest in something happening further down the carriage and swaggered out of the compartment. The rest of the journey passed pleasantly enough. Mr Donahue read his paper, Seb dozed and the honeymooners spent the next hour or so whispering to each other. Before he knew it, Seb felt the train slowing down as it approached Leeds Port. The steel grey sky hung low and ominous. There was trouble ahead, he could feel it.

CHAPTER 31

Flo came to at the foot of the stairs, surrounded by a group of anxious-looking citizens. Seb's train had gone and she was confused, angry and in considerable pain. Someone had pushed her, but she knew she had to keep her suspicions to herself.

"Can you hear me?" someone asked.

Flo groaned. "What happened?"

"You fell, or tripped, I think," the same person replied.

"I know her," said someone else. "Let me through, please." Even in her confusion Flo recognised that voice. "I didn't actually see her fall, although I'd noticed she was acting strangely just beforehand." Flo blinked and looked around until she located the speaker.

"Miss Pugh. Do you know what happened? Where were you?

"Seeing off my nephew. I'm so glad I was still here. We need to get you looked at by a medico and then taken home, dear." She looked sternly at a young station official. "Don't just stand there, boy, go and fetch help!"

He ran off quickly. "Well," Miss Pugh went on firmly, "while we're waiting I'll just check you over myself. Don't worry," she added seeing the expression of horror that rapidly crossed Flo's face. She bent down to check Flo's pulse. "Nothing much wrong there, I think. But you've got a couple of nasty lumps coming up on your head." The teacher frowned. "How many fingers am I holding up?"

“Three,” Flo answered wearily. “I’m fine. Honestly. I just want to go home.” She struggled to sit up, but a huge swelling on her elbow made her arm stiff. Miss Pugh looked at her and tentatively prodded the bulge, making Flo wince.

“You’re fine, are you? Move your fingers, please. Good. Now the other hand. How about your toes? Can you move them?” She peered at Flo’s feet. Flo wiggled her toes very cautiously, and although her butt ached with the movement she pretended not to feel it. At last, Miss Pugh helped her to her feet. “All right, dear. Nothing broken. No need to wait for the medico, so I’ll be off. I’m sure someone here can get you home.”

Flo was surprised that her teacher, who had recently been so interested in her well-being, should now just abandon her, but in no time at all she found herself being lifted into the back of a trolley-bus by a few strangers, and on her way home. Flo twisted round, looking for Miss Pugh, but the woman had already faded into the crowd.

The back of Flo’s head throbbed and was sensitive to the touch; even the feel of her hair moving in the breeze sent a shiver of electricity across her scalp. Her left arm hung swollen and immobile at her side. She knew she should probably be checked over by someone more professional than her history teacher, but feared the clinic would contact George. No way was she letting George know about this.

The trolley driver asked his horse to take her all the way home. It wasn’t a big detour from the standard route, but nevertheless she was embarrassed at putting out the other passengers.

Everyone was very friendly, but she was irritated by the way they spoke about her as if she were deaf.

"I heard she had some sort of fit at the station and flung herself down the stairs," she heard someone whisper.

"Oh, that is sad," said another. "So young, too."

"I heard she'd said goodbye to her boyfriend and then tried to throw herself under a train," said a third voice.

"Yes, that's true. I saw her do it," a fourth said proudly. Flo wanted to laugh. So this was how rumours started; all of a sudden she was an unstable, lovesick, suicidal loser, and so, so tired. Right now all she wanted to do was rest. She staggered home from the trolley stop, crawled up her stairs and lay down carefully on the bed. "But I must not nod off…"

"I was pushed," she told Lonce some hours later when she woke up to the sensation of Lonce's tongue licking her forehead. "I was deliberately pushed by someone who wanted to keep me quiet. I'm sure of it. The crates were there, Lonce, I saw them. I'm sure they were the ones from my dreams. But I couldn't properly feel the animals inside. I just felt this awful, awful pain and fear."

They risk killing you. You take more care. George worries like old female. This second time you are hurt. George will smell trouble. Lonce carried on licking her grazes.

"You're right, Lonce. You know him so well. He'll get involved and get all motherly and then that'll be that." They sat in silence for a few minutes, contemplating the latest turn of events.

Suddenly Flo cried out, “Lonce, what have I done? Everything is out of control! I can’t bear it. I keep thinking about Seb. If someone did push me, it means they think we’re on to them, so they’ll know about Seb too. I can’t believe I’ve let him go off on his own like this!” Lonce began to form a response, but she cut him off. “We have no way of staying in touch long distance, we don’t know if we’ll manage to get to the island as we planned, or if we do get there whether he’ll be able to join us.” She paced round and round her apartment, while Lonce watched her impassively. “Why do I keep doing this sort of thing, Lonce? Why? Why do I get an idea in my head and can’t let it go until…” She was lost for words, as she tottered into the living room. “If he didn’t like this plan he should’ve said so earlier.” She was cross now, and seeking justifications. “It’s not my fault! He didn’t have to go! He was meant to have got in touch with his parents before he left, but he couldn’t, or didn’t, or wouldn’t! Oh, Lonce, I don’t know… This is terrible, this not knowing what he’ll be facing.” Lonce kept quiet. “I know Jack knows what’s going on. I can’t believe he just abandoned the research he was doing with my mother. But maybe everybody was right. Maybe I should just give up too.”

She heard Lonce’s mind voice. *The dreams stronger now. I see things too. I hear calls for help. We help them.*

“It won’t be easy to get hold of Jack, but I don’t know if we can do this without him. I can’t ask George for help. I love him, but he’s pretty useless. He’d just want me to call the Guardia. But if mammals are being transported by train, it means people from the rail company are involved. The Guardia might be involved too. I don't know who to trust. Someone pushed me down those stairs." Her throat suddenly constricted and her eyes pricked. She flopped down next to him on the floor and touched his forehead with her own, her good arm around his thick neck. "Someone wanted to kill me," she whispered.

Do not be afraid. You need help, yes. I am with you.

As she lay beside him on the floor she felt her courage returning. He licked her face in approval.

"All right," she said aloud, wiping her cheek. "In that case, Lonce, you go and check out the station."

That evening Lonce set off for the station, where he bounded effortlessly up and on to the beams high above the platforms. From there he could observe without being seen. He enjoyed the task. It didn't strain his wound.

Silent move through shadows. High above station. Clanking, ringing, and echoing of night train. Fat, sleepy pigeons. I shut mind and watch. I wait...long time. Flo told me, look at train, look at station. I look, I leap. Like hunting, but not hunting... not hungry now. Pigeons safe. Dropping shaken feathers and shit. I stop above loading place. Sensing, scenting. Some smells fresh, some old. Now I know. I see what happened here.

I curl up and wait. Uneasy. I understand "Evil". I shiver. Suddenly I feel crushed by it.

CHAPTER 32

New Era-London, Guardia Station, Interrogation Room 5

Witness Statement 1.3 of Melissa Gryfe née Harcourt
Species: Human
Sex: Female
Affair: Rosendale
Signed in the presence of K9 Officer Dante.
Wednesday 3 August

Dante's assistant prepared the Perd for the third session of interviews with Melissa Gryfe. If he found these sessions at all disturbing, as Dante did, he didn't show it.

Dante nodded to Melissa to begin.

Melissa was tired too and sat for a few moments in silence. When she began, she spoke slowly.

"Normally I never went on his business trips, but for some reason he wanted me there on Rosendale. He hinted there was something impressive he wanted to show me. I could tell he was excited about it, but perversely the thought made me want to spoil his fun. Perhaps I hoped it would make me feel better about myself."

Dante leaned forwards and interrupted her, keen to move along, *Did you ever have any idea why your husband hated the Coalition so much?*

"Not really. I'd never questioned him. But finally, a few weeks before we were due to travel, I did. He seemed a bit puzzled, like he'd misheard. Then he started with the insults. He said I was even dumber than I looked, and accused me of never listening to him or Father."

So? Did he ever tell you?

"He said it was a question of personal freedom. He believed the Coalition with its unelected officials stifled men like him, gave them no room to breathe, work or create. Everything was regulated to ensure mammalian equality. But he just didn't think we are equal."

Didn't you contradict him? Dante asked. For some reason he found himself really hoping she had.

"Of course I did. But he wouldn't listen. At the time he wasn't interested in discussing his reasons. But he was keen to explain how unstable our government is and how easy it would be to overthrow."

Dante was fascinated. *How so?* he asked.

"He explained that it was because we have an integrated political system. The local councils feed in representatives to the National Council, then the nationals elect representatives to the regionals and so on, all the way up to the World Council, which controls the One World Militia and ultimately all the rules we live by. Because everything is interconnected, he explained, it would all fall apart really easily if it was destabilised in any way. The Coalition works because it is a simple system. One world - one army - one set of laws for everyone - and one police force to enforce those laws."

Gaining control of the World Council, would give him control of the lawmakers and law enforcers. The implications shocked him.

"There are no backup systems."

There has never been the need, Dante said. Suddenly feeling he'd heard enough for the day, he gestured for his assistant to stop the recording.

CHAPTER 33

The train pulled into Leeds Port and the weather, which earlier had seemed only vaguely threatening, now decided to let rip and unleash a full-blown storm. Seb took one step out of the station into the rain before turning on his heels and heading back inside. A jolly man in a little booth was offering the new arrivals information on local attractions and places to stay. The two bullies from Seb's compartment headed off to one of the larger and presumably more expensive hotels. It was obvious to Seb that the booth man had been keen to push them into taking rooms there, and he quickly concluded that the man was working on commission.

Pasted over the entire booth were dozens of fliers, stickers and posters advertising seasonal activities and excursions. By far the most popular, by the look of it, were the glass-bottomed boat tours to see the sunken cities of York and Hull. Seb smiled at the idea of Flo taking one of those trips. He knew she'd hate them; not only because she suffered from seasickness, but because she couldn't stand the idea of 'all those deads down there' in the drowned houses.

"Hello," he said, when he reached the head of the queue. "I'm looking for a room for one night. Somewhere near the port if possible." The booth man gave Seb his best smile and started shuffling brochures. Seb cocked his head to look at them. They appeared a bit fancy so he hastily added, "Nothing too grand. I have rather a limited budget." The fake smile instantly drooped and the man reached for another, smaller pile and fished out a cheaply printed flyer.

"You could try this place on Boar Lane," he said, sounding irritated. "It caters to people with limited budgets." The last two words had been delivered in a surly tone with a side order of sarcasm.

"Is it far to walk?"

"No."

"Is it close to the port?"

"Close enough to see through the portholes from your bed."

"Ah, good. I can tell you highly recommend it. Thanks for your help."

As Seb trudged along the road in what he hoped was the right direction for the guest house, he was joined by a boy of about his own age, who'd apparently overheard the conversation at the booth and decided to try his luck at the same B&B. He introduced himself simply as Ellis and fell into step beside Seb, both boys concentrating on staying upright in the wind as they trudged in unison along the road. Icy rainwater trickled slowly down Seb's neck and he sighed. What was he doing on this adventure?

A chatty woman called Gladys Parker ran the guesthouse, and it turned out to be much nicer than Seb had expected.

"Just fill in the register, my dears," she said. "I don't need to see any identification. I can't be bothered with all that. It's just one of those little rules the Coalition likes to impose on us hoteliers.

Seems like an awful invasion of privacy, if you ask me. You look like nice boys, both of you. Do you want to share a room? I've got a nice twin free at the back of the building. It'll save you some pennies if you're on a budget, dears. Otherwise, I've got two singles at the front overlooking the port. They are a bit noisier, but if the weather clears the views are lovely. On a fine day you can see all the way across to Rosendale. That's why the rooms cost a bit more." She paused to take a breath and Seb plunged in while he had the chance.

"I'd like a single room, please. I don't mind paying a bit more, and I like the sounds you get in ports. Back home I live near a marina," he said, before adding, "My name is Timothy Richard Watts. Where do I sign?"

"Right here, love. Timothy, what a nice name. Old-fashioned. No problem. I'll put you next to each other on the first floor, but you'll have to share facilities." She managed to simultaneously lower her voice and emphasise the word 'facilities', delivering it in a peculiar nasal whisper and blushing as she did so at the crudeness of the term. "All my rooms have to share facilities. That's why my prices are so low."

"It's fine. I don't mind sharing," Seb whispered back, winking.

"My brother James is staying with his son on the second floor. That's where I have the family rooms. They're over from Rosendale, you know. Young Josh is about your age." She looked the two of them up and down. "I'll get him down later and you can chat. You'll like Josh. Everyone does. Makes friends easily. We all do in our family. Can't help it. We're people people. Well, Josh and I are." She laughed. "I do wonder about my brother, though. His wife's got the patience of a saint. I should know; I had to put up with him for twenty years when we were growing up! Anyway," Seb started to realise, with a sinking feeling, that his landlady never stopped talking. His mind drifted. Luckily she paused for breath and Ellis jumped in.

"Thank you ever so. But I'd like to go straight to my room if you don't mind." He leant across the counter and primly plucked both sets of bedroom keys from her hand. "Which did you say mine was?"

"Oh, number three is yours, dear. I am sorry; I do go on, don't I? I expect you want to get out of your wet clothes, don't you? Both your rooms are just to the right at the top of the stairs."

Ellis glanced down at the keys and tossed Seb the set for room four. "See you later." Seb watched him heft his bag and make towards the staircase.

"Well I never!" the landlady exclaimed, turning back to Seb with a slight frown and a shake of her head, her arms crossed tightly across her chest. "I expect he's tired."

Even though Seb had no connection to Ellis he still found himself embarrassed by the boy's abrupt manner and could see that the woman's feelings had been hurt. "Is there any chance of some food here tonight, Mrs Parker? I don't really want to go out again tonight. But I don't want to put you to any trouble either. Perhaps a sandwich?"

"Just call me Gladys. I must say, you're better brought up than that friend of yours."

"Oh, he's not my friend, Mrs - Miss - Gladys. We met on the way over here. But we are both going to the vacation camp on Rosendale."

"You'll have a lovely time there, dear. All my nephews have done it, except for young Josh upstairs, of course. But I expect he'll go next year. You can come down in about half an hour and I'll set you something to eat with us. Your friend can join us too if he wants, unless he'd prefer sandwiches in his room."

"He's not my friend."

At dinner later that evening, Seb found himself sitting at the large dining table with Gladys, her brother James and nephew, Josh and Ellis.

Mr Atkinson was a big, confident man who liked his food. "So, you're off to Rosendale then, are you, you two?" he said. "You'll enjoy it. My two eldest boys have both done it. Of course…" he reached for the salt, "normally it would be too pricey for the likes of us, but…" He kept the boys waiting again as he ladled more potatoes on to his plate, "as a courtesy to us islanders, Grey lets our younguns go for less." He smiled affectionately over to his son and ruffled his hair. "Josh'll be going next year, won't you, lad? You've been waiting to get old enough for ages, haven't you?"

"I don't know why they have these age restrictions," Josh grumbled. "Joe and Jason told me about what they did there and I reckon I could handle it. I can't wait to go. You're so lucky."

"Who organizes these vacations?" Seb asked as nonchalantly as possible. "I don't really know much about it. I just won a free ticket and thought it sounded like fun while my parents are away." The others all stopped eating to look at him. "I mean," he continued, "I'm really into sport, but I've never really considered who manages it. I assumed Rosendale was a government thing, but I guess by the sound of what you are saying it's probably, um, private." He trailed off. Gladys and Atkinson exchanged a knowing look. Seb nearly laughed at the theatrical cliché of it.

"I heard it was run secretly by the HSL," chipped in Ellis cheerfully, apparently oblivious of the tension that had suddenly filled the room. "But I don't really care who runs it. Anyway," he added as he ate another forkful, "my mum says there's nothing wrong with the HSL and they are perfectly entitled to disagree with the Coalition."

"We don't discuss politics at the table, dear," said Gladys firmly. "Have some more pie."

The next morning the weather was still bad and the 10 a.m. ferry for Rosendale was not running. Ellis and Seb spent most of the day in the lounge area playing cards and chatting with Josh while the rain beat relentlessly on the windows.

"So, Josh, you live over there, on Rosendale? What's it like? Isn't it really quiet?" Seb asked him as he dealt another round. "I'm from N'Era-London and I couldn't imagine living anywhere else. What do you do all day?"

"Well it's not the city, that's for sure. I wouldn't like to live in N'Era-London. Leeds Port is big enough for me. I've heard you've got more than thirty thousand people there. I couldn't bear that," Josh said simply. Ellis, who had been concentrating on his cards, suddenly laughed. It wasn't a mocking snort, just a laugh of genuine amusement. "More like ninety thousand, you mean, Josh. It's not that bad, is it, Tim? There's always something to do, places to go, people to meet."

"Is there any work on the island apart from at the vacation camp? I mean," Seb said, "how do people live?"

"There is some work." Josh replied enthusiastically. "The vacation camp employs a few people. Then there's the heather collection. You can earn a bit doing that, in season. Kelp collection is okay, as long as we don't go over the quota the Coalition agreed with the Aqua-Oceania Council. That job pays the most. We collect brown, red and green seaweed for chloroform production. Who'd have thought people would need so much chloroform?"

That was the last thing Seb had expected to hear, even after meeting Mr Donahue on the train. "Chloroform? What do you do with it all? You can't possibly use it all on the island?"

"Some is used at the Panopticon, and the rest is sent around the archipelago to all the hospitals," Josh replied. "Anyway, mostly people get by by doing odd jobs and growing their own food. Quite a few have moved over to Leeds Port and work on the ferries or in businesses here. Like my Aunty Gladys. But my dad has a good job at the Panopticon, so we won't have to leave. My mum works as a cleaner for some of the holiday home people, and my uncle Bob works with my dad."

Ellis yawned loudly. Clearly he didn't have a curious nature.

“What’s the Panopticon?” Seb asked as nonchalantly as possible. He didn’t recognise the word, but it sounded sinister.

“A sort of clinic,” Josh replied, suddenly looking a little shifty. He was getting uncomfortable with all the questions and was glancing frequently at the door, but Seb persisted. He’d come all this way on this crazy, creepy mission and wasn’t prepared to back off just to spare the boy’s feelings.

“What do they do then, your dad and uncle?” he asked.

“Dad’s chief of security and Uncle Bob is a guard. It pays quite well, so Dad says he’s going to get my brothers jobs as guards too. He says they’re in with a chance because they did so well in the vacation club.”

“What do they need guards for at a clinic?” Seb asked just as the lounge door opened and Mr Atkinson appeared, glaring pointedly at Josh.

“Come on, Josh, enough of this mucking around, disturbing your aunt’s guests. Go upstairs and get packed. It looks like there’s going to be a break in the weather and we’ll be able to get home this afternoon after all.” He turned to Seb and Ellis. “You two had better get a move on. I heard the ferry’s leaving at five o’clock. You’ll be checking into your suites at the camp by six-thirty at the latest.”

Ellis headed obediently out of the room, but before Seb could follow him Mr Atkinson laid one of his enormous hands heavily on his arm. “We’re private people here, Timothy, and you ask a lot of questions. If you want to get on at the camp you’re going to have to learn to obey orders, not query everything. Don't bother my son any more. He's not sophisticated like you city folks." He gave Seb's forearm a squeeze. "Now off you go. The ferry ain't going to wait for you."

CHAPTER 34

Three men dressed in military-style uniforms greeted the ferry when it finally docked at Helmsley, Rosendale's main port. Seb stared at them, trying to figure out which one was Flo's attacker, as he'd only caught a fleeting look at him as the man had fled the flat.

Harold Grey stepped forward and identified himself to the group, before starting his introductory speech. "Everything is ready for your survival exercises, first-aid instruction and other things, which you'll hear more about in the second week." He gave a brief parody of a smile, "Those of you who make it through the first week, that is." There were about around thirty-five new recruits and Seb could feel the undercurrent of excitement and the intake of breath as Grey continued. "Make no mistake, anyone failing to make the grade will be shipped off home. There are no second chances here. Just like in life."

There was no time for chat or speculation as they were shown to the dormitories, where bags were hastily thrown on to bunks before their owners headed eagerly for the mess hall. Ellis and Seb were billeted in different quarters. Seb watched sympathetically as Ellis headed off to his dorm which was already occupied by the bullies from the train.

The meal consisted of meat, meat and more meat. He and Flo had forgotten all about eating when they came up with the infiltration plan. He'd been vegetarian all his life; it hadn't occurred to him that people might eat meat. Did Non-Comms generally eat meat? Who knew? As he stood in line in the communal eating hall, he felt sickened. He knew he'd have to eat it – and keep it down – to keep up his disguise as a Non-Comm. At the other tables, apart from one or two boys, the majority of 'vacationers' were as horrified as he was.

If he could have walked away right then, he would have done. But then, Flo would have killed him.

Later that night Seb sneaked to the latrines to vomit up the meat he'd eaten. Similar sounds were coming from other cubicles. Clearly some of his co-vacationers, Non-Comms or not, were having the same problem. Without waiting to see who came out,.he quickly made his way back to his bunk and spent the rest of the night horribly aware of his bubbling guts and hoping his stomach would 'acclimatise' quickly.

The following day Captain Grey greeted them at muster. At second glance it was clear that this was the man who had barrelled into Seb at Flo's apartment. Seb found himself wondering exactly where Lonce had dug his claws in, and hoping the injuries still hurt. To his disappointment, Grey appeared perfectly fit as he carefully surveyed each new recruit, meeting their eyes and trying to intimidate them through the power of his gaze.

As the man made his way slowly down the line, Seb could feel his heart pounding and his palms beginning to sweat. He would be spotted as a fake, he was sure of it. When Grey stood in front of him and looked him up and down, time stopped. Seb held his breath, waiting for the inevitable flash of recognition, or quick challenge, but it didn't come. Grey moved on to the next vacationer and Seb could breathe again.

"This is not, nor has it ever been, a training camp designed to undermine the government or any law enforcement agencies," Grey announced when the inspection was over. "There will be weapons training, but only to facilitate protection protocols." Seb listened attentively to every word. "We're not a bunch of extremists, but we must be prepared to help our fellow citizens. There are two reasons why we are open only to humans. The first," he held up his enormous hands, "is because we have opposable thumbs. They are a fundamental requirement for the exercises you will be doing this week." He paused, and Seb found his mind drifting to all the other creatures with opposable thumbs and wondering whether any enthusiastic great ape or koala wishing to vacation here would be welcomed, but Grey had started speaking again. "Secondly, attitude. We believe it is our duty to manage the planet, to rule over it. We are the dominant and superior species, and as such we are the earth's caretakers." His voice became conspiratorial. "Unfortunately for them, there are still a few species that don't quite see it that way." After the laughter had died down, he continued, "Over the next few weeks your holiday activities will grow to include weapons training, patrolling techniques and radio protocol. Essentially how to shoot, move and communicate. But this first week will be establishing your level of fitness, whipping you all into shape and getting you to function in teams. You will also practise hand to hand combat as well as search and rescue first aid."

Seb's night was long and restless. There was much to ponder and take in. Not least the question at the back of his mind; did all Non-Comms feel this way? Did they truly believe they were superior to other species and were just biding their time? It couldn't be. He had Non-Comms in his class; while not particular friends of his, he'd never considered them to be either threatened by or a threat to society. But now, remembering that shiver of excitement among his co-vacationers as Grey had been speaking, he began to wonder.

CHAPTER 35

Seb had been gone a couple of days before Flo managed to track down his parents. At the phone hub, she started the conversation off with a little white lie. The line was bad, full of crackles and it threatening to disconnect at any moment. She couldn't decide if this made lying easier or not.

"Hi, Laura. Seb's asked me to call you about our school project. He's gone to visit some metalworkers somewhere up north as part of the research for his academy application, so he didn't have time to contact you directly. I hope you don't mind."

"Not at all, love. I'm glad he's knuckling down to it at last. I was worried he would miss the deadline. What's the project about?"

"Well, it can be about any aspect of pre-Siklus society, or the Siklus itself, and how it connects to us today. So initially we thought we'd do floods."

"That's interesting, particularly in light of your hatred of deep water. How far have you got?"

"Well, that's the thing," said Flo, ignoring the reference to Pukey Flow. "We've actually finished it and handed it in already. I was having difficulty getting inspired, as you can imagine, so Seb did most of the work. But now we're looking at a second project and I've persuaded Seb to tackle something a bit more unusual, something I know Mum and Jack were particularly interested in."

"Sorry, I missed that. I only heard the words 'tackle' and 'Jack'."

"Animal experimentation," Flo shouted down the phone.

"Wow, Flo. That's a big and nasty subject. Are you sure you wouldn't rather just stick to floods? I mean, you'll find experimentation upsetting. I know your mum did. Even Jack did, and he's as tough as they come."

"No, it's OK. I've already discussed it with George. I know what I'm getting into. He's even shown me her research notes, which he's kept." That wasn't too big a lie.

"Claire had only got as far as collecting quotes from various people," said Laura. "She hadn't got round to writing up the finished piece before she died." There was a moment of silence, as if Seb's mother was trying to collect her thoughts and remember what she could about her friend's work ten years before. "Look, I'll see what I can send you. I'll have to ask Jack. "

"Thanks so much, Laura. Just one more thing," Flo was winging it completely, "I already have a lot of Mum's notes on the history of experimentation. What I'm really after is what she was working on with Jack, the stuff about what's happening now. We're going to start the project by looking at the pre-Siklus world and conclude with what's happening in our time." The line crackled, but Flo ploughed on. "George told me everything. I know about the HSL's involvement." She could just make out Laura's sharp intake of breath.

"I can't tell you that," said Laura. "We shouldn't even be talking about it. I'm surprised at George; he had no right to discuss any of this. Look, Jack abandoned the project after your parents were killed. I'm not saying I think they were killed because of their work. The accident was a coincidence. I'm sure of it. But Jack just lost heart. Then he got involved in other work and time passed." A second or two of silence was broken by her deep sigh.

"There's another thing, Laura," Flo said quickly, scared she would hang up. She took a deep breath before continuing. "What about the dreams? I have to know, because I'm having them too. We're all getting them, even our friends at school, and whatever they signified then, they signify now. I know they aren't normal dreams, they're a form of telepathy. Even George agrees. Are we all evolving?" She could hear nothing on the other end of the phone. "Laura, are you there?"

"Flo." Laura's voice was suddenly stern and serious. "Don't pursue this. Don't investigate the dreams on your own. Do you understand? This is too big for you. Wait until we get back. Just a couple more weeks and we'll explain everything. You and Seb cannot do this alone. Promise me, Flo!" There was urgency in her voice now. "Drop it. It's dangerous."

Suddenly Jack was on the phone. Flo had never heard him so angry.

"This is an order, Flo. You will not pursue the dreams until we get back!"

"But, Jack, I have a right to know. You and Mum found evidence of animal experimentation happening ten years ago on Rosendale. I think it is still going on and the nightmares are connected. Don't you want to stop it? I think the HSL are trying to eliminate interspecies communication at a genetic level!"

"Drop it, Flo. Wait until I get back. Let me talk to Seb."

"I can't. He's gone."

"What? Where?"

"Rosendale," she said, as a sudden wave of fear washed over her.

"Get him back! I'll talk to you later!"

Then the line went dead. All Flo could hear was the distant fizz and crackle of static.

CHAPTER 36

Before seeing George again she made sure the bruises from her tumble at the station had faded completely. The poor man's heart would not take another shock. In the meantime, she organised her own journey north. Jack and Laura's words had frightened her and she worried constantly about Seb. There had been no word from him since he'd left. His father's words - "Get him back!" - still rang in her ears.

But first she had to deal with George. Luckily the subterfuge about the fictitious journey north was getting easier to tell with each repetition, and on her next visit she confidently embellished it for him.

"So," she began, "Seb's off on his trip up north. But he left you this." She handed him one of Seb's Damascus metalwork creations. It was an exquisite letter opener in the form of a bird. The tail formed the blade.

"I'm lost for words," said George as he turned it over in his hands.

"George, you're not getting soppy are you?"

"Not at all, not at all. I'm just touched. The two of you are very dear to me."

She put her arm round his shoulder and kissed him on the cheek. "Lonce and I are going up north to meet Seb. We might even all take a trip down the coast to Nottingham and Derby."

"That's a good plan," said George. "I'm glad you're giving yourself a chance to get away from all your worries about the dreams and so on. I'd love to come with you." Her heart sank at his confident assumption that he was invited. "I could do with getting away for a bit too. But I'm a bit behind at work, so if you don't mind I'll stay here, although I would like to treat you to a first class sleeper ticket to Leeds Port, if I may. Quite frankly, if you've never been on one of those Pullman-style sleepers, you haven't lived."

Flo packed lightly. After all, she was going to have to carry it all. But packing turned out to be a frustrating and annoying process, and it took longer than she'd expected. Spring had arrived without her noticing, but she guessed Rosendale would still be cold at night. That made packing doubly difficult.

She went over the plan in her mind. Before Seb had left, they'd studied a map of Rosendale long and hard, in the end picking a sheltered bay next to Hodge Beck Promon tory as their meeting point. She had enough cash to bribe a local sailor to take her across to the island with Lonce and, she hoped, enough to offer him a considerable reward for picking the three of them up four days later. With any luck their unofficial arrival would go unnoticed. Seb would be waiting for them in a hiding place on the hill overlooking the bay, and once they'd combined forces they'd work out what was happening on the island and alert the necessary authorities. Or at least, that was the idea. But she still hadn't heard from him and she couldn't help but worry about his silence.

That night Flo again found herself inside the strange body of someone called Finch.

Flo/Finch was pulled from the crate and on to the floor of a cold, stark room. Her head was spinning and she felt sick. Standing up immediately provoked a fit of vomiting. When it subsided she looked around for something to drink; anything to take the taste of vomit away. There was nothing. Not even a bowl in the corner. She stretched out her front legs, bent her head between them, nose to floor, and flexed her spine. She raised her head again and sniffed. She smelled death. She listened, and heard cries. She reached out with her mind and felt fear.

Once more Flo woke exhausted and crying. She knew time was running out.

CHAPTER 37

From the first day Seb arrived on the island he'd been surprised by the overtly military structure of the camp. The boys were required to wear uniforms and tp keep themselves and their barracks spotless and ready for inspection at all times. More than once, they were forced out of bed in the middle of the night to mop the floor or perform another equally banal task. Try as he might Seb couldn't detect any sensible reason for this, other than a power trip for the leaders Grey and Blue.

He was still unsure about why he'd come. Flo had better appreciate this. A fact-finding mission, yes, but then what? He kept notes, hoping they might be useful one day. Finding a hiding place for them proved a little tricky, and he didn't like the thought of what they'd do to him if they found them. But he settled into the camp routine quickly enough and was confident that no one suspected him. Meat would always be a problem, but it had been days since he'd actually been sick. Nevertheless, the more time went on, the more uneasy Seb became. He continued to make notes daily, but even he had to admit they made boring reading. *Nothing connects to abductions. No suspicious activity.* He repeatedly checked his note stash but it appeared untouched each time. Still, with every passing day, his doubts grew.

It had started with a push-up challenge the week before. Grey's second in command was a sadistic, controlling man with more muscle than brain. Seb had taken an instant dislike to him, and by the day of the challenge he was beginning to suspect the feeling was mutual.

At the sergeant's whistle thirty boys dropped simultaneously to the ground. Half of them started their push-ups as quickly as possible, barely completing each descent before pushing back up, technique sloppy. Most of them tired quickly and it soon became a direct competition between Seb and Owen, one of the bullies from the train. Seb swore angrily under his breath. He'd seen Owen and his friend, Liam, around the camp. Their characters hadn't improved since the journey up from New Era-London.

Seb had started slowly and paced himself. He was fit. He knew he could do this. By focusing only on the clock he could ignore the others and find his natural rhythm. He was up to twenty-five by the end of the first minute. But next to him, Owen was showing surprising discipline and strength.

"Watts!" Blue's boot crashed into his spine and Seb found himself pinned to the ground. "You're doing it wrong! Start over!"

"What?" Seb turned his head and glared at the man towering above him. "How can I be doing them wrong?"

"Are you questioning the drill sergeant?" shouted Blue. "I said start over!"

Seb began again. Before long, Blue started counting off the remaining seconds.

"Ten. Nine. Eight."

It was getting harder. Seb was getting slower. Sweat ran down his face. Owen was struggling and finally stayed down, face red, eyes closed.

"Five. Four. Three.

Arms shaking, Seb flopped down, exhausted.

"Two. One," said Blue, finally. "And the winner is Owan Gladwell, with thirty-eight."

"What? I'd done twenty-five before you stopped me, and then I did another fifteen. That makes forty!" Seb couldn't believe what was happening.

"True," said Blue with a half-smile, "but the first twenty-five didn't count."

Week 2. Every day the following week, the boys were tested to their limits though obstacle courses, challenges and forced marches carrying full kit. Suddenly things fell into place. Seb wrote:

Finally! I'm on to something! We were doing stuff on the far side of the island. I have no idea how far it is from the camp. We came across it quite late in the day and we'd been charging about the place for hours. In the distance was a wide river plain between two lines of hills which went right down to the sea. There was this weird-looking ring-shaped building, just like the one from our dreams. I reckon you wouldn't see it at all from certain angles. We didn't get too close, but I could just make out bars on the narrow windows. Grey said it was abandoned. If it hadn't been for the distress calls I'd have believed him. Alarm bells were ringing in my head. I've never felt anything like it before. Everyone else is a Non-Comm, so I was the only one who picked up the calls. I had to pretend not to notice anything. This is the place and the dreams really are calls for help. Flo, you were right all along! Now I have to find a way to get back to that place. Bad things are happening down there.

Week 3. Every evening in the days that followed, the boys came back exhausted. But Seb was now sure he'd been singled out for special treatment. He knew he couldn't complain without drawing more attention to himself, but each day brought a new frustration. The drill sergeant definitely had it in for him; Seb hoped it was just a natural aversion rather than suspicion. Somehow only Seb's equipment turned out to be faulty or missing parts. At the end of a particularly long and hard forced march, he discovered someone had added extra weights to his backpack. Instead of the regulation twenty, he'd been carrying thirty kilos.

"Pugil sticks!" Blue yelled one afternoon. There was a murmur amongst the boys. Few had heard the term before. "Pay attention!" Blue shouted. "This is a pugil stick for combat training," Blue held one up above his head; then, bringing it down to waist height, he demonstrated a few sweeps and thrusts. "As you can see, it's not complicated. Even you, you sorry lot, will be able to use them!" The long pole was thickly padded at both ends, with hand guards in the middle. "Partner up. Winners from each bout will go through to the next and so on until only two are left. Make it controlled. Make it accurate." There was a buzz of excited chatter as the boys helped themselves to protective gear and chose their first partners.

The bouts were swift and brutal, and half an hour later only the two finalists remained. Ellis was one of many who went down in the first round. Liam lasted a bit longer until his mate, Owen, floored him once and for all.

Seb groaned. He'd won every round easily and now found himself in direct competition with Owen again. Damn! Why the hell was it always him?

The two boys barely acknowledged each other. Owen swung first and landed the initial few blows. He started hard, fast and vicious. Seb, caught by surprise at the aggression, tried to get in a few broadside swipes, which were swiftly met with brutal jabs to his head and belly. More than once, Seb was winded or lost his footing. Owen was relentless; a human battering ram. He was trying to annihilate Seb, and Seb glimpsed Blue watching, satisfaction written all over his face. Infuriated, Seb rallied. It wasn't going to end this way. He would fight fire with fire. Breathing hard, he smashed the pugil stick into Owen's diaphragm, then delivered a sharp upper cut to his chin.

The impact snapped the bully's head back and Seb used that split second to finish the job. He put all his weight and momentum into a final devastating smack into the side of his opponent's head. Owen went down like a felled tree.

Seb dropped his stick and bent double. Panting. Exhausted. Satisfied.

CHAPTER 38

Flo and Lonce entered the first class 'Pullman' train carriage the following evening. A framed repro-advertisement depicting the wonders of twentieth-century train travel hung on the wall directly in front of them, but the reality was even better. A luxuriously furnished lounge area stretched out ahead.

"Oh my, Lonce, look at this!" Flo exclaimed excitedly as they got on board. She continued to enthuse with every new discovery. "Can you believe this place? Thank you, George!" Uneasy about having deceived him, she silently promised to make it up to him. "Lonce, just look at that wood panelling and those chairs!" She spun round, mouth open. "Wouldn't George love this stuff for his apartment?"

Lonce looked a bit bemused. *They are chairs. All chairs look same.*

"But just look around! Have you ever seen anything like it?" Deep, soft, patterned carpeting covered the floor, inviting her to wiggle her toes in it. Lonce again gave a cursory glance around and sniffed.

It is train. It smells of train.

"Can you sense anything else? Remember we're looking for crates too. Can you feel anything yet? I can't. I'm getting nothing at all."

Nothing yet. Too many new smells. New sounds. Confusing. They carried on through the lounge, nodding greetings to the other travellers. If most of the passengers were surprised to see the world's last known snow leopard aboard a train, they were too polite to make a fuss about it. As they walked through the compartment Flo had the opportunity to see Lonce through their eyes. They were looking at him as if seeing him was one of the greatest moments of their lives and yet also one of the saddest.

At the far end of the lounge Flo spotted the compact stainless-steel kitchen. Going over for a closer look, they could see an oven, a hob and a grill stacked bottom to top immediately in front of them. A notice on the wall next to them claimed that all their dining needs would be taken care of from the buffet. "From simple snacks and beverages to complete three-course meals, the entire menu will be tailored to your satisfaction."

The chef smiled at them expectantly. A few other passengers were already settled in the armchairs and sofas, looking over the menu cards and chatting quietly. Flo imagined that most of them had travelled this route before, so the luxury of the Pullman didn't impress them, but she continued to gawk at everything and kept running her hands over the wood and metalwork. Everything looked so smooth, shiny and expensive.

"If you aren't hungry, Lonce, I think we should check out our compartment."

Not hungry. Impatient. Curious. Not hungry. His emotions flowed through her. Feelings of shame threatened to spoil her enjoyment of the moment.

"Let's find our compartment now, and then we can look for a freight car once everyone else is asleep. It there is one, it'll be just behind the engine, like the one I saw on Seb's train."

Their personal porter had already carried her bag to the sleeping car, but luckily hadn't unpacked it. The contents would have raised an eyebrow. Instead of her own nightwear, she found a comfortable pair of guest pyjamas folded neatly on her pillow, the Pullman logo embroidered on the lapel. Flo was again overwhelmed.

"Look at these!" she cried out loud. "It's all pure pre-Siklus style! This is so cool! Just think, Lonce, people must have travelled like this all the time." The craftsmen had done an exceptional job of recreating the comfort of the old Pullman carriages, and the train's accommodations hadn't been designed exclusively for humans. To a certain extent each compartment could be adapted to the particular needs of non-human travelers, and Lonce immediately claimed possession of the fold-down upper berth. He leapt straight on to it, and circled round a few times, kneading the mattress with his enormous paws, before lying down and promptly going to sleep. Flo explored the space some more, and located a private bathroom, with both toilet and litter tray, hidden discreetly behind a door within the polished wooden panelling. Back in the bedroom, she also found a folding writing desk, a fan, heating controls, a reading lamp and a call button for the porter. After fiddling around with a few of the buttons she managed to set the in-built alarm clock next to her bed. The generous double bed folded back into a comfortable sofa during the day, but right now it was calling to her. I'll just relax for a little while, she told herself, and fell asleep immediately.

The two friends woke up simultaneously and fully alert to the sound of the alarm at about three in the morning. A minute later, Flo opened the sliding door and stuck her head out of the compartment. There didn't seem to be anyone about, so they quietly stepped into the corridor and slid the door closed behind them. The roller blinds were down and anybody passing would assume they were doing nothing more than enjoying a luxurious and relaxed night's sleep.

Lonce led the way. Their carriage was towards the back of the train and they had to make their way past several sleeping compartments before going through the lounge and past the galley in order to see what was beyond. The lounge was mercifully empty; the luxury of the sleeping compartments had enticed even the most hardened lounge lizards to their beds and in the galley the cook had fallen asleep at the counter with his head cradled in his arms. He didn't even stir as they crept past. They got to another articulated platform between the cars and Flo peered through the little window into what she realized was the baggage car. She could see the porter asleep in a chair, his legs spanning the narrow passageway between the piles of luggage and his crossed feet resting on a large trunk. But at the far end she could make out another set of doors on either side of the articulated platform: the entrance to the freight car, if there was one. Somehow they had to get past the sleeping porter and through to the next door.

The train rocked steadily, with only the occasional unbalancing tilt as the track curved. One particularly strong lurch caused the porter's feet to slip off the trunk and he partially woke up with a start as his feet hit the floor. Flo ducked down before he could see her, and waited. Lonce glared at her and indicated that they were running out of time. Their position was vulnerable and anyone finding them would be instantly suspicious. If crates of animals had been loaded on to this train, then all the staff on board were probably complicit. If they valued their jobs, even if they personally didn't condone any illegal activity, they weren't likely to betray their employers.

She peeked through the glass again. The guard had gone back to sleep with his feet resting on a smaller case. Flo opened the door and the hydraulics made a quiet hiss. She stood still for a second to be sure he hadn't heard.

"OK. He's still sleeping. How on earth am I going to get past, Lonce? His legs are in the way!" She was grateful most telepaths couldn't pick up or send messages while sleeping; he couldn't 'hear' their thoughts. Not unless he's a dreamer too, she thought and shuddered. But the sleeper slept on.

They crept in and the door hissed closed behind them. Flo stared at the porter and noticed he'd stuffed his ears with cotton wool.

Lonce leapt easily over the porter's legs then waited for Flo to do the same. She hesitated.

"There's no way I can do this. I can't get over him or round him."

Go under him!

The porter had covered himself with a blanket which dangled down on each side and swayed with the rhythm of the train on the tracks. But his legs were clear of it and she judged there to be just enough room to get under them without disturbing their gently snoring owner. She got down on her hands and knees and crawled towards him, then lay stomach down on the floor to slide under his knees. Her face scraped against the dirty wooden floor as she pushed herself along inch by inch with the tips of her toes and elbows.

Somehow, she got past the porter without waking him, scrambled to her feet and joined Lonce at the next set of doors. She pulled at the handle, but it didn't budge. It was firmly locked. Once again she peered through the glass and could just make out the window in the freight car door. There was nothing to be done. There was no way they could open the door. She stopped struggling with it, frustrated.

"Can you feel anything?" she asked silently.

One mammal barely awake, others sleeping. So sad. So alone.

"We can't do anything. We can't get in… we can't rescue anybody… we can't stop the train…we have no idea where we are… and we have no idea what they'll do to us if they catch us." All of a sudden there was a change in the rhythm of the wheels on the tracks, but her watch showed there was still an hour to go before they were due to arrive. "Lonce, I think the train is slowing down. We've got to get back to our compartment. Come on. Quickly!"

Lonce leapt again. Flo took a deep breath and ducked down on to the floor. The porter snorted a couple of times and she froze. Luck was still on her side and she got through without waking him. The train was definitely slowing down now and they still had to get back past the galley, through the lounge, and along the corridor to their compartment. In the galley, the cook had woken up but was standing with his back to them preparing breakfast for the passengers. Flo bent at the waist and ran awkwardly past his counter, doubled over as far as she could go. They raced through the carriages. Flo could see light seeping out from between the blinds and the doorframes of some of the compartments, meaning other passengers had also been woken up by the change of pace.

They flung themselves through their door and on to their beds just as they heard voices approaching from the other direction. Flo slid into her bed, fully clothed. Her heart was pounding but she was fairly confident they hadn't been seen. She listened hard for any telltale sounds to indicate what was happening outside, and she heard the odd clang and scrape as if heavy objects were being moved with great care. She was just about to pull back the covers and peer out of the window when she heard a noise close by. She snuggled further down under her blankets and tried to peek through half-closed eyes. Then a guard slid their door open and looked into the room. His silhouette was just visible against the dimmed corridor lights. He took a step inside and Flo struggled to keep her breathing regular, as if she were fast asleep, but when he bent down and picked up her shoes to examine them, a sense of outrage replaced her fear and she pretended to wake, startled by his presence in the room.

"What's going on?" She hoped she'd got the tone right.

"Don't worry, miss," he answered. "All part of the service. Shoe cleaning. Part of the Pullman experience, miss."

"I don't need them cleaned."

"Certainly, miss." He started to back out of the room. "Excuse me, though, miss," he continued in the same falsely servile tone, "but is there a problem with your pyjamas? I couldn't help noticing you hadn't used them. Were they not to your liking?"

"No. Thank you. They're lovely. But I feel happier sleeping in my clothes while travelling. You know. In case of emergencies."

"Very good, miss. Good morning. Sorry to have disturbed you. We will be serving breakfast soon, prior to our arrival at Leeds Port. Have a safe onward journey, miss." He shut the door.

That usual? asked Lonce, puzzled.

"How should I know? Weird, though." Flo looked over at her shoes. "I can't believe the company would risk waking paying customers in order to shine their shoes. Maybe I'm being paranoid, but I think he knew what we'd been up to. But first things first. We have to see what's in the freight car. As soon as we arrive, we've got to get to the other side of the train, to the loading platform." He nodded. He knew.

They disembarked separately, both intent on finding answers.

CHAPTER 39

Flo hefted her backpack on to her shoulder and set off down the platform towards the exit. Lonce had already gone. She mind-called him silently while trying to spot him. He'd completely disappeared.

Look down. Keep walking.

She looked down to the track below and glimpsed his tail as he crawled quickly across the tracks under the belly of the train.

"Brilliant. Hang on." She knew she couldn't follow him, but speeded up and got to the front of the train. People were pouring through the exit, uninterested in her. A tall wooden gate, standing at right angles to the track, blocked the passage between passenger and freight platforms. Flo ducked unnoticed through it, silently thanking the station worker who had forgotten to lock up. If anyone asks me, I'll say I'm looking for the lost property office.

Once she got past the two buffer springs at the head of the track, she stopped and bent down slightly, to peer round the side of the train. This platform was completely empty, and although she couldn't see the freight car, from this angle she knew it was just behind the engine. She had to find a safer spot and a better view. Any minute now someone would notice her. Lonce was completely invisible; either he was still on the rails or he had managed to hide on the platform somewhere. She mind-called him again.

Look up. She looked up and spotted him on a girder above. *I like stations. Many good places. High places.*

But that didn't help her. Across an open expanse of about a hundred and fifty feet she spotted a pile of cardboard boxes. Perfect - if I can just get there. Some porters were coming out now from the doorways in the wall parallel to the track, heading to the train. As they moved to open the sliding doors of the freight car, Flo seized the moment to dash across the open to the shielding boxes. Crouching down behind them, she silently cursed the weight of her backpack. It made movement difficult and prevented her from squeezing further back into the shadows.

The porters worked in teams. One group unloaded the regular freight: the bags of mail, the heavy cases and parcels. They worked efficiently, flinging the lighter objects between them, hefting the heavier objects with only the occasional grunt. There was none of the normal cheerful workers' banter. They worked without talking. Like automatons.

The second team wheeled up a sort of mobile conveyor belt to the open car door. It sloped down at a sharp angle from the lip of the door to a waiting trolley cart. Two men hoisted themselves up into the freight car, while another two prepared to receive whatever came down the rollers. One by one, wooden crates were manhandled on to the belt, and trundled down to the trolley. Even though the rollers had been well greased, Flo could imagine the terror of the creatures within as the crates tilted, bounced and scraped along.

She tried reaching out to the occupants, but got nothing back. No mind connection, no flicker of telepathy. She asked Lonce whether he could sense them.

No. I sense little. Confused.

"Sorry, what do you mean? You are confused? Or whatever's in the crate is confused?"

Me confused.

Suddenly Flo remembered a detail from her nightmares. Chloroform. They're asleep. Drugged. That's why we can't feel them."

She still had no evidence of foul play, of kidnappings. All she'd seen was a few wooden crates being unloaded from a train. She had to get closer. She had to see into a crate. She had to get proof. But how? She had no idea how long it would be before the last crate was unloaded and they were on their way out of the station. Once gone from her sight, she hadn't a clue how she'd find them again. She paused for a moment.

"You'll have to distract them, Lonce. You'll have to get their attention, make them worried. Make them chase you." His doubts were palpable. "It's all right. They won't catch you. Stay up there - just move so they see you, or something. Use your imagination!"

Lonce sprang. The Ghost of the Mountains lived up to his ancient name. He leapt effortlessly from one rafter to another, fifty feet at a time, his thick tail helping him keep his balance. At first he was too quiet and the men didn't notice him, so he jumped back until he was above them again and gave an irritable growl. At the unexpected sound, they looked up, shocked, and at once he jumped on to the roof of the train and bounded along it, leading them away from Flo. The men gave chase.

Flo wriggled out of her backpack and dropped it down next to the boxes. She ran towards the crates still poised on the conveyor belt. A few had already been loaded on to the trailer-bed of the trolley cart, but she couldn't reach them without climbing on to the vehicle, which would take time. She could still see the men, but she could also see that Lonce was far outrunning them, and any minute now they'd start to head back, frustrated by the futile chase. She needed more time.

She aimed for the easily accessible crates on the conveyor, which had come to a standstill with no humans to shove them along. The first one appeared completely sealed except for a few miserable air holes, too small to see through. She tried to contact whatever was inside. Nothing. Moving on to the second crate, the same: no means of gauging what was inside. The crates were well made and would need a crowbar to open them. Desperate, she looked around in vain for anything she could use.

The third crate at the top of the conveyor was her last chance. There were still no gaps visible in the woodwork. But she had a feeling this was the one; the one that would prove her point. Ducking again, she clambered under the sloping belt, stepping over and between the metal struts which made up the underside of the contraption.

There it was. There was the loose board. Whoever was in there had kicked up a fuss. Literally. The board had been bashed from the inside and a nail was loose. Tugging at the nail itself only hurt her fingers and made no difference, so she grabbed the bottom of the board and pulled. It gave a little and the nail protruded a little more. She tried peering into the interior. Too dark. But she smelled the unpleasant tang of a captive animal. Sweat, fear, urine, and worse. She remembered her travel torch tucked into one of her many pockets, and tried to shine it inside. But the gap in the woodwork was too narrow for her to see anything.

"Lonce," she mind-called him. "I need more time. Do anything to get me more time!"

Lonce obliged. Like an enormous furry spring, he jumped from the roof, slashed at one of the men and then, in the same movement, leapt back up on to the train and off the other side. In a fury, the eight angry men ran past the last carriage, jumped down on to the tracks and crossed over. They scrambled up the other side, heaving themselves roughly up on to their bellies, knees and then feet. Panting. Furious. Frustrated now as the huge cat was nowhere to be seen.

One eye pressed to the crack, the torchlight illuminating an inch at a time of the interior, Flo could make something out. It was a mangy pile of fur, but it moved; the tiniest movement of all. A slow, shallow breath. She called out silently but there was no response. There was a short length of bent wire on the ground, not thick enough to prise up the plank, but she could use it to wake the sleeping occupant. She poked it through the gap, her knuckles scraping the rough wood, and kept up a constant reassuring mind-call, reaching out to whatever consciousness was in there.

The wire was too short and the angle too awkward to do anything more than tickle the animal within. He - or she - didn't stir, and Flo was on the point of giving up, when the end of her wire touched something else. She heard a tiny metallic clink. Working furiously now, she tried to capture whatever it was. Again and again she felt the wire scrape something before sliding off. With her other hand she tugged harder at the plank, trying to gain a fraction more space for manoeuvring her probe.

Finally, it snagged. She pulled her booty carefully, an inch at a time, until it came to rest next to the opening. It was some sort of metal cylinder. Flo tugged again at the wood, and as the bottom nail came away she carefully eased the plank to one side. It pivoted stiffly on the top nail. She looked behind her towards the end of the train. No sign of the men, but she knew they'd be back soon. They wouldn't leave these crates unattended for long. Her heart was thumping now; she knew she was on borrowed time. A few more inches was all she needed. Finally! She pulled the strange little cylinder out and read the writing on the side.

She shone the torch in again, desperate to wake the drugged animal. "Wake! Wake up, please. I can help you if you'd just wake up!" There was still no response. "I'm sorry. I have to go." With no time to lose now, she scrambled as fast as she could back through the undercarriage of the conveyor belt. Once out the other side, she ran full tilt until she got back to the pile of boxes, retrieved her backpack and scuttled past the buffers, through the gate, then out of the passenger exit and into the main concourse of Leeds Port Station.

As she reached the ferry port Lonce reappeared at her side.

"Oh Lonce! I saw one of the animals! I saw him and I couldn't do anything. He was asleep. I couldn't reach him. But I did it, Lonce," she whispered. "I got the proof." She patted her pocket for the reassuring shape of the cylinder. "A canister of chloroform. I told you."

CHAPTER 40

Although Seb had been on the island for more than three weeks, he'd never had the chance to explore much inland. The near daily marches were tightly controlled and there was no time for any deviation from the assigned trails. The village port of Helmsley was only allowed for shopping, posting letters or visiting a local bar, and the boys were actively discouraged from going further afield. But no one objected to swimming, so Seb took to the water whenever he got the chance, thinking at least he'd be able to learn quite a lot from the coastline. He might even manage to discover the relative positions of the ring-shaped building he had seen and the bay where he had arranged to meet Flo and Lonce.

"Where are you off to?" called out Ellis one morning, just as Seb was heading down to the beach. Seb cursed under his breath. "Can I come?" Ellis added breathlessly as he jogged up to join him.

"Sorry, Ellis. Another time, maybe. I'm not swimming for fun. I'm training for a competition in a few months' time. When I'm in training mode, I like to push myself hard and swim quite far. I don't think you'll be able to keep up, quite honestly." Ellis's face dropped, so much so that Seb added quickly, "I promise I'll take you another time. I've spotted a couple of good places for a picnic. We could do that."

"Sure, whatever you say." Ellis sounded disappointed and resentful. Seb watched him stomp back up to the dormitories, which for once were virtually deserted. Most people had gone out, making the most of their time off. A couple of stragglers were just leaving.

"Where are you off to?" Ellis asked. The other boys looked vaguely irritated by the question.

"We're heading into Helmsley for the afternoon."

"Can I come?"

"The thing is, El," the boy's voice dropped to a near whisper, "we've each got a date with a local girl. You get yourself a girlfriend and you can come with us next time. Promise."

After watching them leave, Ellis shrugged and proceeded to get on with his favourite occupation of all. Snooping, sneaking and peeping, rifling through other people's things. He went through every bag and every locker, looked under every mattress, and finally, satisfied he'd found all the obvious treats, he started searching for the less obvious. This required a little more effort and ingenuity. But it paid off. Within an hour he had uncovered something which he was sure would earn him a huge reward.

Quickly forgetting all about Ellis, Seb launched himself into the water and headed out to the far side of the bay, trying to remember whether his objective was round the second or the third headland.

But today, for some reason, the swim was harder than before. Perhaps the currents were stronger here. Certainly the water temperature was much lower than he'd been used to. He was sharply reminded of how unforgiving seawater could be. He struggled to keep on course, thinking of Flo and the importance of this mission with every stroke he took. Flo should be on the way soon. Something was going on, she was right about that, but they had to find a way in to that weird building.

The morning was crystal clear, so at least he could see where he was going, but by the time he heaved himself on to the shingle at Hodge Beck point he was exhausted. He lay on the beach, letting the morning sun gently warm him, but was still shaky when he finally stood up. As he struggled to his feet he was aware of muscles that hadn't been exercised in all the days of training. He felt weak, and ached in parts he'd forgotten even existed. Straightening up, he heard a footfall behind him, but before he could turn round he felt a blow on the back of the head and knew no more.

When Seb awoke he was lying on a metal cot with a thin mattress and a rough blanket in a cell-like room. He registered that one of the walls was slightly curved, and his heart sank; he knew where he was. He was inside the Panopticon, the building he'd first seen in his nightmares all those weeks ago and spotted again during the exercise on the far side of the island a few days before. He got slowly to his feet, and gently probed the bruise on the back of his head with his fingers. He was relieved to discover, even though the contact made him wince, that there was no blood. Cursing quietly, he shuffled like an old man to the barred door and peered out. He could see he was within a circular structure, built around a large tower. This seemed to grow up, dark and brooding, from the central arena-like yard. Dozens of other cells lined the outer structure, while metal walkways ran round the inner circumference and staircases gave access to all floors. His cell was on the second floor.

The tower was capped with some sort of closed inspection platform giving a 360-degree view of the yard and all the cells. It resembled a squat, old-fashioned lighthouse except that instead of transparent glass at the top they had used two-way mirrors. If it was designed to be unnerving, it had succeeded.

As his full range of senses came back, Seb became aware of the noise. The sounds reverberated around the hard, reflective surfaces. The resulting cacophony was almost deafening. As his ears adjusted to the onslaught he started to identify individual sounds. There were clangs and scrapes of metal on metal, coughing, moaning and crying, as well as pathetic yelping and howling. He could feel his stress level rise as he took in the misery of the place. He sank back down to the floor.

Overcome by rage and frustration, he thought back over the last few weeks and tried to figure out what had gone wrong. Someone had seen through him.

CHAPTER 41

New Era-London, Guardia Station, Interrogation Room 5
Witness Statement 1.4 of Melissa Gryfe née Harcourt
Species: Human
Sex: Female
Affair: Rosendale
Signed in the presence of K9 Officer Dante.
Thursday 4 August

We are now at the most recent events, Melissa. Take your time and tell me everything you remember about your trip to Rosendale. Dante checked the Perd. Everything was ready for the day's session.

"Our journey north was completely uneventful. We travelled by train and spent most of our time in our private sleeping compartment, having all meals and refreshments delivered. Marcus spent most of the time reading while I passed the hours re-examining my life, and gazing out at the countryside or at my own reflection. I found myself thinking about events and characters from my past I hadn't thought of for decades."

Like what? he asked, keen for every detail.

"I don't see how my thoughts back then are relevant now. But if you must know, I was remembering all the different nannies I had had as a child. Looking back, there was a ridiculously high turnover of staff. I suppose none of them liked working for my mother. I wasn't particularly bothered by their hasty departures, until Anna. Now, of course, I'm almost embarrassed to admit this, but I remember I used to devise little tests for all the nannies, designed to discover whether they actually cared about me or not. As nanny after nanny failed the tests, I put myself into more and more dangerous situations, until finally Anna got the most shocking test of all. I ran into the middle of a busy street and stood there daring something to hit me. Anna launched herself into the stream of vehicles, grabbed my hand and pulled me to safety. Once on the kerb she gave me a slap which could be heard on the other side of the street. I threw my arms round her neck and hugged her."

Sometimes human reactions puzzle me. Why did you do that?

"Because I'd finally found someone who'd risk her own life for me."

Talking about Anna, Melissa became more and more animated. Dante watched fascinated as her face revealed a range of emotions in quick succession.

"Anna and I quickly became close," Melissa continued. "She introduced me to Toby, a young dog. He could never come to the house; we all knew my parents well enough to know that wouldn't have been a good idea. But we managed to meet whenever Anna took me for a constitutional walk in the park. With Anna's help I gradually became adept at mind-sharing with him. I couldn't believe my luck; finally I had companions to fill my lonely days."

Your parents were always very controlling. Didn't they notice?

"My parents were more concerned I'd become overly fond of walking. They didn't consider it a good pastime for a young girl like me. They would have preferred me to stay at home and learn the piano or some such thing. I know now they had their suspicions about Anna and her way of caring for me. But I didn't care. I just wanted to see Toby as much as possible. I thought nothing of their constant enquiries into where we went each day."

So let me get this straight, said Dante, *Anna introduced you to Toby. A dog. But you were a Non-Comm? How? What possible-?* He was at a loss for a moment, trying to understand the sort of relationship Melissa, with her background, could have had with another species.

"I remember the first time Anna tried to explain sharing to me, I found it confusing and slightly frightening. I mean, my parents were so rude about telepaths."

Dante listened, fascinated.

"She talked me through the process of emptying my mind and then linking it to Toby's. I was to practise forming a sentence or a mental image in my head and then visualise it arriving in his. After trial and error I found I didn't need to use my physical voice any more; mental imagery was enough. At first she got me to practise giving Toby instructions. Simple ones, like suggesting certain actions. She warned me that if I simply said in my mind, 'Don't sit on that cushion,' I'd have a picture of that cushion in my head and that's where he'd go! I made so many mistakes at first. But Anna also explained that the purpose of sharing was not to control Toby, but to empathise with him and exchange experiences."

Telepathy or mind-sharing was such a natural part of his life that Dante had never questioned the mechanics of it. This was the first time he'd had the opportunity to discover how a human could 'learn' to do it. He was riveted. Perhaps the government should consider compulsory lessons for all Non-Comms if it was as easy as that. Surely that would help with interspecies relations and put an end to all the violence?

He snapped back into the present as Melissa continued, "When, finally, I could pick up his messages, they came in a sort of," she paused, searching for the right term. "It was a kind of universal language; something my brain could translate into images, emotions, thoughts, even actual words. It was the most amazing experience. For the first time ever I felt connected with what Anna called the fabric of life. I felt I had grasped something important, something my parents didn't understand and were the poorer for not understanding."

Dante felt her joy.

"Anna explained that all life on earth is made of the same stuff; that we are all more similar than we appear, yet we each vibrate at a unique energetic frequency. After the Siklus, most people found they could automatically 'tune in' to the frequency of another mammal. That 'tuning in' became known as sharing or telepathy. Nobody understood why or how they could do it, they just could.

"She told me that a long time ago people believed everything was made of two things: matter and energy. But they were wrong. There is only energy. That means everything we can sense physically is energy, and even the things we can't sense directly are made up of energy too. Of course," Melissa added, "I didn't understand how something could be there, if you couldn't sense it."

Dante nodded. This was by far the most interesting interview he'd ever conducted, and this Anna sounded like a remarkable woman.

"But think about it. Anna was right. You can't see wind," continued Melissa. "But you can see the effect of wind on the grass and the trees, and feel it in your hair. For hundreds and hundreds of years people have made instruments which can measure things we can't see, hear, touch, feel or smell." She counted off those five senses on one hand, remembering the lessons from her childhood. "But now we know that even our thoughts have a frequency that can be measured and can be passed from one life form to another."

Interesting. It is something I have always taken for granted, confessed Dante. *Where is Anna now, I'd like to meet her.*

Melissa slumped. The excitement of a few minutes before was replaced with intense sadness. Dante felt her pain, as he had felt her joy.

"One day I woke up to find that both Anna and Toby had disappeared and I never saw either of them again. I spent days looking for them. I was upset that Anna had gone, and guessed my mother was behind it, but I couldn't quite believe she'd send her away without even letting me say goodbye. But losing contact with Toby was tearing me up inside. I missed him so much. In my worst moments of paranoia I even became convinced Anna had taken him away from me out of jealousy."

Dante, curious, leaned forward.

"Only during my tenth birthday breakfast did I finally learn the truth. Mother appeared holding a hideous urn. She had known about Toby all along. She came forward and placed the urn in front of me." Melissa started crying. She rocked silently back and forth in her chair.

"Then she told me… I'll never forget… It was terrible."

Dante shuffled impatiently, eager to know what happened, finding he actually cared about this human and her story.

"She told me Toby had been hit by a car and she'd had him cremated. His ashes were in the urn." Melissa stopped speaking, yet Dante could see she was still reliving the past. She was staring at her hands as if they still held the urn.

Gently, Dante approached her. *I understand now.*

"No. No, there is more!" she wailed. "You wanted to know what happened to me. How they crushed me." Dante nodded. "I was sent away to school. To a hard, cold, non-comm school. I bet you didn't know there were any.

"At first, I dreamed of Toby every night and woke up calling his name. Perhaps the girl in the next bed was tired of being woken by me, or maybe she believed it was her duty to report me. I still don't know if she hoped to help me or to get me into trouble…The teacher seemed sympathetic at first. She encouraged me to talk about Anna and Toby… about how much I missed them. She asked me about

Anna's lessons in communication and how I'd gradually got the hang of it. She seemed genuinely interested. I was so happy to talk to someone about Toby that I told her everything.

"She said she understood, but that I should forget him and that she - and only she - could help me. She took me by the hand and led me to a room I'd never seen before. She gave me a thin cotton dress and told me to change into it. I remember folding up my clothes and laying them carefully to one side, curious about what was going to happen next. She told me to bend down and grasp my ankles. All the time she talked reassuringly, about how this would help me. I had to concentrate on breathing, that this was a proven method of helping with homesickness. Then I was birched.

"You look surprised. Haven't you heard of birching? Bundles of twigs, four or five foot long, which were kept soaking in brine for just such an occasion. There were hard little buds still on the twigs for added effect. They beat me with those until I bled. For every dream of Toby I would receive a birching. At first I couldn't control my dreams, but my neighbour made sure I didn't miss out on my 'treatment'. My ability to communicate with any animal was methodically beaten out of me, one stroke at a time."

CHAPTER 42

It was late afternoon before Flo and Lonce found a captain of a small 50-foot solar-powered catamaran prepared to take them out to Rosendale. Locals seemed reluctant to go over there, and the ferries going to the island were all privately owned by a firm based in N'Era-London. In Leeds Port it was generally assumed Rosendale was better left alone. However, Captain Gaines, mercenary to the core, was more than happy to take them once he knew his exorbitant asking price would be met.

"Will it get us there, Captain Gaines? Surely it's not powerful enough?" Flo asked, beginning to feel sick just at the idea of climbing aboard. He folded his arms over his chest and began reciting in a peculiar mix of pride and boredom what 'his girl' was capable of.

"She's got twin hulls integrated to the deck, which makes her light, and thirty-five square metres of solar panelling on her roof. Take my word for it, missy," he concluded, "she's got more than enough power to get you anywhere you'd care to go."

Flo barely listened. She was dreading the crossing. Only the idea of Seb alone on Rosendale and the horrifying collection of facts recorded on her mother's Perd gave her the strength to climb on board.

There was no avoiding the ordeal; the captain was eager to get going. A cold front was coming in and the winds were picking up. Rosendale lay about fifty nautical miles from Leeds Port which, at a top speed of around twelve knots, *Sunrider* would cover in just over four hours. They cast off, and before they had even left the harbour Flo had thrown up twice. She spent the first part of the journey hanging over the side, much to the amusement of the captain.

In the event, Gaines was fairly accommodating throughout. He didn't ask too many questions. In her mind she had manufactured an elaborate story for whoever helped her, but Gaines seemed so uninterested she didn't bother. His main concern was being paid and getting back home as quickly as possible, and he only spoke to tell his unusual passengers more about his precious boat. Flo still had no idea by the end of the journey whether he was married or not. But she knew a lot about *Sunrider*. Her fault, of course, for asking the first question our of politeness.

"What sort of batteries do you use?"

"Saltwater Envias," he said proudly. "Fully charged they'll get us there and back without the need for sunshine." Flo was sceptical. He continued. "In any case, there's a pair of fold-up emergency wind turbines that'll start generating power as soon as the wind gets above eight knots." He looked up at the skies. "Which it will, by the looks of it." Whatever the technicalities, he didn't seem too concerned about his return journey. He pointed to something over her shoulder and gestured with a nod. "We're here. The bay you wanted," he said. "Not much here though. I could have taken you to the port at Helmsley just as easily."

"It's all right. Our friend knew we'd be coming here and will meet us as soon as he can. Thank you for bringing us. Are you sure you won't forget to pick us up in four days?"

“No problem, lass. Watch out; the sea bed drops steeply a couple of feet from the beach so I can get her in quite close, but you’ll have to wade ashore.”

Flo took off her boots, hitched up her trousers and hopped off into cold, calf-deep water. Lonce’s longer leap had landed him in a much shallower spot. By the time they’d both got out of the surf and twisted round to wave goodbye, Gaines had already turned about and was silently heading back towards Leeds Port.

Flo and Lonce sat on the beach at the base of a shrub-covered hill to dry off. It always seemed a contradiction to Flo that Lonce’s raspy tongue was good at grooming off excess water. He licked himself dry, while Flo had to make do with wet trousers.

“OK, Lonce, it’s getting late. We need to let Seb know we’re here,” she said eventually. “Can you sense him?”

No. He’s not near.

“So the only thing to do is to get to higher ground and try a mind-search from there. Maybe we could do our old trick of linking our minds to make the call stronger? If he’s within radius, he’ll pick it up.” Lonce never expressed irritation with her and Seb’s inability to communicate properly with each other, but who knew? She’d certainly picked up a flicker of exasperation once or twice. Telepathy was one thing, but frustratingly you couldn’t know everything in an animal’s heart and mind. Secrets were still possible.

The shrubby hill rose up quickly to become slightly untidy woodland. It was already getting dark, and the stars were beginning to appear. According to George the skies were more polluted and duller back in pre-Siklus times. How sad for the people then. Now they were out of the city she could appreciate the full glory and majesty of the galaxy above them.

"Look, Lonce, there's Jupiter!"

Lonce shrugged, unimpressed by the small lights in the sky.

Starlight's not enough for you. You will fall. Strap your bag to my back and follow. The light from her torch wasn't adequate either and she stumbled, hit her shins and got scraped by brambles, but thanks to Lonce they made it to the summit within an hour. The trees had thinned out halfway up and by around fifty metres from the top they'd gone altogether. As far as she could tell the top of the hill seemed fairly flat. They searched the horizon for any telltale signs of habitation. Nothing. No lights. No sounds, except for the occasional hoot of an owl.

"Lonce, try again from here. Can you sense him?"

No.

"We'll have to do a mind-meld, then. Maybe that'll work."

With normal interspecies communications there were limits to what could be done. Minds couldn't be read without permission. Predators couldn't find their prey purely telepathically, just as a prey animal couldn't avoid detection by sending out disruptive signals. But a mind-meld involved joining two minds together and seeing through the eyes of a third. It worked well enough within a radius of five miles, but it required patience and lots of energy, and often resulted in headaches and nausea. It was so powerful that they'd had to agree to use it only in emergencies. Flo had no idea if she and Lonce would be able to track Seb now, as they didn't know how far away he was. She simply had to pray it would be less than five miles.

Lonce looked at her expectantly.

"Lonce, we have to do this, but not now. I can't now. It's the middle of the night and I haven't slept since the train. I'm hungry and tired, so let's rest first."

Rest first. Be stronger, he agreed. He had eaten a rabbit on the way up the hill and was already curling round himself in preparation for sleep. *What happened here? This land empty.*

"Well, I did a bit of reading about Rosendale before we left N'Era-London," she said quietly, beginning to delve in her backpack for some of the food she had brought. "Before the Siklus there were quite a few villages and hamlets scattered across this region – before it became an island. The larger towns on the coast were all submerged and the survivors fled to the upland villages. The influx of townies from the coast put a tremendous strain on the inland villagers." Flo could picture the scene in her head. Perhaps the heather carried the memory of it all. "There were fights and resentments… I mean, they were killing each other… then, as the Siklus got worse, there was famine too. Once the sea settled down, the remaining inhabitants escaped starvation by coming down to the new coastline and establishing fresh villages. But until they could get a deal with the Aqua-Oceana authorities, they ate nothing but seaweed for the first few years." She turned to Lonce, but he'd gone to sleep, uninterested, and perhaps unsympathetic to human tragedy.

Well, I don't blame you for not caring, Lonce. We brought it on ourselves.

Finch returned more strongly than ever to Flo's dreams that night.

Barred doors slid back and two men grabbed her roughly. She tried to talk as they dragged her out of the cell and onto a waiting gurney. They strapped her down brutally, their rough hands pulling the straps so tight it hurt. She tried biting them and received a blow to the jaw for her trouble. She whimpered with pain and tried to send out a distress call. A vision of her sons surfaced and then sank in her mind as once again a chloroform-soaked rag was pushed into her face. As the darkness descended Finch wondered if she'd ever wake up.

Flo lay for a while trying to shake off the dream, while her sleeping bag, normally so snug, felt damp and clingy about her. Typically for the region, the clear night had changed to an overcast and blustery morning. The heather wasn't in bloom yet; it wouldn't start flowering for a couple of months, by which time the moors would be overrun with collectors from Ripon. The heather was famous for the coloured dye that could be extracted from it, and was popular with cloth manufacturing cooperatives, who would pay handsomely for well flowered specimens. But now the dull grey pastures undulated like sullen waves under cloudy skies, and did nothing to alleviate her sense of foreboding.

She moved away from the makeshift encampment to pee, then built a small fire by gathering up handfuls of bone-dry heather and twigs from the few wind-blasted trees which dotted the moor. The pile caught quickly and she managed to boil some water. Finding water on Rosendale wasn't a problem: numerous streams criss-crossed the landscape and the water was some of the best she'd ever tasted.

Now she was rested, she could focus on finding Seb. It dawned on her that they hadn't planned for anything like this. Back in N'Era-London it had all seemed so easy. He was to infiltrate the HSL camp and see whether the kidnapped mammals were being sent here. Then, according to the plan, she and Lonce would arrive. At this point the plan got a little fuzzy. She had to find her parents' killers, she had to discover what was happening to the disappeared citizens, and then? What then? So far the nebulous plan involved meeting in the bay and all together saving the day. But how? Right now it didn't look straightforward at all. They hadn't even managed to find each other yet. How dangerous was it to take on the HSL? There was a sick worried feeling like a weight in the pit of her stomach. Who knew what else could go wrong?

CHAPTER 43

Security Chief James Atkinson was very proud of his team. They were all island lads, recruited from the villages, not the privileged sons of HSL supporters. Only one, William Bateson, ever had any complaints about the job.

"Listen, Will," Atkinson said, "real wage-earning jobs are scarce up here on the island and we've all got families to support. I've got a wife and three sons, you know that. I admit I don't always like what they ask us to do. None of us do. Scares the crap out of me sometimes, to be honest. But then I think about payday. It isn't exactly hard labour, is it? There are twelve of us sharing the work. What are you complaining about?"

"Well, I'm not complaining really. The pay's good and so on. But you know how you've worked out a rota, two shifts a day, six men on each shift?"

"Yes, you stupid sod: as you said, I worked out the rota. So what?"

"Two men in this tower at all times, right? The other four monitor the cells. We take it in turns."

"Get to the point, will you?"

"OK. My point is, I don't want to do the prisoner transfer stuff any more. I want to stay here in the tower. Full time. For my entire shift. There, I've said it. I can't stand it. I can't stand the smell; I can't stand the look in their eyes! That last dog ..."

"You're asking me to rearrange everyone's shifts because you don't like the smell?" Atkinson roared. He glared at Bateson. He'd known him all his life; he'd put his name forward for the job in the first place. It was a cushy number. It was one of the best-paid and most secure jobs on the island. Better than the backbreaking seaweed harvesting, or heather picking. Security Support Officers patrolled the building; carried out the transfers of inmates from the upper cells down to the holding pens and on into the lab itself. Each unit of twelve men worked for periods of two months at a time, living and eating at the Panopticon. At the end a boat would come to pick them up and drop the next twelve.

Atkinson looked at William's face, took in the expression of desperation and said, "OK, you moron. I'll see what I can do. The others won't like it, though."

"Thanks, boss."

"Just to be sure, though, you want to do this every shift? Sit here on your fat behind in this tower with me, drinking tea?" They were having their third cup of tea of the day.

"It doesn't have to be with you, boss." Before Atkinson could roar with rage again, Bateson laughed, and the chief relaxed.

"Yes, well, it may all be irrelevant now. Professor Feldman sent word down that the boy from the beach is to be transferred down to the pens later. The lad's due for surgery, apparently." Atkinson winked. "I imagine you don't want to do that transfer either, do you? Can't have you freaking out because of his spooky eyes, can we?"

"Why are they cutting the boy?" said Bateson, ignoring the jibe.

"It'll be the new treatment the doc's come up with. It's make or break today for the professor. Gryfe is coming and expecting results. You'd better hope Feldman can come up with the goods, or we'll all be out of work and having to farm kelp for a living."

"You're not serious, are you? It's not really as bad as that?"

"Do you live in a bubble?" Atkinson was exasperated. "Don't you listen to what's going on around you, or what? Feldman has to show Gryfe the sort of thing he's been up to recently. He's angling for a new machine, but he won't get it unless he can show he's been making progress. He's been at it long enough. It was all right at the beginning, but recently the prof's hardly made any headway. Gryfe's getting pissed. No joy today and he'll shut it all down."

They sat in silence, Bateson wishing he'd asked for a change of shift years ago and Atkinson wondering about the joys of seaweed farming.

"Who is this lad anyway?" Bateson asked at last. "He's not an islander, is he?"

"No. A mainlander. I recognised him as soon as they brought him in. He was one of the lads from my sister's guesthouse. Tim, he said his name was. My youngest, Josh, seemed to rate him, although I had my doubts about him from the start. I don't want to imagine what they're going to do to him."

Bateson nodded sadly. "It won't be pretty," he agreed. "It's the first new human subject in a long while, isn't it, boss?"

"Yup. Certainly the first time we'd ever had one so young. Because Josh liked him, I feel a bit bad about what's going to happen to him. Stupid kid. What did he think he was playing at?"

The two men lapsed into silence again. A few minutes later a messenger delivered a file from Captain Grey: background information on the lad from the beach. As Atkinson read it, any sympathy he might have had for the prisoner evaporated.

"Bateson, listen to this. This'll make you feel better. This isn't some innocent HSL kid visiting the vacation camp for legitimate purposes. No, this is a Coalition agent, no doubt sent by the government to spy on us. At Gladys's place I thought he was a bit too nosy, too smart for his own good. You know, one of those city lads trying to show us all up as country bumpkins. Now I know he was out to destroy us, the swine." He was interrupted by a loud banging.

"That'll be him then," said Bateson. "He'll have just woken up. Probably with a bit of a headache, I reckon."

"Well," said Atkinson as he stood up. "Someone is going to have to pay him a little welcome visit. Don't worry, Will. I'll not ask you to go, you big pansy. I'll go myself. I'm quite looking forward to letting him know he's been rumbled."

CHAPTER 44

At first, Seb sat slumped on the floor of the cell and waited. After some time, he became so uncomfortable he shifted position to lean his back against the cot and stretch out his legs. He'd stopped berating himself for getting caught and now he just listened and waited. There were a few regular noises which were probably the humming and clanking of machinery, interspersed with the occasional clang and scrape of doors opening and closing. He tried to identify the mammals from their cries. He could hear some large primates and several human voices amongst the cacophony, but other calls were trickier to identify. Information coming directly into his mind was confused and he could make no sense of it.

His stomach started a rumbling protest. He hadn't eaten anything since leaving the camp. The long swim had depleted any energy he'd had, so now he was ravenous. He stood and shuffled over to the door and took some deep breaths. He knew better than to hope for room service, but thought that if they had wanted him dead they would have killed him by now. He shook the bars in frustration. It was a tentative shake at first and then he decided to really go for it. He was in deep trouble anyway, so what had he got to lose? He started shaking and kicking the bars then began to yell.

"Oi! Someone! Oi! Is anybody there? Oi! Can you hear me? Bring me something to eat!" He shouted until he was hoarse. His toes hurt after all the kicking and he slid back down to rest on the floor, his back against the door.

A few moments later there was the sound of footsteps climbing slowly up the stairs. The heavy, slow tread of a large man. If ever there was an example of footsteps sounding grumpy, this was it. Seb waited. The footsteps reverberated on the metal walkway, approaching his cell. Outside all noise seemed to stop. It was as if all the other occupants of the cells were holding their breath in anticipation.

"Oi yourself! Orders are no food! Get it? No food till you get back from OR. So you can shut up. You start makin' a fuss again and I'll take the hose to you. Understand?" The speaker hit the bars with a wooden truncheon. Seb felt them judder against his back. What did he mean, OR? Seb was scared again.

"What are you going to do to me? What's OR?" He tried not to sound as frightened as he felt. He twisted his neck round until he could see the speaker was Mr Atkinson, Josh's dad. He didn't look pleased.

"Mr Atkinson, it's me, Timothy." Seb was relieved. "We met at your sister's boarding house. I made friends with your son. Don't you remember me? Why am I here? This is a mistake isn't it?"

Atkinson peered at Seb balefully. "Your name ain't Timothy. I know that. You're here because Captain Grey wants you here, and he wants you because the professor wants you. You've been a naughty boy, haven't you, Seb Dyer?" Atkinson spat the name. "I told you back at my sister's place you ask too many questions, didn't I? I warned you that we don't take kindly to busybodies, didn't I? So what did you expect, you stupid git?"

"People know I'm here. If I go missing, they'll come and find me."

"No they won't. Don't kid yourself. By the way, OR means operating room, you dummy. Don't they teach you anything in your fancy city schools?" He smirked at Seb. "The professor wants to have a go at fixing you."

Fixing him? What did he mean by that? "Well, tell your professor I'm not broken! He can let me go right now, or there'll be trouble. My parents will -"

Atkinson cut Seb off before he could finish his threat. "Your parents will nothing. They're a long way from home right now, aren't they, Seb? Besides, what can a couple of journos do all the way over in the Americas?"

Seb didn't like the way he spat the word 'journos'. Nor did he like the fact that this guard at a secret prison facility on a remote island in the New British Archipelago seemed to know all about his parents. But that wasn't his most immediate problem.

"OK. So you know who I am. Very clever. So I guess you can tell me why your professor wants to 'fix' me? Fix me how?" He tried to keep the panic out of his voice, but he could feel his throat constricting and his heart thumping in his chest. Atkinson was eager to tell him everything. Seb just wasn't sure he really wanted to know.

"Well, you see, lad, the prof and his mates have worked out that this telepathy business is actually an illness. It's not natural and it's very dangerous.

Imagine it's like a virus you've caught. For thousands of years mankind got along quite nicely, thank you very much, without being able to talk to animals. Then along came the Siklus. See. Siklus, sick. Get it? People like you have been sick all along and it's the job of people like me and the prof here to cure you." With a sudden jerk of his head, Atkinson gestured to movement on the other side of the building. A stream of men in hospital robes were wheeling rickety gurneys along the walkway opposite Seb's cell. As a gurney hit bumps in the floor, a limb or tail would sometimes fall out from beneath blood-spattered sheets. Seb's heart sank further. "Can't have you infecting any more people, can we?" Atkinson continued with a smirk. "Can't let you breed, can we? Can't let you spread your infected genes to the next generation." He was glaring at Seb through the bars, but as Seb met his eyes he had an overwhelming feeling that the man was jealous of him. Suddenly Seb had a revelation. This man resented everyone who could communicate with other mammals simply because he couldn't do it himself. It was as ridiculous as that. This was behind the HSL. Simple jealousy. They felt excluded. Shunned. Like second-class citizens. They felt they hadn't been given the 'gift', the 'magical gene' which had made it all possible. It didn't matter that the Coalition government regarded everyone as equal, telepath or Non-Comm: the Non-Comms didn't feel it themselves. The intensity of Atkinson's bitterness was frightening. Jealousy and hatred were raw emotions which overrode conventional morality, and Seb felt a chill run down his spine as it dawned on him that he was in deep trouble.

"What are they going to do to me?" His voice cracked a little as he asked the question.

Atkinson smiled down at him, looked him in the eye and said coldly, "First they are going to take samples from you. From your brain, cut bits off. Then they are going to start injecting you with the drugs they've developed. The thing is, all this treatment is still in the experimental phase. Not even the prof knows exactly how you'll react to the injections. So unless he gets the new machine he's ordered, the only way he can tell if the drugs are effective is to drill directly into your skull through your eyes and take a look at your brain." He turned abruptly to leave, satisfied that he'd scared Seb enough. "That's why the no food orders. Can't have you puking your guts up in OR."

He turned back with one last quip. "Make the most of your illness while you still can. Enjoy your last little mind chats with your neighbours. By this time tomorrow it'll all be over. You'll be lucky if you can still remember your name, let alone talk to anyone, by the time we've finished with you."

This time when he walked away he didn't turn back, and Seb slumped over on the floor. He suddenly felt unbelievably cold. Cold, alone and very, very scared.

CHAPTER 45

Seb didn't know how much time had passed since Atkinson had gone, but at last he tried his best to calm down and send out a general call. He had no idea if it would work, as distracted as he was, but during a lull in the noises outside his cell he grabbed his chance. He knew Flo was much better at this than him, but he had to try.

Can you hear me? Can anyone sense me? I'm Seb. There seemed to be a pause in the cries outside, and his third attempt provoked a definite response. It was foggy, as if the sender's mind was befuddled with drugs, but it seemed to originate from the occupant of the adjoining cell.

You bring bananas?

Seb smiled with a mixture of triumph and relief. *Whoever you are, get to your cell door.* He hoped that if he could look out, the curve in the building would be enough for him to see his neighbour. He heaved himself to his feet, and pressed against the cold bars of the cell door. He squinted through the bars to the right and was rewarded with the sight of two large, long-fingered black hands clutching the bars of the neighbouring door. The palms were deeply lined and slightly shiny, the backs covered in coarse dark fur. As far as Seb could see the thumbs were differently angled from those on his own hand. As he'd already guessed. Primate, maybe chimpanzee.

Reach out, touch me! Seb said in his mind as he stretched out his arm. A hairy, black, scarred arm did the same and for a brief moment they managed to hold on, fingers entwined, before a long ear-piercing whistle sounded in the cells, forcing them to drop hands and cover their ears.

"No physical contact permitted!" barked the voice over the tannoy once the whistle had stopped.

But those few seconds had been enough.

My name, name, Moe.

Seb managed to tune into Moe's mind relatively easily, now the initial connection had been made, but found that Moe's thoughts tended to wander and become quickly confused. Rather than the stream of consciousness Seb had hoped for, they flowed in little trickles which emptied randomly into murky pools. Moe's mind flitted over his memories like a butterfly, briefly touching down on one idea before flying jerkily to another. There was no logic to the process, just an erratic meander through the past. Seb had difficulty following the sequence of events Moe projected into his head, but slowly, bit by bit, the chimp managed to tell his story.

I arrived with my mate, Millie. They did things to her. Seb felt Moe's pain. *Sometimes the humans would do things to me and watch how Millie reacted; other times they do things to my Millie. I miss my home. Regents Forest, nice place. You should go. But they are doing bad things here. They fed my Millie things to make her sick. One day she was taken away. They strapped her down. I never saw my Millie again.*

Their connection faltered as the chimp became distressed. It was incredibly frustrating. Seb desperately needed to link minds with someone more lucid. He moved over to the opposite side of the door and tried again, straining to hear any sign of life in the cell to his left and feel any connection there. Alone, he stood no hope of reaching Flo's mind. Would mind-melding with strangers work, even if he was sure he could do it? He toyed with the idea of setting up a relay call from one mind to the next until it reached her, but he knew the moors from his time at the camp, and there weren't many higher mammals conveniently roaming around. No, it had to be a group effort by the prisoners here. If he could orchestrate it, it could produce a single, powerful beam of thought. He peered through the bars of the cell door. "Well, there are certainly lots of captive minds in this place. Let's hope they can focus," he muttered.

CHAPTER 46

Flo was desperate to reach Seb. She and Lonce had woken feeling fresh enough to attempt a mind-meld, but if this failed to bring results they planned to make their way down to the holiday camp to find him. This meant heading west and then down towards Helmsley. Flo had no idea about the inhabitants of the little port town. Were they all supporters of the HSL? She imagined most would be, particularly if they were making money out of the 'vacationers'. The wind rustled the short heather and she shivered with apprehension.

Everything seemed impossibly difficult right now. She felt the familiar disappointment of a plan going wrong. Seb had to answer their call. He just had to.

"It shouldn't be like this. I should have been with Seb by now. I'll never forgive myself if anything happens to him, Lonce." Lonce stretched out and rubbed his head against her thigh in sympathy.

Flo sat cross-legged on her sleeping bag with Lonce at her side. She placed her left hand on his head and closed her eyes. She felt the stillness descend and the soft external noises of the moors retreating, leaving Lonce and her alone. They became points of lights in a sea of mist. She concentrated and willed her light to join his. Slowly, an inch at a time, they coaxed them together. As the points finally joined they created a bright beam, like a lighthouse, which swept around them, illuminating and scanning the mist, coming to rest occasionally on the timorous mind of some small creature. They scanned further and further afield, picking up the mind traces of countless scurrying creatures. Flo even had her first tantalisingly short connection with what felt like a raven and her heart leapt. But still they could not find Seb. If he were within range they should have sensed him by now.

Eventually, their minds focused on a point of collective fear and anger. They heard crying and howling, but neither managed to connect directly with Seb. It felt as though they were communicating through mud. A sharp pain in her head broke her concentration, her mind separated from Lonce's, and she felt a rushing sensation before she crashed back into her physical body. It was the most intense experience, and the worst pain, she'd ever had in a mind-share. She rolled over, clutching her head, and lay like that for a while, battling with the pain, trying to control it, willing it away. How long it took, she didn't know. No more than a couple of minutes, she guessed. She opened her eyes and met Lonce's. Concern was written over his brow. He licked her head. She'd never felt quite so physically drained before, nor so ill at ease.

"Agh!" She was furious. "Where did that come from? I've never felt anything like it. No, Lonce, I'm fine now. But I'm so annoyed with myself for breaking off. If only I'd held on just a little longer. But I couldn't, Lonce. I couldn't. I can't tell if it was him or not. What do you think? Did you feel it too? What if it was Seb's pain I was picking up? We have to get going. We have to find him!" She stood up, staggering slightly. But her head felt clear now.

The pain had gone, and so had the sense of panic. Now all she had was a cold, hard, rational determination to get the job done properly. Lonce too was ice calm.

Remember plan. We go to camp first, he said evenly.

"Yes, it isn't so far. It's near an old ruined abbey place. I saw it on the map Seb was given." Lonce was confused, so she tried to explain. "An abbey was a big building where people thought they could talk to God, but that isn't important right now."

Let us go, said Lonce, suitably unimpressed.

"According to this," she said, waving the map she'd copied from Seb's vacation welcome pack, "it's about seven miles straight across the moors west from where we are now. The HSL compound is just north of Helmsley." She pointed vaguely west. "But we came up the eastern side of the valley from Hodge Beck Point. So we've got two choices." She checked the map again. "We could go down the steep bit over there to the bottom of the valley, climb up and over the other side and then approach the camp from behind. Or we could go back the way we came and work our way round the coast."

Lonce pictured crows flying. The image made her smile.

"You're right; the crows have the definite advantage when it comes to mileage. Either way, it's going to take us the better part of a day." Lonce projected an image of him running effortlessly. "Sorry. It'll take *me* most of the day." He was right. He would have no trouble whichever way they chose, so in the end it was for Flo to decide and she chose the easier but more visible route via the shore.

As they scrambled back down the way they'd come the night before, she was amazed she hadn't broken an ankle.

"How on earth did I do this in the dark?"

I am good guide. I keep you safe.

"Modest too!"

Going down hurt her knees and she frequently slipped, cursing as she landed heavily on her behind. But they did it, and within only half an hour were back on the beach. Without wasting any more time they struck out towards Helmsley, keeping as close to the base of the hills as possible. There was no point in advertising their arrival by strolling down the middle of the beach, and becoming two moving targets against the pale background of sand and shingle.

CHAPTER 47

George woke up at his usual time of seven thirty. After a quick trip to the bathroom he padded in slippers and pyjamas to the kitchen. There was a definite advantage to Flo's living in her own apartment: he could potter about like this, making breakfast, humming to himself, or even singing, without being teased by her. He wondered vaguely how she was doing, and smiled to himself at the mental image of her reaction to his gift of the overnight train ride.

Before his second cup he went to the front door to see what, if anything, the postman had delivered. He enjoyed getting the post. Colleagues from around the world shared their finds with him, so that nearly every morning something new about the past arrived. It made fascinating breakfast reading.

The *Coalition Gazette* was there, but nothing too impressive in the headlines as usual. Under the paper lay a couple of official-looking letters and another from George's counterpart in West Virginia. A fourth letter, addressed to him in Jack's distinctive handwriting, was waiting at the bottom of the pile. Forgetting he should be bending at the knees, he let out a faint grunt as his back protested when he bent over to pick it all up. What was Jack writing for? He never wrote. Whatever the reason, it couldn't be good. George settled down to read it over a cup of fresh Caffeinix.

As usual he took a second or two to smooth the envelope before opening it. He was surprisingly nervous as he carefully slid his new bird letter opener along the flap and pulled out the contents. It was another letter, the envelope grubby and creased. He squinted closely at the postmark.

"What on earth?" Looking more closely, his confusion deepened. "Why send me a letter more than ten years old?" He then took a fortifying sip of his favourite stimulant before slowly unfolding the crumpled paper.

Dear Mr Gryfe,

This is just a quick note to update you on our research.

Over all, work is going well. We've been examining a group of mammals and humans who were displaying exceptionally effective telepathy. As you well know, this ability to mind-share between species is an extremely dangerous condition; however we believe the damage caused by the genetic awakening of the Siklus to be ultimately reversible.

In brief, trans-species communication without the need for physical verbalisation or illustration has only existed for a relatively short period of time. When the phenomenon was first observed, initial theories suggested it had an electromagnetic origin, with the brain detecting and interpreting electrical patterns in other individuals. Later studies showed double-stranded DNA had the ability to recognise similarities in other DNA strands from a distance. Once the theory of a genetic basis for telepathy became generally accepted, the search to identify the particular gene responsible for it began, one we could eliminate or deactivate over time - "breed it out of the equation", so to speak.

Our scientists took blood and tissue samples from all the test subjects to analyse their genes. Samples have also been taken from pure individuals, who exhibit no signs of telepathic ability or genetic contamination whatsoever. Through comparison studies we have discovered a few dozen short sequences of genetic material which seem to be causing this telepathic transfer.

I won't bore you with the specifics (a more detailed report is attached) but needless to say we hope this finding will lead to earlier identification of telepathic human children so they can be trained or treated to overcome their condition, whilst the process of gene elimination is perfected.

If we had not had so many candidates available to us for testing, our research would have taken decades longer. Thank you so much for arranging a steady supply of fresh specimens. The rail and sea delivery system you devised works very well.

I hope we can count on your continued support in this research. The new laboratory facilities you've provided on Rosendale are potentially ideal and we have fifty test subjects currently in residence, as well as my team of scientists and research assistants. We look forward to many happy years of collaborative research.

Yours sincerely,
Ulrich Feldman

As George read, his heart sank. Although there were no attachments, clearly this was the letter which had sparked off Claire's investigation more than a decade ago. This was the document which had got her killed. Jack must have had it for a while, though, so why he would be sending it to him right now? He thought of Flo's recent conversations about evolution and visions, and remembered her odd behaviour. Had she somehow seen the letter as well? He knew Jack felt Flo should know more about her mother's research, but surely he wouldn't have shown her this too? Little clues and inconsistencies began to make sense. Like the mysterious chip on the rim of his key pot. He suddenly felt stupid and naïve. She must have been planning something for a while.

Forgetting breakfast, he rushed along the corridor to the office, where he quickly accessed Flo's Finance Co-Operative account. It had been completely drained in one large withdrawal. Enough money to last a month had vanished in a day.

CHAPTER 48

New-Era London, some years earlier

Ulrich Feldman's official scientific career, heading the government's own laboratory, was short-lived. In fact, it ended after barely five years in the post. He was called to the head office for dismissal.

"Dr Feldman, your work here is of an exceptional standard. We are not calling into question your technical abilities as a scientist. It is just," the official paused to peer at him over his glasses before continuing, "it is just that you have yet to demonstrate any natural empathy or sympathy towards your fellow man, let alone to any other species." He felt uncomfortable under Feldman's impassive gaze. "Dr Feldman… Ulrich… I'm afraid we are going to have to let you go."

"It is because I'm a Non-Comm, isn't it?" Ulrich stated flatly.

"No, no, no. Not at all, not at all. You know we are not allowed to, we don't, discriminate on the basis of telepathic ability… or lack of. The Coalition is a government for everyone… for every living inhabitant of the planet and their preferred environments. All residents of this planet are all equal in the eyes of the law. All laws, Gaia's and ours." He tried to smile reassuringly at the man sitting opposite him. "Let's just say, your character simply does not fit the post."

Ulrich glared at him. "Was my work not adequate? Did I not get results? You knew I was ahead of the others in my research. I will complain to the Ministry…I…"

"The Ministry asked us to terminate your contract. There have been too many complaints about your apparent enjoyment of inflicting pain or humiliation on your subjects, and in one or two cases, on your fellow workers." The official stood up, indicating the end of the meeting. "I'm afraid we are unable to provide references at this time. Please clear your desk before lunch. Goodbye."

It was clear that the original choice of Ulrich for the post of director of the ComGen Laboratory in N'Era-London had been a flawed one. He'd been given the job simply because of his skills as a persistent lobbyist. He was a scientist in the most prosaic sense, and he lacked several necessary qualities for greatness and for the task at hand, namely, care for his fellow beings, social responsibility, open-mindedness and humility. In his view, though, mere technicians had the presumption to complain about him to the authorities and he found himself ousted by a petty bureaucrat and on the streets looking for work. Finding it was easier said than done, and he spent a few dark, resentment-filled years on the fringes of the scientific world. It never occurred to him to question his own role in his demise; it was far too easy to blame discrimination against Non-Comms on the part of 'we're all in it together' fakers of the Coalition.

But Ulrich was a survivor. He always had his own interests at heart. He was interested in power, and power, he knew, came from knowledge. Over the years he'd made an effort to cover his back by building a network of supporters from his contacts in the HSL. Turning his back on his former colleagues, he ended up seeking funding for his own lab, and the HSL were only too happy to provide it.

He had always relished playing God, and ever since he was a small boy he'd enjoyed taking things apart to see how they worked. When he was about twelve years old he had fun extracting DNA from his own cheeks. This led inevitably to attempts at extracting the DNA from anything else he could get his hands on and many unpleasant experiments took place in his mother's garden shed. Dozens of small creatures involuntarily supplied their DNA to his cause. As a child, of course, his equipment had been pretty basic: washing detergent, rubbing alcohol, his mother's supply of food colouring, some water and salt - but he'd come a long way since then, and finally his HSL bosses had spared no expense in providing a state of the art laboratory complex in the old Panopticon building on Rosendale.

Ulrich's mother believed he was a genius, so her little boy could have all the food colouring in the world as far as she was concerned. Her husband had died when Ulrich was only six years old, so 'little Ulrich' became the only man in her life. As a single mother it had been hard bringing him up. He was such an unusual boy.

"Nothing is too much trouble for my little Ulrich," she told a lodger one day. "He's special. You just watch. He's like a rocket that is going to light up the sky!" The lodger didn't quite know what to say. How can you contradict a mother's love? But as far as most people were concerned, Ulrich was a weird, unpleasant kid and you were wise to check whether you still had the correct number of body parts after meeting him.

Sybil Feldman, had inherited a grand house and even grander debts on her husband's death and had been forced to take in lodgers to cover the bills, but she'd been happy for Ulrich to carry on his experiments in the shed. Every now and then her lodgers complained about strange noises and unpleasant smells coming from it, and once a neighbour bravely suggested that Ulrich might have mammals imprisoned there. Sybil would firmly explain that her son was carrying out important work and walk away. If she ever heard the screams herself, she never let on.

So Ulrich grew up with no friends and no father, and a mother who indulged him and protected him from the rest of the world. In turn, he absolutely worshipped her. When he wasn't in his shed torturing small animals in the name of science, he was furtively watching her every move. This strange life continued for several years, until he landed his post at the New Era-London lab. One evening he had been walking back to the house he shared with his mother when he noticed a commotion ahead.

"What's the delay up there?" he asked someone.

"Don't know, mate. I heard a carriage had turned over." Ulrich carried on walking towards the gathering of mixed citizens, vaguely curious about its cause, until he was near enough to hear some snippets of conversation and excited chatter. It seemed a horse-drawn trolley carrying shoppers back from the market had overturned. Apparently the horse had been spooked by something, but was still too upset to be coherent about the accident. A couple of people had been injured and one killed.

Ulrich wasn't particularly interested in, or bothered by, the commotion. He continued on his way until something caught his eye. A fluttering scarf could be seen poking out from under one of the carriage wheels. He stopped, recognising its pattern. Then he caught sight of his mother's distinctive shopping bag lying on its side, the contents spread across the ground. He pushed his way forward through the crowd and saw, in unnerving detail, that the only fatality of the accident had been his beloved and most cherished mother.

CHAPTER 49

Rosendale, May

The methodologies at the Human Supremacy League laboratories were similar to the ones used in the state-run labs, but the final goals were diametrically opposed. Both sought to understand telepathy, but on Rosendale it was in order to eliminate it. Over the last twelve years Professor Ulrich Feldman had built up a team of like-minded, technically proficient but eerily unsentimental staff. As far as he knew they were all clear of the mind-sharing contamination which plagued the world outside.

As he walked through the lab he passed banks of hooded technicians, repetitively pipetting or placing trays in machines, their role to collect, organise and prepare data for use by the geneticists. Some of them were loading high-speed centrifuges, or putting equipment into the sterilising autoclaves. The machines, meanwhile, hummed and beeped or glowed green and blue. Two technicians were working on DNA electrophoresis, the standard method of sorting DNA molecules by length. Ulrich acknowledged the equipment had come a long way since he suspended his first strand of DNA in salt water in his mother's garden shed. Here they were suspended in a coloured gel and subjected to an electric field, causing the strands to migrate towards one end of the tray and separate out into bands of differing lengths. He gazed at them, almost lovingly, momentarily mesmerised.

Further on he passed the banks of holding pens where subjects were kept for immediate use, and then past the stairwell leading to the cells on the floors above. The pens ranged in size according to the species of the intended occupants and many had beds with restraining straps for the larger mammals and humans. As he peered into the pens his distaste for other living creatures was palpable.

Normally he would take a relaxed walk through his domain several times a day, but today he rushed along, accompanied by a mysterious sense of unease. Today the atmosphere in the lab felt highly charged and he was unusually nervous as he hurried past the holding pens. As he passed, the occupants became silent and watched him, some even managing to turn their heads to watch him go by.

Once in his office at the far end of the laboratory complex he shut the window blinds and the door, sank gratefully into the comfortable swivel chair at his desk and tried to calm down. He considered calling his head of security, Atkinson. But what was the point? What could he possibly say? "Hello, I'm feeling a little nervous today, do something about it"? Or "I think I'm being watched and I'm hearing whispers"? No, he couldn't do that. He did a quick mental check of possible causes of his disquiet. The few local communities dotted around the island's shores had pretty much been bought off by the HSL. There might be a few individual Coalition supporters out there, but the village elders had all benefited from the arrangements Gryfe had put in place, so that wasn't the issue. A fleeting worry that he might somehow have been contaminated with telepathic material crossed his mind, to be dismissed as ludicrous a second later. Who knew what other illnesses these animals carried?

He glanced down at the papers on his desk. Amongst the usual in-house progress reports lay a brief memo from one of the HSL's chief informers in N'Era-London. It stated that there had been an increase in reported nightmares amongst citizens around the time of the last major extraction of test subjects from the capital. Ulrich had dealt with this particular informant before and had found her to be reliable. Her position gave her access to hundreds of families. However, there was nothing in her current report to worry him particularly. These round-ups and transportations to the island had been going on for years, each time accompanied by a reported increase in REM activity amongst the telepathic citizenry. But as long as no one put two and two together, Ulrich was not bothered. Far more unsettling were his own feelings that morning.

Then he remembered something which temporarily took his mind off his personal worries. The boy. Just yesterday his guards had picked up a possible Coalition troublemaker. They'd found him on the beach, presumably after he had swum ashore from a boat. Ulrich didn't know the details yet, but was confident that one boy wasn't much of a threat to his research programme. Rather, his arrival was a stroke of luck. He would be the ideal specimen for the procedure Ulrich had been perfecting over the last year. Finally, he'd have something tangible to show Gryfe and his wife, the lovely Melissa. As he contemplated their imminent visit, Ulrich's nerves started up again. Immediately, the cause of his mysterious sense of unease became clear, he was simply nervous about this 'inspection'.

He gathered some papers together and hurriedly booted up his computer. He had to prepare for his sponsor's arrival. He hadn't made much headway since the last visit and wasn't looking forward to the inevitable storm, but he hoped his latest report might do something to deflect Gryfe's anger. He'd known the man for well over a decade now and had learned enough about politicians to understand that his choice of words was vital. He had to use expressions familiar to them. He wouldn't talk in terms of outright "failures", but rather "limited successes". The language also had to be as simple as possible. "Words of one syllable, dear," his mother had always advised him to use when talking to politicians. "They are not known for their intellects." He needed to focus on the potential of the new research rather than the disappointments of the old. The capture of the boy was perfect. He rubbed his hands together before cracking his knuckles happily. Yes, this boy was going to save his lab.

Ulrich was stressed by the prospect of Gryfe's visit because deep down inside he feared being revealed as a fraud. The reality was that after so many years of experimentation – of introducing an assortment of enzymes and viruses to the test subjects, operating and torturing – they were not much closer to discovering the cause of interspecies telepathy or the cure than they had been at the beginning. Of course, Ulrich wouldn't say as much to Gryfe. He wasn't going to jeopardise his cushy job and comfortable salary. No, Ulrich was many things, but he was not stupid.

"Gryfe barely understands the concept of genes. How can I explain enzymes too?" he muttered to himself. With a shrug, he started to compose his welcoming speech:

What is an enzyme? he wrote. *Simply put, it is a catalyst, something which causes change without being changed itself. Enzymes are the catalysts for chemical reactions. Our bodies need chemical reactions to live. There are naturally occurring enzymes in all living tissues, and they are highly specialised.* That's simple enough, even for Gryfe. He hastily scribbled a few more notes. *Our working hypothesis has always been that an enzyme was released into the environment during the Siklus which acted a catalyst or trigger, setting off interspecies communication.* He paused and gazed around his office. Not bad. Surely Gryfe will be able to follow that. He's heard it all before. The trouble was, could Gryfe actually appreciate the complexity of the task Ulrich had been set?

"However, given the sheer numbers, pinpointing the exact enzyme … or the exact gene… responsible for telepathy is, quite simply, a nigh on impossible task. For this reason," Ulrich muttered, practising what he intended to say, "I have concluded that direct surgical intervention will ultimately prove to be the most effective solution to the problem." He was relying on the scanner which Gryfe was bringing to facilitate this "surgical elimination" of the problem. Ulrich planned to subject the boy to a series of traumas by inflicting severe pain on several of the captive mammals. With the aid of the brain scanner he would be able to pinpoint the exact portion of the human brain activated by such stimulation; it would then be a simple procedure to lobotomise the affected area. The lobotomies he'd already carried out had been inaccurate. More often than not they resulted in complete idiocy, or worse. Too often death, if he was being honest. They'd lost too many subjects over the years to clumsy surgery.

The bitch, Finch, was the most recent casualty. The one who'd upset the guard with her eyes – what was his name? He paused, irritated he couldn't remember a detail like this. Bates, Bateman, something like that? Atkinson had reported the incident to him but had pleaded that the guard - a protégé of his, it seemed – should be given one more chance. Ulrich had reluctantly agreed. He tapped his pen distractedly on the desk… he'd been too lenient. The bitch's death had been unfortunate. She'd been a healthy, relatively intelligent specimen and could have provided a lot of interesting data had she survived. Most specimens were in a sorry state by the time they arrived at the facility, let alone when he started working on them. This one, however, had been in exceptional health, considering the length of the journey. Such a waste of money and resources, he thought bitterly. It was getting more and more difficult to obtain suitable subjects, and there was the constant worry that the authorities would hear rumours about what was happening and somehow discover their programme.

However, things were about to change. The boy was a perfect subject, and with the scanner Gryfe was supposed to be bringing Ulrich would be able to look into his brain as he gradually shut it down. If that didn't get answers, nothing would. He picked up the handset of the in-house phone.

"I want the prisoner down and prepped for surgery by four o'clock. Understood?"

"No problem. I'll see to it, sir."

CHAPTER 50

Flo's calf muscles began to ache after about an hour of walking on the mix of sand and shingle and a couple of times she nearly twisted an ankle. For the most part Lonce ran on ahead, scouting the area and occasionally chasing seagulls. It was his first major adventure outside N'Era-London and he was enjoying himself. He seemed to take particular pleasure in bounding up and down the rocky cliffs which overhung the beach, scent-marking sheltered patches. The city might be full of green spaces and wild forests, but it wasn't like this.

"The air has a different taste and smell up here, doesn't it?"

I feel free, he answered. *Yes. The space good.*

"This isn't a holiday," she reminded him, although she too felt almost hypnotised by the rhythmic pounding of the waves on the shore, the cry of gulls, the breeze, and the smells of the coast.

She had to call a halt. Her legs were burning and she was getting hungry. They found a sheltered spot where the shrubland vegetation came right down to the beach and she flopped down into a sandy dip. Her first priority was food. She pulled out four cereal bars from her pack and ate them one after the other, washing the last bites down with fresh spring water. Lonce stalked herring gulls, but settled in the end for a meal of two smaller oystercatchers.

As they sat there they discussed the practicalities of finding Seb. Flo had started to worry that he'd been found out and was being held somewhere. She was sure there was still a laboratory facility here on Rosendale, even if she didn't know who was in charge of it, and she had to assume the locals would stop at nothing to protect their own interests too.

"Lonce, we can't afford to be seen. You're better at moving around at night than me. Your vision is better, you can climb better, you can talk to species that I can't and, let's face it, you're better in a fight."

Lonce couldn't disagree. Accordingly, they planned to get as close to the small town of Helmsley as possible, then Flo would find a suitable hiding place on the outskirts and Lonce would go on alone. He would search the town and locate Seb, and if Flo was right they'd figure out a rescue plan.

After a short rest she was eager to get on with it. They still had a few miles to go. The coastline wasn't a straight one; it zigzagged back and forth, occasionally broken by jagged rock formations which they had to scramble over, or slippery rock pools they carefully skirted. By Flo's reckoning it would take them several more hours before they got to Helmsley; she hoped they wouldn't meet anyone on the way.

They arrived at Helmsley as night fell, and found an empty, slightly dilapidated barn on the edge of a large farm property where Flo could hide.

"This place reeks of neglect. Hopefully the farm's abandoned." She settled herself comfortably into the straw, and prepared herself for a long wait. Lonce nuzzled her head before heading off silently to scout round town.

Alone, Flo lay down in the straw, enjoying being horizontal at last. Her muscles ached and she desperately needed the rest. Her eyelids began to droop as she succumbed to her exhaustion, but she'd only been lying there for a few minutes when she was suddenly bombarded by a very clear distress call from someone nearby. She hoped it was from Seb, but that was the problem with generalised calls for help… they didn't come with calling cards. The cry originated from somewhere on the farm, she was sure of it. She did a quick mental scan and pinpointed its origin; it seemed to come from someone tied up at the back of the main house. He sounded so upset that Flo had no choice but to try to find him and help him if she could. Hoping she'd get back before Lonce returned, she set off.

The farm had a sinister feeling unlike anything she'd encountered before. Itwas not a happy place and there was an undercurrent of violence in the air, but she couldn't ignore the call for help. Whoever it was had managed to visualise his surrounding and was sending her directions. As she crept forward she disturbed a group of chickens roosting in a hen house. Their gentle chuffing turned into loud agitated clucking and other calls as she went by. "Shut up!" Flo couldn't believe her bad luck. What if they bring someone out to see what's wrong?

She found the dog tethered at the back of the house. He'd been straining at the rope and had hurt his throat. He told her his name was Atticus, and he'd been there for weeks.

I'd rather be beaten than tied up like this. I'm going crazy here, he went on quickly as she struggled to unknot the rope. *I haven't been fed for days, and if I bark to remind them that I'm still out here they come and beat me. My throat hurts from this collar. Help me get it off. Hurry!* He was desperate.

"What have they done to you? Why? Who brought you to this place?" Flo asked, as she battled to untie the leash.

Everything was fine at first. I worked as a guard dog for them, but then in the winter they brought another dog back. Her name is Obi and they like her better. She lives inside. Alerted by the mention of her name, Obi started yapping excitedly from within the house. *Talk of trouble and it will come,* Atticus said bitterly. He strained on the rope. Flo looked round frantically for something sharp to cut the cord, until she remembered Seb's knife and patted down her pockets looking for it. The yapping from the house was getting louder and a light went on upstairs. Her fingers fumbled and she dropped the knife as she pulled it out of its sheath. Dropping to her knees, she blindly searched the ground. It had to be there somewhere. She could hear noises from the house, and the chickens were still clucking restlessly. Any minute now she'd be discovered.

By some miracle her fingers closed around the smooth sheath. Pulling out the blade, she slashed as hard as she could across the taut cord. Liberated, Atticus started running and Flo raced to catch up with him. Together they made it to the barn and Flo flopped back into the straw, breathing heavily, her heart thumping. She could hear a voice shouting over the sound of her rasping breath.

"Shut up, Obi, you stupid animal! Just shut it! We're trying to sleep!" There was a high-pitched yelp and then silence. The light went out and they were in the clear.

CHAPTER 51

Lonce moved swiftly and silently through the sleeping town. He didn't like this place. It felt wrong.

Avoid waterfront and port. Bright lights and movement. Too much noise. Avoid humans in town. Leap in and out of small, dark gardens and slink down unlit alleys. I find a small group of felines, and snort to show I peace-come. Not hunting. I share our story. They are quick learners, and they understand my fear. Their leader, Zero, shares same feelings, same fear. He tells me of big meeting outside town this night, in old place humans called abbey. Flo told me about abbey.

I go back to Flo.

Lonce returned to find Flo and Atticus lying together in the straw. She was stroking the dog gently while studying the lacerations which covered his back and throat. Lonce chuffed a greeting to them both and padded over quietly to inspect this new member of their team. The two males sniffed each other warily, gleaning basic information. Atticus explained his story.

I headed a team of dogs specialising in cancer detection at a hospital in N'Era-London. I was happy there but the work was wearing me down so I left last year. I wanted to find something completely different. I have, I had, a special friend. I wanted to find a place for a new life with her, so I accepted the job here. I was going to send for her. I thought it would be a good change of pace. Being a security dog on a semi-derelict farm doesn't take a lot of brains, does it? He looked mournfully at them both and hung his head. *It wasn't long before I realised I'd made a dreadful mistake. Most of the people on the island are Non-Comms.*

Lonce settled down on the straw next to Atticus and started to gently lick the dog's wounds. His saliva would be the best medicine for the parts Atticus couldn't reach himself. He then proceeded to share with them his discoveries of the evening. Flo was impressed by Lonce's speed in contacting the local feline community, and could hardly wait to join his new friends at the abbey. She pulled out her map from her bag and used the torchlight to study it, estimating the ruined building to be about a mile away. The rendezvous with the felines was due to start soon and they still had to get there in the dark, but Atticus was weak from lack of food. Suddenly, Lonce got up and trotted purposefully out of the barn. A few minutes later he returned with a chicken hanging lifelessly from his jaws.

Eat! he commanded Atticus. *You come with us. You need strength. Eat,* he said again.

Without needing to be told twice Atticus guzzled down the chicken. A few minutes later there was nothing left of the hapless bird except a few stray feathers clinging to his chin.

Flo and Atticus hurry now, to abbey. Flo led the way, while Lonce silently shared their story with Atticus, who was eager to help.

As they approached the ruins Flo glimpsed a group of creatures standing in what would once have been the abbey cloisters. Several cats, half a dozen dogs, some weasels and a few crows were waiting patiently for the meeting to begin.

Welcome all of you, began the leader, Zero, as soon as Lonce and the others arrived. *Tonight we greet a new friend, Lonce. We greet also his human companion, Flo. I see Atticus too. Welcome to you all.* Zero anticipated the concerns of the group gathered around him. *Do not fear this human. She is friendly to us.* Flo felt dozens of pairs of eyes fix her with penetrating stares and felt gentle exploratory probes in her mind as she opened herself to them. They had accepted Lonce's and Atticus's participation easily, but she was treated with suspicion. The reason slid into her consciousness: they were afraid of the human residents of Rosendale. Now she felt their surprise as one by one it dawned on them that she was open to communication.

Zero acted as the mind-voice for the Rosendale crowd. *Since the time of our fathers' fathers, the island humans have changed. Money has arrived, more than before. Still they want more. We do not understand it. They have everything they need to live. They have food. They have shelter. We do not understand their need for this thing called money. Our life here is difficult. Atticus is not alone in suffering. Many of us suffer. We watch what happens. We have been watching the humans at both the camp and the Fearful Place. Enough! Enough! We will stop the bad things.*

Flo could see that Zero had done a fine job of gathering information and support, but he needed an outside catalyst to really motivate his followers to do something. Now she, her friends and their stories became that catalyst. One thing bothered her more than all the rest, however. "The Fearful Place", Zero had called it. What on earth was that?

Flo stood on the ruined wall between Lonce and Atticus as they took it in turns to communicate with the group. She could feel the residual mistrust of the group gathered in front of her. However, Lonce testified on her behalf and managed to convince them of her sincerity. She was the sort of human they could trust, he insisted; not like the Non-Comms of Rosendale. Together the two of them shared their recent experiences: their lives in N'Era-London; their fears for the status quo; the death of Flo's parents and the spate of mysterious disappearances down south.

"But my immediate problem, tonight," Flo added, "is that my best friend Seb is missing. We need your help to find him." She pictured him in her mind. She knew every detail of him, and the image was crystal clear as she shared it with the crowd. Instantly her mind was bombarded with questions, information and images. Everyone wanted to feed her information.

He has been seen many times at the HSL camp. He asked questions about the Fearful Place, the humans call the Panopticon, said Zero. *He is there now.* He went on to tell them that Seb had been taken there unconscious.

"What is this Fearful Place?" Flo asked. "What happens there? Why are you so frightened of it?"

We do not know what happens inside. We only know that apart from the humans that work there, no one else comes out alive.

"So help me! Help me find Seb and together we'll save -"

We will help you, Zero interrupted. *There is a way for us all to be helped.*

CHAPTER 52

Marcus Anthony Gryfe and his entourage arrived by boat a good two hours earlier than expected. He'd done it deliberately, of course. It was his way of checking up on his employees. His team consisted of his wife Melissa, and Captain Grey and Drill Sergeant Blue of the training camp. It was several years since Gryfe had bothered to visit the facility and it certainly impressed him more than it had the first time. Earnest men and women were doing complicated things with pipettes and Petri dishes. Lights blinked and machines hummed. It all looked very efficient and professional. As he marched through the laboratory he stopped from time to time to question the operatives. He didn't often follow their explanations about the technology and procedures but, like the long dead politicians of the twenty-first century he tried to emulate, he'd learned how to fake the appearance of intelligence and understanding. He'd also done some reading on genetics on the journey up, enough to make the right sort of noises, at least. He had decided to leave the scanner on board until he was sure the lab workers deserved it.

"So tell me, where do you keep your micron arrays?" he asked the nearest technician, Larry, who stood with a pipette in hand. After a split second of surprised confusion the young man gestured to the workbench he was standing at.

"Well, er, sir, here is one."

"Ah yes. I'd expected a bigger one," said Gryfe, hiding his embarrassment. "Perhaps you could explain to my people what you are doing here."

A look of horror flickered across Larry's brow, and he looked nervously around the group. This was his first meeting with the great man himself and he wanted to make a good impression. He took a deep breath and launched into an explanation of his work. He was sharp enough to know his presentation should be clear and concise but avoid patronising his audience. Pre-Siklus, he'd heard, children learned basic genetics in school, but now most people's knowledge of genetics started and finished with Lush's famous communication gene. Everyone had heard of it, but few people understood it.

"The first thing you need to know is that genes influence physical characteristics and behaviour," he started. "That is, with very few exceptions, most physical traits and behaviours are influenced by at least one gene, sometimes several." His audience nodded wisely; they seemed to be following him. "But genes are not destiny and they can be changed or even removed completely." Larry gestured to the bench. "Here, you'll see what Mr Gryfe has correctly identified as a micro-array. But it is, of course, only a small part of what we do." He smiled at them, warming to his subject. "These arrays are the fastest and simplest ways of conducting genetic tests. On each glass slide there are rows and rows of things called DNA probes, which test for specific DNA sequences or mutations. If the mutation or sequence is present in the DNA being tested, a specific spot will glow under special light." He paused, worried he was losing them. “Er, you can think of it as a sort of ‘scanner’ or ‘reader’.” He waved them forward, closer to the bench. They all leaned forward obediently. “In this example, the green represents the control DNA and the red represents sample DNA. Both have been hybridised to a target DNA. Yellow is a combination of control and sample DNA, also hybridised to the target. Black, of course, represents areas where neither the control nor sample DNA have been hybridised to the target. So you see -” A sharp cough from Gryfe interrupted him.

“What on earth are you talking about, man – red, green and whatnot? Captain Grey and the others are not interested in every damn detail, and you can’t expect my wife to follow this rigmarole. Just tell us, in plain English, what you are doing here. And hurry up about it. I haven’t got all day!”

“No, sir! Yes, sir! Of course, I’m sorry.” Larry took a breath before continuing more slowly. “Each spot on an array is associated with a particular gene. In our case, of course, we are looking for the genes which cause the mental illness commonly known as interspecies telepathy. Our task is more complicated than normal because we are dealing with so many different species, and there is so much genetic similarity between species. The cross-referencing alone is a nightmare, and you have to factor in errors and so on.” He tailed off as Ulrich appeared at his side. The director had been monitoring Larry’s performance from his office, and although he couldn’t hear every word he could tell by the body language that his young assistant was floundering.

"Forgive my tardiness." Ulrich came forward, smiling, and shook first Gryfe's hand and then the hands of the others in the party. "Larry here is one of my finest technicians. And the most dedicated to the cause. But let me briefly explain some other aspects of our work." With a nod, Ulrich told Larry to get back to work, and then gestured to Gryfe and his team to follow him. "As you know, our main purpose here is to identify a means of switching off whichever gene is responsible for interspecies communication through telepathic transfer." He nodded, and his audience automatically nodded back. "We have various research strands working simultaneously. Apart from our lab work, we do other sorts of experiments in order to pinpoint the exact part of the brain involved." His audience stared blankly at him. "We've had some interesting results in this sphere of research," Ulrich continued. "I now believe surgical elimination is the way to go."

"How did you come to that conclusion? It's a fairly big leap, isn't it?"

"We reproduced an old Soviet experiment with a mother rabbit and her eight kits."

"What was that?" Melissa asked suddenly, interested in the idea of rabbits.

"We fitted the mother rabbit with electrodes and took her eight babies several miles offshore and killed them one at a time. It was fascinating," beamed Ulrich. "Each time the mother's behaviour changed dramatically at the exact moment of their death." He smiled widely at the group. "With the scanner you've brought us we'll be able to pinpoint exactly which portion of the brain is activated by such trauma." He looked pointedly at Gryfe. "And then it will be a simple procedure to lobotomise the affected area of the brain."

"So you think it's as simple as that to eliminate telepathy? This is good news," said Gryfe. "Finally," he added under his breath.

"But the baby bunnies?" Melissa asked. "Was it really necessary to kill the babies? That poor mother."

"Good grief. I don't have time for this," Gryfe barked. "Where is your office? Melissa, you stay here. Look around. Or go upstairs, check out the holding pens. Forget the damn bunnies! Go pet the cute little animals you are so fond of. Grey, Blue, come with me. Professor Ulrich and I need to talk."

Once in Ulrich's office, Gryfe idly flicked through papers on the desk before saying sweetly, "I'm having a bit of trouble with our HSL supporters. They don't appreciate the long drawn out nature of scientific research. Not like me." Suddenly he slammed his fist down. "They want results, don't they? They want to see that the money they've donated hasn't been wasted!" Grey and Blue stood silently by the door, effectively blocking Ulrich's exit. "They've threatened to stop all funding unless we give them solid results within the month. You know what that means, don't you? I may well lose my position within the party. You would certainly lose all your funding, *and* my protection, and believe me, you don't want that to happen. Without my smokescreens the government will be on to you like a ton of bricks, shut this place down, arrest you and throw away the key."

Years of suppressed paranoia filled Ulrich's wiry frame. A vast chasm opened before his eyes and he was back to the dark days of humiliation and unemployment. This time it would be worse, because he'd been caught doing "wrong". He wouldn't simply be unpopular with colleagues; he would be considered a danger to society and locked up. The strain of the last few years was suddenly too much for him and he felt himself sinking. He desperately needed to reassure Gryfe. He needed the brain scanner Gryfe had brought. With that one machine he knew he could change the world. He could cure the world of its mental affliction. Humans would rule again. Gryfe must understand that once Ulrich got his hands on the scanner, there would be no more delays.

Gryfe ranted and raved while Ulrich whined about the difficulties they'd had with substandard technology and the size of the task they'd been set. In fact, Gryfe had invested too much time and too much of his career to have any intention of stopping the programme now: it had to succeed. But he wanted Ulrich, the slimy little toad, to sweat a bit. However, one thing was sure. If it was destined to be a failure he wanted it to be Ulrich's failure, not his. He listened half-heartedly while Ulrich babbled on. The man was clearly unhinged and Gryfe was losing patience.

"So, you see," Ulrich gabbled, "what we really need now to bring our research forward is the scanner you've secured for us. That one piece of equipment will revolutionise our work here." He grabbed Gryfe's arm in desperation. "We have a first candidate in mind and with the scanner we can watch his brain as we subject him to various tests. He'll be in theatre by four. If you get the scanner in, we can set it up quickly. We've isolated a few substances which may impact on his telepathic abilities; various bacteria and enzymes, for example, which stimulate genetic recombination. I'm also sure that triggering emotional responses will be effective. It is amazing the effect emotions have on our subjects. You'd be astonished. With your scanner we can pinpoint the exact part of the brain responsible for telepathic transfer, and then it's just a case of lobotomizing the subject and retesting. We're not entirely sure what collateral effects will be achieved, so all test subjects must be both physically fit and expendable. This lad fits the bill perfectly."

CHAPTER 53

It was two in the morning and Helmsley appeared deserted. As they made their way through the back streets Zero explained more of the town's recent history.

Over the years, our town has grown. More and more humans arrive from places far away. We know nothing about them because they do not talk to us, or communicate with non-humans in any way. I think they do not even see us, perhaps because they do not wish to. Some of these people do not stay long. They come like birds, only when the weather is good. His eyes glinted viciously. *I wish they were as easy to deal with as birds.*

They arrived finally at another outlying farm on the edge of the town. It was smaller and better kept than the farm where Flo had found Atticus.

Be careful here. Behind the stable is the killing place, Zero said solemnly.

"The what now?" Flo stopped walking, thinking at first she must have misheard. "Don't tell me. Another charming name… but I can guess what happens here." She shook her head. "I'm sorry, Zero; I'm having difficulty grasping all of this. It's all so far removed from the way life is in the city. I just don't believe there are so many HSL supporters, or that killing actually still happens. Have I spent my life in a bubble?" She turned to Lonce and Atticus. "Did you know? Did you have any idea?"

Atticus hung his head. *No,* he said. *I had my suspicions when I arrived on the island, but no, I didn't.*

There was no reason for Atticus to know, interrupted Zero. *It is a well kept secret. Even the farmers do not talk about it. It is against the Coalition laws. If the farmers were to be caught killing and providing meat, there would be trouble. So no one talks... not even to each other.* He started walking again, towards the stables. *We must continue. Come now. Quietly. We must find Torigon. Without her you will never help your friend.*

"Why have you put up with this?" asked Flo as they walked swiftly through the back streets. "Surely you can stand up for your rights? Contact the Coalition authorities?"

We no longer believed help would come. We no longer trusted humans. Zero hung his head with embarrassment but didn't stop walking.

With a shudder, Flo followed him. She felt more and more out of her depth. This wasn't the sort of adventure she had planned. The Fearful Place, the Killing Place? But there was no way to rewind and start again. She was beginning to appreciate how complicated life was and how precariously modern society was balanced. Carnivorous animals hunted in order to survive; this was acknowledged and accepted by all, even by prey species. It all connected to the great circle of life. But the killing of other life-forms simply for pleasure, profit, or when not absolutely necessary for survival, was universally frowned upon. She sighed. This was something she needed to think about. Right now, however, Seb needed saving. The HSL needed stopping – because whatever they were up to, it wasn't good. She needed to finish what she had started.

There were a couple of lights on upstairs in the main building, but the stable block and the Killing Place beyond it were both dark. Flo could just make out that the quality of the building was much higher than that of Atticus's farm. Clearly the owners had a lot more money. The HSL must be paying top rates for their meat. The stable had the sort of folding concertina doors in highly polished wood which would not look out of place in the city. There was a small round window in each of the gleaming panels, but these were sealed, with no means of opening them. Flo grabbed one of the handles, expecting to stride right in. She could sense someone inside willing her to enter.

"It's locked. The door is locked. I can't get in," she said to Zero, surprised, unused to the concept of locking animals up.

So unlock it, he replied, misunderstanding the whole concept of doors.

"It's not that easy. I need a key." She looked around for inspiration. There was no way she'd get through the porthole window. It was too high and too small even for her. Someone needed to get in there to try the door, but she was probably the only one present with a chance of working the handle from the inside. There was no point asking the occupant to kick the doors down, easy as that might have been. The noise would have woken the entire town, and the thought of the darkened Killing Place was an effective deterrent.

Atticus came up beside her, stood on his hind legs and sniffed the glass.

I can get through, if you open it.

“There is the problem of the handle on the other side; a slight issue of thumbs, Atticus. How can you open the door?”

I worked in hospitals for a long time; do you think I never encountered a closed door before?

“Yes, but not like this,” she started to say, but Atticus raised a quizzical eyebrow and she wasted no more time arguing. With every passing second they risked detection. She picked up a large stone, took the scarf from her neck and wound it round the rock. The thin pane broke quite easily, but the noise seemed likely to wake the household. She stood stock still, listening. Only silence. Apparently killing was tiring work. She pulled the remaining shards of glass out of the frame, more aggressively than she intended.

Atticus took a few steps back and then leapt through the empty porthole, landing almost silently on the floor of the stable. They heard some scrabbling of his claws on the door before it slowly folded open. Flo unlatched the other segment of the concertina and led the others inside. To the right, something metallic glinted. Lonce stiffened. He recognised it.

“Oh, I know what this is,” whispered Flo excitedly. “It’s a hydroride. Very cool and very fast. Is this what you chased in N’Era-London, Lonce? No wonder you couldn’t catch it.”

Can you ride it? asked Lonce, ignoring the pang of failure. The other animals looked on apprehensively.

“Well, I know how to in theory… but no, I can’t. I wish I could.” She peered further into the gloomy interior of the stable. She could make out familiar shapes of riding tackle hanging over a stall. A soft whinnying accompanied the warm welcome which filled her mind. There, at the back, stood a creature she could ride. Her name was Torigon.

CHAPTER 54

Hours had passed since Seb first tried to communicate with the occupant of the cell to his left. Whoever it was seemed very distant and mistrustful, and it was probably going to take some time to establish a working bond. First of all, Seb needed to find out what species he was dealing with. It didn't really make that much difference to mind-sharing, but it was more polite, in some way, to know. Moe seemed to be sleeping now and Seb had no wish to disturb him. He assumed whoever was to his left was sleeping too. That would explain why he couldn't reach them.

Seb must have fallen asleep as well, because he suddenly found himself slumped over on his cot, his mouth open, and what passed for a pillow slightly damp where he'd dribbled on it. He woke with a crowd clamouring inside his head. He was bombarded with information, questions and demands, urgent shrieks and cries of raw fear. Moe was awake too, and for the first time apparently completely lucid. Seb also felt a call from his mysterious other neighbour, urging him to wake up and come to the cell door. Once again he pressed his face against the bars and squinted to his left.

He'd got the impression she was a female, but had no idea of her species until he caught a glimpse of her. The young adult was startlingly familiar. She was Lonce's double.

Seb, like everyone else, had always assumed Lonce was the only snow leopard in the archipelago, the final and solitary descendant of an original captive pair, so was completely stunned by the sight of her. He knew what a healthy snow leopard should look like, and this one had clearly been in captivity for quite a while. There was an air of misery about her. Her coat was patchy, as if she had been over-grooming, and her face poked forlornly out between the bars as she stretched out a foreleg.

My name Uncia, she said and he knew instantly, that although she was in poor physical condition her mind was still sharp. Maybe she would be able to help him set up the mental beacon he needed. Lonce and Flo would have figured out by now that something was wrong. They'd be trying to find out where he was, but for that they'd need help. He had to think of a way of reaching them. Uncia had evidently coped better with captivity than Moe. Snow leopards were solitary beings anyway, unless they were with their cubs. Moe, on the other hand, was a social animal who needed to live amongst a group of friends and family, not stuck by himself for months at a time in a bare cell.

He fully expected a loud alarm bell and an angry voice over the tannoy system as soon as he reached out to touch her, but nothing happened. The guards' attention must have been elsewhere. Seb wasn't about to complain. Carefully, he took hold of her paw. Now they were linked forever.

CHAPTER 55

New Era London, Guards Station, Interrogation Room 5
Witness Statement 1.5 of Melissa Gryfe née Harcourt
Species: Human
Sex: Female
Affair: Rosendale
Signed in the presence of K9 Officer Dante. Friday 5 August

Melissa, today I want you to talk about Rosendale. What you found there. Your impressions. Can you do that for me?

"Mm-hmm. Yes. I understand." She paused. "I found the Panopticon deeply disturbing. I hadn't expected anything like that. By the look of it the lab had been going for years, but the more I heard about it the sicker I felt. I spoke to some technicians while Marcus was with the head of the laboratory and the two men from the holiday camp. The scientist was the same creepy little man I'd met years ago, when I got engaged to Marcus.

"I looked into the holding pens. I felt sick, but I took my time peering into each one, forcing myself to absorb every detail. This wasn't a clinic where cleanliness was important; clearly it was just a glorified prison. I noticed traces of dried blood and faeces the so-called cleaning staff had missed. It smelled of ammonia… urine, I suppose. I saw the odd scuff mark along the skirting boards and rips in the curtains. But worst of all, I saw the eyes of the penned 'subjects' as they looked back at me. Not one moved or uttered a sound and yet it was the noisiest and most violent place I'd ever experienced. I forced myself to walk slowly the entire length of the pens and look carefully into each; it was part of my rebirth.

"I found the stairs, next to the lift shaft, leading to the upper level of cells and started up them, emerging from the stairwell onto a wide metal walkway which circled the huge interior yard and led round to all the cells. Similar walkways ran round the second and third floors above me. There must have been around twenty-five doors on each level. Unlike the holding pens on the ground floor, which had been eerily quiet, here the level of audible noise was staggering. As I stepped onto the walkway the cacophony was deafening. Then, gradually at first, I found little by little I was beginning to understand the cries and whimpers inside my head."

Melissa met Dante's eyes. "You can't possibly know how I felt then. You've always been able to mind-share; but at that moment, on the walkway, in that dreadful place, simple noise became some sort of 'communication'.

"Without warning, the calls and cries abruptly halted. As the silence outside my head grew louder I could see an increase in the guards' activity in the courtyard; they appeared to be as unnerved as I was by the sudden quiet. The air seemed heavy, or maybe it was just my perception. I could still hear the guards' shouts, but they sounded much further away than the ever increasing cries inside my head. I was bewildered for a while and staggered a little.

But I had to know what was in those cells, so I kept going along the walkway. I heard some guards clanging up the stairs behind me, but I carried on towards the first cell. Then two guards pushed past me and I flattened myself against the wall and stopped. The guards ran to the first cell door and peered inside, then on to the next and then the next. I could make out two others checking the cells on the floor above. As one of them passed me for a second time I could hear him reporting back to the tower guards."

Melissa looked across to Dante again. It was hard to sit here, day after day, explaining her life as a Non-Comm, as the wife of Marcus Gryfe, to this gentle, compassionate dog. She was embarrassed, humiliated, and strangely defiant.

"I know you think I'm weak and pathetic. I know you can't understand why I married him, why I did what my parents told me to do. But you don't know what it was like. Only now do I understand it myself. I had so little self-esteem at the time. My parents thought I was a disappointment, but, at least I could be a means to an end. I wanted them to love me. I believed if I did everything they asked of me, they'd love me. I thought… oh, I know this sounds like just an excuse for a life wasted, but I thought that if they saw him happy with me, I would gain their respect and their love. That's all I ever wanted. To be loved, you know?

"But there I was, waking from a dream into a nightmare. The burning invasion of my mental space shocked me. The voices in my head were so anguished, so pained; yet hearing their pain made me feel alive. It connected me to something bigger than myself. For the first time in my life, I felt purposeful and unafraid. I came to the first cell door. I forced myself to look inside. There, sitting in the middle of the floor, eyes closed, was a solitary macaque. I walked on to the next cell. Another single large primate sat silently on the floor, eyes closed. The cells were dirty and smelly and the inhabitants looked ill and maltreated. I'd only ever seen healthy animals around N'Era-London, so I couldn't believe the difference. I walked on again, picking up speed now, the full horror of the place finally dawning on me. Pigs, sheep, and many other smaller creatures all sitting forlornly in dirty cells. The idea that Marcus could be involved in it turned my stomach. It was worse than simply enjoying his bloody steak every evening; there he was complicit in torture.

"As I peered through the bars into yet another cell I was horrified to see Toby, my old friend; the only creature who had genuinely, unreservedly loved me. Of course it wasn't him; I know that now, but at that time my chest felt constricted and for a moment I was completely unable to breathe. Was this Toby? I'd believed the Toby of my childhood long gone, but could this pathetic creature, shivering in the cell, be him? As I peered through the bars at him I became more and more sure I'd found my old friend and I looked around in vain for a way to open the cage door, some sort of switch or button.

"I didn't find one, but finally I saw the truth of my life; all those lies I'd been told and the lies I'd told myself; my complacency, the surrender to my parents and to Marcus. I saw him then as dangerous and depraved and I wondered how much my parents had known about his activities there."

Dante had to ask. He didn't want to; it was more than professional curiosity; he was intrigued.

Did your parents know what was going on?

"I can't believe my elegant, upper-class mother could have ever condoned that facility. But then again, she'd condoned selling me to Marcus in the first place. She agreed to send me to that school. But my father must have known; I can see that now. So, yes, Daddy knew what was happening there. His money probably funded it. I was finally awake to the fact that my life had been a sell-out, the pathetic delusion of an unquestioning mind. I hated myself. Why had I wasted my time begging for love from people who didn't even deserve my respect?" Melissa looked to Dante as if he could explain it.

A major part of this investigation concerns the disappearances over the years of various mammals. Do you know anything about them?

"I was seeing the 'disappeared' right there! Some were tethered to cots, others to the walls, but they were all sitting, eyes closed, waiting. But no, I didn't know about them before."

CHAPTER 56

Knowing Seb wasn't needed in theatre before four, Atkinson sent his men on a quick tour of the cells with orders to fetch the boy on their way back down because, as he said to William, something was happening which he needed to investigate before they did the transfer. Feldman would have to wait a few minutes.

"That silence is getting louder, mate. We need to check it out," he'd said to William. "I know you, you lazy sod; as far as you're concerned, the quieter the better. Idiot!"

"I wouldn't worry about it," Will answered, pouring himself more tea from the ugly brown pot which sat between them on the desk. "Doc's probably given them something to sleep. I like it, I do. I get sick of all the yowlin' and carrying on all the time. Can't hear myself think most days."

Atkinson couldn't fault his logic. "Yeah, you might be right, but can't hurt to look though, can it?" He looked out of the window. His brother, Robert, and another guard emerged onto the walkway of the first floor. They had brought a gurney ready for the boy. He clicked on the radio. "Oi. Bob. Have a good look at what's happening in the other cages." Knowing he was being observed by his brother, Robert waved to show he'd heard rather than radioing back, and quietly passed on the orders to the others patrolling the floor below. From the tower Atkinson watched the two youngest men abandon the gurney and break into a sprint along the walkway.

"Them two like pretending they're in a real prison, not a zoo. Look at them running around like that, silly sods." William had joined his boss at the window, casting a lazy eye over the walkway. "Hey, look, chief, they just nearly knocked over Gryfe's missus. What's she doing up there?"

"Gryfe and his party have got security clearance for the whole place. They can go where they want."

Atkinson's younger brother, Robert, loved his job, partly because it was one of the best paid jobs on the island and partly because, with his brother in charge, he knew he would advance rapidly through the ranks. Most of all he liked the control he had over the prisoners. Dealing with pathetic animals was one thing, but having his hands on a young human male was something else entirely. He looked forward to bringing the upstart traitor downstairs. He didn't know what was in store for him, but he hoped it would hurt. Robert had had enough of bleeding-heart telepaths banging on about species equality. For the moment, though, he had to concentrate on the other prisoners. Something was going on, but who knew what?

It had started quietly enough. The inmates were just sitting there in their cells, eyes closed. But then the air started to vibrate, and shortly after that every surface did the same. Each material vibrated at a different rate and pitch, the faster the rate the higher the pitch, and the glass was the highest of all. Robert's teeth were immediately set on edge and he clamped his hands over his ears. The other young guard cowered from the sound. Like a thunder-cloud gathering momentum it grew, brewing its energy from deep within, until both men wanted to hide from the storm.

They scurried onwards, instinctively ducking from the fury. Robert could see the big spotty cat thing up ahead, reaching her front leg through her cell bars towards the boy. The two guards speeded up. In passing, Robert bashed at the cat's leg before coming to a stop outside Seb's cell. He peered in.

"Hurry up and get this door open will ya, you stupid sod!" he hissed to the other guard. "This is freaking me out. What the hell's going on? D'you think he's doin' it?" He pointed at Seb. "Look at him! Look at his eyes, man! Let's just get him out and downstairs quick!"

"I'm trying. Can't find the bloody key, can I? You just get the cuffs ready and shut up, will ya!"

Robert smashed his truncheon through the bars onto Seb's head. It was a satisfying moment. Seb fell forward, stunned.

"What have you done?" gasped the younger guard, "Didn't the boss want him in one piece?"

"He'll be all right. I didn't hit him that hard. But we'll have to drag him out. He won't be walking on his own for a few minutes."

After a few more seconds of fumbling the two men got the cell door open and grabbed Seb under the arms. Panting, they pulled him face down along the metal walkway towards the gurney, his legs trailing behind and the toes of his shoes sometimes snagging on the uneven surface, making their task more difficult.

Suddenly, around the building, the glass, stressed beyond belief, shattered. Metal screamed and twisted on itself. Cell doors buckled and floors reared up like angry waves.

There was a sudden roar behind them. Robert turned, and his blood ran cold.

CHAPTER 57

Flo's backside, thighs and knees all screamed for a rest. Her spine objected to each thump of Torigon's hoof-fall. The exhilaration of riding had long worn off. Her arms were tired, and her hands hurt from holding the reins so tightly. Torigon pressed on determinedly, jumping easily over logs and large stones. Flo stayed loose in the saddle to allow for these sudden jumps and changes of direction. She glanced quickly over to the others. They were struggling to keep up. She called a halt.

As soon as they'd stopped, Torigon wandered off in search of something to eat, and Flo did some stretching exercises while Lonce and Atticus lay panting in the heather. A few minutes later, they were on their way again. Flo lost track of time. It seemed they passed hours in the same pattern: run then rest…run, rest. Some rest stops were longer than others as exhaustion took its toll on all of them. Flo was cold, tired, hungry and worried about Seb. Her head had begun to hurt. Torigon and Atticus seemed to be coping, but Lonce was really only at his best at dawn or dusk, and Flo was beginning to worry about him too. He was not built for sustained running and his age was telling against him.

This is it, said Atticus. *That must be the building you are looking for. The Fearful Place.*

Flo shivered. "I see it!" From this height she had a clear view of the Panopticon and could see how it nestled and blended into the landscape to become, from certain angles, almost invisible. Lonce and Atticus stood in silence, lost in their own thoughts. The four friends pondered the immensity of the task at hand. The solidity of the ring-shaped building dampened any previous bravado.

“We need to try another mind-meld, Lonce. Between the four of us surely we can make it work? We’re so close.” But adrenalin made her jumpy and her head felt worse. It took her a while to calm down, and when the connection was finally made it felt different. There was no bringing light and minds together, softly and gently. This wasn’t a subtle connection. It was immediate and brutal, and they found themselves instantly looking out through Seb’s eyes.

He was in a room with a curved wall opposite a barred door. Through the bars they could see a long metal walkway. It ran in either direction past his cell and around a central void. At the centre of this void loomed a tall, sheer tower. Seb looked down, and as he did so they saw his right arm stretch out through the bars. As they watched, another hand appeared from the neighbouring cell. Large, black, hairy fingers completely enveloped Seb’s.

The pain in Flo’s head was even worse now. Again and again she was aware of her concentration slipping as she felt the sweat trickle and drip. But she refused to break away. They were picking up more than visual images; they were completely inside Seb’s head and knew what he knew. They understood this hand belonged to Moe and they knew who Moe was.

The friends saw Seb gently pull his hand away from Moe's. They felt him reassuring Moe that it was 'all coming together', that he had to just keep concentrating. They felt Moe's struggle. Still looking through Seb's eyes, they felt him turn. Flo's concentration slipped again; she was panting with the pain now. Her heart raced. She saw Seb stretch out his arm and grasp the hand of the mammal next door. Except it wasn't a hand. It was a large, furry, grey paw; exactly like Lonce's.

Lonce's concentration wavered. Again, as they saw Seb making contact, information hit them like an energy wave. As it crashed over them, Flo's pain increased. This was another snow leopard. A female called Uncia.

As Flo watched the scene through Seb's eyes, she suddenly saw two pairs of trousered legs at the barred door. Seb looked upwards and Flo gasped in horror as she caught a glimpse of something flashing through the bars. Seb's head exploded with pain, while simultaneously she and Lonce were brutally shocked apart. The connection with their friends was severed completely. Lonce immediately stood, turned, and was gone. Flo cried out with shock and hurt. But Lonce would not stop.

"We've got to go. Now!" she shouted to Atticus as she climbed back onto Torigon. The mare reared. They glimpsed Lonce bounding down the hill and it looked as if he had shed years. He was more determined and energised than she'd ever seen him in her life. She knew in an instant that their relationship had changed. She wasn't the only female in his life any more. For the first time ever, the difference between their two species seemed to matter, and she knew his loyalties no longer lay primarily with her.

But action was needed now. There was no more time for reflection. They had to follow Lonce and get to Seb. Without warning, another mind blast hit her, and she slumped over Torigon's neck. Unable to stop herself, she slipped further down, until gravity took over and pulled her to the ground. The thick heather broke her fall. She lay still, giving herself over to the strange assault of information and images while Atticus and Torigon nuzzled and licked her in distress. There should be no way of acquiring such a rush of information without being connected to Lonce. But something was different; perhaps the energy from Seb and the other prisoners had changed her. She didn't know, but as clearly as she could see the moors and the hills around her she had a vision of the inside of the Panopticon. She saw the guards, the technicians and the geneticists at work.

She had to pull herself together. She rolled over onto her knees and slowly, gingerly, eased herself into a standing position. The pain was still there, but already she was getting used to it, accepting it. Atticus stood by, ready to help. Finally, with some effort, she managed to remount Torigon and urge her on, and together they flew down the hillside. Atticus ran beside them, taking short cuts by jumping off high rocks. Potential suicide. It was all Flo could do to keep her eyes open. She felt a scream of pure exhilaration build in her throat ready to burst out. Ahead she could see several large birds of prey circling above the building. Were they there to help, ready to attack? Had Zero contacted them?

She had no idea. To her right, in the middle distance, she could see Zero's motley group of allies pouring over the crest of the hill and sweeping down towards the menacing building. An aerial attack combined with the ground assault would work. The talons of an eagle were effective weapons.

Now she was on a level with it, the Panopticon looked larger and more intimidating, and she could hear the sounds of a battle. Men were screaming, as their former prisoners scratched, bit and tore at them. The scientists and guards were overwhelmed. Most were simply trying to stay alive. Any thought of containing the prisoners was long gone.

Flo could see Lonce ahead, about to enter the building. Beyond it she glimpsed the sea and a concrete ramp leading down to a jetty below. Her senses exploded, but there was no more pain. Everything was amazingly clear. She urged Torigon into a flat-out gallop, and together they hurtled towards the gate.

CHAPTER 58

Seb's head was on fire. He flickered in and out of consciousness, aware that he was being dragged along by two men. He also knew he'd successfully linked his mind to all those within the building who could receive such a call. The telepathically disadvantaged guards and scientists had no inkling of what was going on with their prisoners. But Seb knew help was coming. As his mind cleared, he continued to feign unconsciousness. No point making life easy for the bastards. Beside, he wasn't quite ready to fight.

With Uncia's help contact had been made, and he knew that Flo and Lonce were gathering their forces outside the building. He'd felt them. Perhaps 'forces' was a bit optimistic, but he knew they hadn't come alone. While his body slumped, his mind was working on another plane altogether. The guards' voices seemed to come from a long way off as his focus remained on the other inmates, sending the visual image of what he hoped to achieve. It had to be done together, or it would never work.

And it did. As one, fifty minds came together and simultaneously every barred door was flung open by an energy blast so intense that it sounded like a bomb. Seb abruptly stood up. Taken by surprise and overcome with terror, the two guards lost their grip and scrambled to grab him again. An eerie, high-pitched whine reverberated through the building as metal bars twisted and all the windows in the building exploded outwards. A second later every able-bodied inmate leapt up and out of their cells, some eager to taste freedom, others to taste blood. They leapt, bounded, crawled, shuffled, and sprang onto the metal walkways.

Moe emerged from his cell, lucid for once. With a blood-curdling roar, he leapt forward, teeth bared, and wrenched the guards away from Seb, tossing them over the metal balustrade. Seb heard their screams come to an abrupt end as they hit the ground below. Having released him, Moe fled, while Seb pulled himself upright and took stock of the situation.

All of a sudden he felt another mind close by. It wasn't Moe or Uncia, it was human and female, and he found his connection with all the other inmates wavering in a moment of confusion.

I'm sorry, her mind seemed to whisper directly into his. *I'm so sorry. I had no idea. It is unforgivable. He must be mad. He must be stopped. I need to save Toby. I didn't know. I swear it. How could I? I was so young when I married him... They told me Toby was dead... I took his ashes to school. How could I have foreseen this? How could I have let it happen? I didn't know. I didn't see it. You must believe me!*

Seb struggled to stay focused. He'd never experienced direct contact with another human mind in this way. Not even with Flo. But he couldn't afford the distraction. He was gambling everything on the next few minutes. His connection with the other inmates must be strong and the unknown woman's mind was intrusive.

The protective two-way mirror in the central tower had been blown out and Seb could see

Atkinson and another guard watching the mayhem with horror. It seemed to take them a couple of seconds to fully realise what was happening. As they leaned out of the observation platform to survey the scene, Seb could see the fat one struggling to draw his gun. Atkinson, meanwhile, was talking into a walkie-talkie, screaming for reinforcements.

Seb grabbed the woman's hand and pulled her towards the stairwell. Mammals were clambering quickly down the stairs and walkways. Most were just intent on getting out, regaining their lost freedom, but some were launching themselves at the bodies of the helpless guards below. The chimps and macaques were particularly vicious and they joined with the dogs in the most aggressive attacks. Their powerful jaws and long, sharp teeth ripped easily through flesh, while smaller animals bit and scratched any available extremities. Seb could see the shocked scientists spilling out of the shattered laboratory trying in vain to avoid the fury of the rampaging escapees.

Seb was battling with the woman, worrying that the delay would cause him to miss Flo. He tried to force her down to the ground floor, but she had her own priorities and struggled against him, still claiming she had to save someone called Toby.

"I can get to him now," she said, tugging her hand from his grip and running off. As he watched her go, Seb heard gunshots above the sounds of screams and howls. A body fell from the floor above, just missing the strange woman. Seb noticed that she barely paused, but ran on, over the debris of twisted metal and broken glass. She was clearly confused. He watched her for a moment as she struggled round the entire floor, peering into each room, before disappearing down a second set of stairs on the other side of the building.

CHAPTER 59

New-Era London, Guardia Station, Interrogation Room 5
Witness Statement 1.6 of Melissa Gryfe née Harcourt
Species: Human
Sex: Female
Affair: Rosendale
Signed in the presence of K9 Officer Dante. Monday 8 August, 2332

This is it, Melissa. Today will be the last time we put you through this ordeal. Let's get this over with. What happened next?

"I met a strange boy on the walkway. A human. But he scared me and I ran. I looked for Toby but of course all the cells were empty by then, so I found another stairwell and headed down to the ground floor. I had to weave and duck as the battle raged around me. Occasionally I found myself pushed over by a hysterical technician or a liberated mammal. More guards emerged from their dormitory and joined in, wielding batons and whips. I got to the heavy laboratory swing doors. The glass panels had been blown out and the rubber seals were shredded. Dust, or perhaps smoke, was pouring out through the holes.

"On the far side of the lab I could make out Ulrich's office, and before heading towards it I picked up a piece of glass from the floor. I was still aware of the screams and crashes around me, and out of the corner of my eye I saw a technician knocked to the ground by something. I felt curiously detached as smaller mammals, maybe cats or ferrets, swarmed over him, biting and scratching. Prisoners were helping each other to escape. I ignored them all and ran on towards the office. Grey and Blue had been shooting from the doorway and there were dead and dying animals in a semicircle in front of them.

"I saw Ulrich as I ran into the room. He was cowering in a corner by the window. It was open. Then in one surprisingly fluid movement he stood up and slid out. I saw him running, zigzagging across the grass outside."

What was your husband doing at this time? Was he helping Grey and Blue?

"Marcus was coming towards me. There was accusation in his eyes, as if he thought I'd caused the riot. I couldn't bear to look at him any more. I hated him. In those moments I realised I'd always hated him. For all those years of being treated like an imbecile - a nothing - I would make him pay. For his conspiracy with my parents I would make him pay. For what he was doing here I would certainly make him pay. I stabbed him in the chest. He fell backwards, but I fell with him. I stabbed and stabbed. I cut my palms. Over and over. I pushed the glass shard deep into him. Deeper and deeper. Until my hands were too slippery to hold my weapon.

" 'Who the hell is Toby?' he asked, and then he died. One minute he was there, the next he wasn't. I was frustrated. I'd wanted him to know why I was killing him."

And?

"Toby was my friend."

CHAPTER 60

Lonce was energised. He had believed himself alone for his entire life. But now he had caught a glimpse of another like him. A female. He could not wait for Flo. The mission to save Seb and destroy the HSL was no longer important. The only thing that mattered was to reach the female, Uncia.

Birds circle above. Swoop and dive at men emerging. In the building I hear screams, smell blood. I call her. Answer comes to my head. I run up two flights of stairs, following her scent. Follow me, I call. We jump together, through the window.

Man on grass outside, running like frightened prey. Ulrich! I hear Uncia cry. We hunt him now. He runs, runs to waterside. Little boat pounces on small waves. Uncia's claws pierce flesh. Uncia will kill him. Man is prey now. His death brings her pleasure. I feel that joy. I want my share too. We tear flesh, rip chunks, we bite bones.

The rest of the place was in chaos. Lonce and Uncia were not the only creatures desperate for blood. The animals from Helmsley were streaming into the building from outside, joining their comrades in the bid for freedom and justice. The humans were terrified. A young guard wildly brandishing a pistol lost his nerve and ran screaming to the nearest window, crashing through it to meet his death a moment later, his throat torn out by vicious teeth.

CHAPTER 61

Downstairs in Feldman's office, Grey and Blue were out of bullets now and using whatever came to hand to defend their position. Grey had swapped a shard of glass for a metal stool and was brandishing it like a shield, occasionally wielding it as a club when necessary. Blue was fighting his own battle just yards away. With his free hand, Grey grabbed a flask of liquid, hoping it would make an effective weapon. The lab technicians and geneticists were losing the war and some seemed to have fled the building already.

"Who knew there were so many bloody animals on this damn island?" Grey muttered. "Go!" he shouted to Blue. "Get to the jetty, start the boat, wait for me there. But if you leave me here, I swear, I will track you down! Go on. Go now!" Blue didn't wait to be told again; he could see they were fighting a losing battle. He ran.

Grey surveyed the room and the bloody mess that had once been his employer. Gryfe's wife, Melissa, still straddled him, her eyes blank, lips curled slightly upwards in a vacant smile. Grey turned to leave. There was nothing for him to do here. The woman was completely deranged. Just then he caught sight of Seb. The boy's eyes were steely with anger as he approached.

"I've known about you all along, boy," Grey couldn't resist taunting him. "Did you really think you could keep notes and send them to your little friend? Did you think we were amateurs?" But he could see there was an unnerving grimness about Seb now, as the boy took a step towards him.

Suddenly, in a move which completely surprised them both, Melissa jumped off the body of her husband, staggered to the window and clambered out. She ran off to the left, heading towards a group of small dogs who were rounding on a technician. Grey used the moment of Seb's distraction to turn and run.

He wove through the smoke-filled corridors towards the main entrance, dodging the hazards of upturned tables, chairs and struggling clusters of inmates and Panopticon employees. He was still clutching the glass flask he'd picked up earlier, but as he ran his eyes searched desperately for a better weapon. Anything would do.

Seb was following him, unused to the layout of the building. Grey turned and saw Seb emerge from a corridor fifty feet away. Grey hung a left and ran down a darkened passage. He knew the huge old entrance doors were down this way somewhere. If only he could get to them before the boy caught him. He'd never appreciated how big the place was. Glancing over his shoulder again, he saw Seb pick up the pace. Suddenly, just before emerging into the light, Grey paused, surprised. There, hurtling towards the building like some manic Valkyrie, was a girl on horseback, accompanied by an enormous dog.

CHAPTER 62

Flo willed Torigon to run faster. She wasn't particularly worried about Lonce; he was formidable in his quest and his rage. They'd almost reached the gate when a man dressed in military uniform emerged from the main doorway. There was something about him that set her teeth on edge. Torigon and Atticus must have felt it too. Torigon sprang forward and virtually flew across the flat. Atticus paced her for the first few yards, then at the last second he simply leapt ahead, and sank his teeth into the man's leg. He gripped hard and shook his head and the man screamed. Torigon got as close to the struggling man as possible, and Flo kicked out and caught him on his left temple with the heel of her right boot. He staggered for a moment and Flo launched herself onto him. She clung on to his neck, swinging her legs round his waist, and with one hand she grabbed a fistful of hair and wrenched his head back. But even with Atticus clamped securely to his calf, he was still able to throw her off. She hit the ground hard, winded badly. The man hit Atticus across the muzzle and the dog fell backwards with a yelp. Even though he was bleeding profusely the man still managed to kick him again and again. Atticus backed off for a second then launched himself at the enemy once more, this time sinking his teeth deep into the flesh of his upper thigh.

Flo hauled herself up, still dizzy and slightly winded, grabbed a rock and swung it with all her might at the back of the man's head. She heard a sickening crunch as it connected with the target, and he staggered. Atticus let go and the man lurched back towards the building, cursing. But for some reason he hesitated. Something or someone inside must have startled him, and she watched as for a split second he appeared uncertain which way to go. The blow to his head had taken its toll and he appeared disorientated. In any case, he was lost. Smoke billowed out from the broken windows. The man turned briefly towards her before taking a few hesitant steps to the left. Flo could see Seb emerging now, a giant ape at his side.

The man glanced down at his uniform. He seemed to come to some sort of decision and pulled himself up tall. His face took on the fanatical, crazed look of a martyr, and his eyes met Flo's as if daring her to attack. He took a deep breath, then raised a liquid-filled flask above his head. What was he doing? He flicked off the cork stopper and stared directly into her eyes.

Flo was stunned by the intensity of the hatred in his gaze.

"I know who you are. I knew your mother too. She was another interfering cow." He spat the words. "But the HSL is stronger than you both. We will not be defeated so easily. We will take our planet back. We will make it great again." He hesitated for a second or two, then poured the contents of the flask over his shoulders and chest. The fabric of his uniform darkened quickly as it absorbed the fluid. "With this sacrifice, I will be known as a martyr to the League." In a dramatic gesture he threw the beaker to the floor. It smashed at his feet. He pulled out a box of matches, struck one, and dropped it into the spilled liquid. It instantly ignited, sending tendrils of flame up his body. His clothes, saturated with chemicals, burned intensely. His head protruded from a collar of fire. As his flesh puckered and burned, his eyes met hers again. His lips seemed to be stretched back into a smile just for her. Then he started screaming.

Moments later there was another explosion, and more acrid black smoke billowed out from the breached walls. Flo flew backwards, blown by the blast, Atticus landing heavily at her side. Something wet trickled down her neck.

She lay there stunned in the sudden silent darkness of unconsciousness.

CHAPTER 63

By the time George's team arrived on Rosendale they found the survivors gazing fearfully at the inferno that had been the Panopticon.

"Leave the dead where they lie," the Coalition forces' captain shouted to the local firefighters. "I'm establishing a command post over between the jetty and the building. That is the point of contact and liaison for all teams."

"Sir," shouted a medico, "we're setting up a temporary triage station at the jetty, to do what we can. The hospital ship will be arriving shortly; then we can start evacuating the wounded."

The captain turned to George and said quietly, "We have to tread carefully. Clearly some of the people from the local emergency services will know people who worked here. There could be conflicts of interest." He raised his voice to issue orders to another group of firefighters. "Look for possible points where the structure might collapse and move any nearby survivors further away."

Flo, Atticus and Torigon were quickly found and taken to the triage station with the rest of the injured. Seb and Lonce were still missing and George couldn't see them anywhere. To avoid further violence, the injured had been separated into two groups, inmates away from their former captors. By now exhaustion had taken its toll and the urge to fight had passed. Once satisfied Flo was in good hands, George set off to find his other missing friends. He painstakingly searched the tents of the wounded until he found Seb, suffering from smoke inhalation and burns, mistakenly billeted with the injured technicians. But of Lonce there was no trace.

Flo didn't know how much time had passed before her vision and hearing returned after the explosion. She had felt herself being gently lifted and carried some distance away from the searing heat of the burning building, and was grateful to whoever had decided to move her out of the pungent smoke, but she was frustrated by her helplessness. After the planning, the attacks and the tension, not to mention the journey across Rosendale and the battle at the end of it, she suddenly felt exhausted and deflated. The image of Grey burning to death was seared into her mind. It was something she could have done without. Her parents were dead. Nothing she'd done would bring them back. Nothing. Would they even know she'd tried to find their killers? The deep, silent ache of loss would never leave her. She knew that. She'd learned to live with it over the years. But this new pain was different, more acute. She wanted them to know what she'd done. How she had taken up her mother's fight and brought it to a conclusion. She wanted their praise, their arms around her in celebration. She wanted them. She didn't feel like the heroine of an adventure and couldn't understand why she was being hailed as one.

"Seb? Lonce? Atticus? Anyone?" she called out, barely audible, suddenly feeling vulnerable in her isolated state. Fortunately, George was able to see that Seb was moved into the same tent. He was still unable to talk and the fumes he'd inhaled had disorientated him.

A medico arrived, rigged him up to oxygen then left quickly, promising to be back soon to check on him. Seb lay there, the hoarseness in his breathing gradually calming. Flo leaned over from her bed and squeezed his hand. *There'll be time later to talk. I'm just so glad you're alive.* She thanked Gaia, and George. Seb wheezed quietly.

Lonce suddenly appeared and licked her face with his enormous raspy tongue. Then, before she could cling on to him, he turned his back to her and went to the flap of the tent. She was left with her arms outstretched, puzzled and hurt. A moment later he returned with his new friend.

This is Uncia. She is my mate. Flo's feelings were mixed and she struggled to hide her emotions. She was delighted to meet Uncia, but also incredibly jealous. The realisation that she was possibly losing Lonce caused her to reach out for Seb's hand and hold on to it tightly.

Don't worry. I do not replace you, Uncia told her. *I understand you are special. You are his cub. Your spirits are joined. I know that. You will not lose him, but he will be with me now.*

"Uncia, Lonce." She struggled to find the words. Images of the life she'd shared with Lonce cascaded from her mind into Uncia's. "Do you see our past? Do you see what he means to me? Lonce is more than just my friend. He is my family."

You were his past and I am his future, replied Uncia firmly. Lonce stood between them now, his heart full to bursting. He struggled to formulate the images which would help Flo accept the inevitable.

Then, just as Flo had shown Uncia his past, he showed Flo his future; a future free in the high hills with a mate and cubs. She understood. But still it was with a fragile heart, stretched gossamer thin, that she finally gave them her blessing.

Several hours later George prepared to accompany Flo, Seb and the others on the hospital boat back to Leeds Port. Torigon was going to stay on the island, so they said their goodbyes in Helmsley.

"Are you sure you'll be all right?" Flo asked her. "We may have destroyed the Panopticon but the HSL still have many supporters on Rosendale."

"Don't worry," George interrupted. "Many local people are shocked by the activities here. They saw no further than the holiday camp story." Torigon nodded in agreement.

"But the farmers trading in meat? What's happened to them?"

"Some were caught as they tried to flee the island. Others gave themselves up, hoping for leniency."

It will be better now, thanks to you, the mare said. Flo's mind filled with feelings of gratitude as the other local animals joined with Torigon in thanking her. *You helped us to stand up for our rights. For the rights of all the animals and birds here. Your human companion too. We thank you both.* Flo was overwhelmed. It was too much. She had done so little. Seb was the hero. Seb was her hero. She squeezed his hand, but he was asleep again.

CHAPTER 64

The Panopticon burned continuously for many days, the fumes polluting the air with a vile black cloud which could be seen for miles. The heat was so intense, and the ancient structure so unsafe, that the firefighters couldn't enter. They concentrated their efforts simply on protecting the surrounding countryside. In time, the fire ran its course and the investigating teams went in. The process of collecting evidence would last weeks. Everything possible was gathered, bagged and tagged. It was difficult, dirty and often disturbing work. The men removing human and animal remains found it particularly hard. Often, individuals had been so closely joined in combat when the smoke overwhelmed them that their skeletons had fused. Bones had melted, seeming to form a new species - part man, part beast.

Flo and Seb, along with the other injured, were shipped out to the mainland, to hospitals in Leeds Port. The handful of Panopticon laboratory workers and prison staff who had survived the battle and subsequent fire, were arrested and taken under guard to New-Era London.

At the Leeds Port Clinic life moved on apace, and before Flo knew it it was time to say goodbye to Lonce and Uncia. She sat in silence beside the two enormous cats. Her right hand rested on Lonce's head as he lay next to her. Uncia sat upright next to Lonce, her thick tail firmly entwined with his.

"I'll miss you, Lonce. Are you sure you don't want to come back to N'Era-London?" she asked one last time. “There’s enough room for Uncia too, you know.” She felt his turmoil and he felt hers. He was torn between the two females he loved, and she knew she had to let him go.

Uncia not trust humans. Never. We need go far from humans. Even you. She wants freedom now. Freedom for our children. We both want hills and forests, not city. No people. The vision of them bounding across wild terrain filled her mind and she knew then he would never return to her. He would always have a place for her in his heart, but Uncia was his future. His old life was over. It was time to say farewell.

Flo stood up. George and Seb were waiting discreetly a few feet away, trying hard not to intrude.

“Come here,” she said. “You both need to say goodbye too.” They approached reluctantly, neither of them looking forward to the parting and both concerned for Flo. Seb dropped down immediately and flung his arms around Lonce’s neck. Flo could tell he was sobbing and gave him a minute. George stood to one side looking miserable. This parting was hard for them all.

“It’s all right,” Flo said. “This feels right. We will still be in contact. Lonce and Uncia are going to Alba, to start a new life there.”

“At the risk of sounding heartless,” said George suddenly, “this is getting too maudlin. We have a train to catch and Atticus has agreed to meet us at the station. He’s coming home with us.”

Flo turned slipped her hand into Seb’s. “I’m ready. Let’s go home.”

Three weeks later, the forensic teams gone, the site was razed. Now the funds from the HSL had dried up, a few canny villagers risked becoming pariahs and sold their stories to the press. For several months, news headlines across the archipelago screamed phrases like Rosendale – Island of Shame! or Blood Money, What Price a Job?

As the investigation into the events on Rosendale went on more and more people were implicated. Back in the city, Flo, Seb and Atticus attended the Guardia offices for questioning. Flo's evidence - the little canister of chloroform from inside a crate - was welcomed by the K9 unit. Together with her statement, it added to the evidence that animals were being transported illegally. It was now up to the lawyers to prove who was behind it all.

"What is going to happen to Gryfe's wife?" George asked Dante one day. "Isn't she under arrest? I saw her being taken away after the fire."

Melissa Gryfe is currently receiving psy-treatment. Meanwhile, she is helping us with our enquiries. There are no plans to arrest her, said Dante.

"But didn't she kill her husband?" Flo asked. "I heard she'd confessed."

Dante looked at each of them carefully before answering slowly, *I am not aware she killed her husband. There are no witnesses who can testify and there are no identifiable remains. There is only her "confession", which has been called into question since she started her psy-assessment.* He stood to go, but Seb stopped him.

"How on earth did they find out about me?" he asked. "I took such care. There is no way they could have pegged me for an outsider."

Well, said Dante. *You'd be amazed by how many people are willing to turn informant. It turns out there was another party involved. She was arrested here in the city and is also helping us with our inquiries. She controlled a network of HSL spies, mostly her own relatives, and regularly provided information about boys attending the camps.*

"But that can't be," said Flo. "No one knew what we were planning to do. I mean, we didn't even know ourselves until right at the last minute." She looked at George apologetically.

Dante continued. *After our meeting with George here, I was authorised to follow up a few leads. Various unionists and members of the public were implicated. It turns out there was a well run network of HSL supporters here in the capital and across the islands. You'd be surprised who was involved. I know I was.*

"I think, after everything we've been through here, we have a right to know who it was who informed on Seb. If this mystery woman has already been arrested it can't possibly hurt to tell us who she is, surely?"

Sighing, Dante pretended to consult his notes.

"But who? Who would do that?" said Flo, frustrated because the officer was taking his own sweet time over revealing the name. "Oh!" The others looked at her, surprised. "I bet I know who it was."

CHAPTER 65

New Era-London Coalition Courthouse. 10 October

Flo held Seb's hand as she watched the jury file into the courtroom. She was eager for an end to this chapter of her life. The trial would give her closure. Although she still bore a few of the physical scars from recent events, her mental ones ran deeper, and hurt more. They were a lifetime deep.

The jury was frustratingly slow at taking their places. Flo noticed many of them appeared nervous. Perhaps the gravity of the case and the weight of their responsibility sat heavily on their shoulders. The human jurors took their places first, but the others took a little longer to settle. She turned, aware of the general hubbub in the gallery behind her. There was standing room only now, but still more citizens were pushing their way in through the doors. She could feel the anticipation and excitement in the air. She felt something else too, and tried to identify it. She looked around. The spectators sat in family or species groups. She opened her mind. Mistrust. That's what she sensed now.

This case had shocked and horrified the world. It had shown a rotten underside to their society. Would things ever be the same again? Would she ever be the same again?

She squeezed Seb's hand and he glanced at her. He'd been watching the proceedings intently.

"Look," he whispered, "over there is where the panel of magistrates will sit. I wonder what's keeping them. The whole thing should have kicked off ten minutes ago."

"Maybe they're waiting for everyone to settle."

"That must be the defence lawyer." He pointed. "I wouldn't want to be in his shoes. Imagine having to defend the HSL."

She looked more closely at the back of the lawyer's head, trying hard to picture what sort of man would take on such a job. He appeared to be entirely focused on the papers before him on the desk, and barely acknowledged the women seated beside him. He was certainly making no attempt to reassure them; if anything, it looked as if he were hoping the ground would open beneath him. Suddenly one of the women turned and Flo caught a glimpse of her profile.

"Oh, goodness. Look, Seb! It's Miss Pugh! I knew it! I mean, I guessed she was the spy. But who's that sitting with her?"

Just then the other woman turned and Flo gasped. She was the exact mirror image of the first. "Look, look, Seb!"

"Good grief, there are two of them! Which is our Miss Pugh?"

"No idea. But shh now, I think we've got some action."

A sharp knock silenced the crowds. As if at some unseen signal, everyone in the courtroom stood respectfully, heads bowed. The judge, flanked by two other magistrates, one pig and one primate, swept into the courtroom and took her place.

After the preliminaries, one of the women was summoned to make her statement to the court. She stood up and gave her name, her lawyer nodded, encouraging her to start. Her twin sat stony-faced, staring straight ahead.

"I had been engaged to Harold Grey for a long time," the woman's statement began. "Although we never formally married, we had two sons. I did hear rumours he was seeing someone else," she glared at the crowded courtroom and smiled confidently, "but that's all they were: vicious rumours. I know you heard he jilted me on the eve of our wedding, but that isn't true. It didn't happen like that.

"We worked together for our independence from the faceless, controlling bureaucrats of the Coalition. We humans have no say in our destiny any more. The Coalition controls everything. That is why it has to be stopped. We were fighting for the little man. Humans were great once, rulers of the planet, and we could be again, if only we could step out from the oppressive yoke of the Coalition 'animals are equal' brigade.

"Harold left me for my own good, to protect me and the boys." She stood tall and defiant. "He explained to me that as a freedom fighter there is always a risk of being captured. That's why he had to leave. He wanted to protect us," she repeated. "So that we would not compromise the league under torture and reveal what we knew." There was a murmur of surprise amongst the onlookers, but it died as she started talking again. "He promised one day we'd be together. But in the meantime, I could help the cause from here." She stopped again and cleared her throat. A clerk placed a glass of cold water in front of her, and she drank it like an automaton before resuming her statement. "He was based on Rosendale, but there were means of staying in touch. There are always means. The arms of the HSL are very long, you know." She stopped speaking and seemed to drift off.

"So how did you help him and the 'cause', as you call it?" the lawyer for the prosecution asked.

"My job was to keep an eye on the boys who were going up to the camp, just in case one of them turned out to be a government spy. I kept tabs on the families of all the candidates. I kept an eye out for any infiltrators and reported them to Harold."

"How did you know specifically this boy Seb would be attending the camp?" the judge asked.

"Good grief! Do you think I'm stupid? I've always paid attention to the goings on at the school. Besides, I recognised Seb at the station even with that ridiculous hair cut, trying to disguise himself and fit in with the camp crowd, and if I needed proof, Flo was on the walkway above the platform. I saw everything, and I told my boy Ellis to buddy up to him."

"Did you push Flo Harris down the stairs at the station?"

George was startled. This was the first he'd heard of the incident. He leaned forward to hear better. Flo avoided his eyes.

"Of course I did," she answered. "That interfering, smug, spoilt, animal-loving brat!" There was a gasp of horror from the entire court. She turned to Flo and pointed her finger aggressively at her. "I know all about you. You think you're so special. Poor little orphan girl. Harold killed your parents because they were getting too close. They would have destroyed years of precious work had they lived. Seb's parents were spared because they were frightened off. You, we should have stopped when we had the chance!"

There was chaos in the courtroom. Her sister hung her head, shamed and horrified by the confession.

Flo leapt to her feet, her hand clenched in tight fists, shaking with rage and shock. Seb leapt up too, a moment later, and grabbed Flo's arm to hold her back. George, Jack and Laura looked horrified and sat in stunned silence.

The lawyer for the prosecution continued. "You indicated earlier that members of the Porters' Guild were involved in loading the cages onto the northbound trains, is that correct?"

"Of course it is. There's no end to the number of real workers willing to help us. The horse porters carry heavier loads and charge less, they undercut the men every day with their unfair advantage. How long did you think humans would put up with that? It isn't real equality. The guilds don't protect their own. I can assure you, there are plenty of people ready to help our cause."

An uneasy silence filled the courtroom. Finally the judge said, "Miss Dorothea Pugh, you are charged with assault and attempted murder. You are charged with conspiracy and crimes against the state. But before I send the jury off to deliberate their verdict, there is something I believe you should know." Her voice took on a steely quality. "The Guardia do not torture. Torture is never sanctioned and has not been sanctioned since the end of the Siklus. That is another part of the old world order we do not wish to revive. It has no place in a civilised society." She paused to assess the effect her words were having.

"Secondly, I think you should know that Harold Grey was married in Helmsley more than ten years ago. He had two daughters." She turned to the jury. "Court adjourned for the day."

Dorothea Pugh was steered from the court, an officer on each side. There was no need for restraints. She was a broken woman.

Madeleine Pugh, her sister and teacher extraordinaire, continued to sit in silence, too shocked by the revelations to move, for once in her life at a loss for words.

EPILOGUE

Several months later, New Era-London, May

"I'm sending you to Grand Columbus. You've been working with me for a while now, Flo, and it's obvious you crave excitement, so here you are." George gently tossed an envelope across the table to her. "Your ticket. A belated graduation present and your first solo assignment."

"George, are you crazy? I'm not ready to go all that way on my own. It's on the other side of the world. What would I do there, anyway? I'm not an expert archivist, so what could I do that you couldn't do better?"

"Well, I think you are ready. You've changed since that whole thing with Rosendale. Matured. You seem somehow calmer now, less angry. You have a quick and observant mind and that's what's needed for this job. I've come to realise my archives here are very amateurish and badly organised. I've been kept on in this role, I suspect, because of my friends in high places."

Flo reached across the table and gave his arm a gentle squeeze. "You're right. I do feel lighter, as if the anger has been lifted off me. You know, I never noticed what a weight I was carrying around. I feel different now."

"I suspect it's because you've actually started living. Interacting with the world and doing something positive to make a difference." Before she could contradict him, he carried on. "Do you remember those New Americans I entertained over here once, the night you burgled me?" Flo nodded.

"Well, I never got round to telling you at the time, but I got the distinct impression they were humouring me. Not mocking me and the archives exactly, they were too polite for that, it's just I think they were surprised at how primitive everything is here." Once again he stopped her before she could say anything. "So I've come to a decision. Thanks to Jack's articles and publicity campaign, we've raised enough money to renovate a wing of the old British Museum, even though we've still got a long way to go."

"That's brilliant, George. I'm so happy for you. You've been trying to wangle that for years. Well done!" She beamed at him. "But I still don't get it."

"Well, you are going to learn everything you can about the archives in Ansted, Grand Columbus. Preserving old documents is all well and good, but it's all a bit pointless, if you think about it, unless you can learn from them as well. Learn from the past. Just look at this whole HSL debacle. We've seen how it divides families; look at the Pugh sisters, for example."

Flo nodded, and then said, "I had no idea. I thought that because most people like the way things are now, because society is fair for both humans and non-humans, there really was no reason to complain."

"Hmm," said George. "I think we've all learned a lot from the events of last year. The majority of people, like us, in fact, have the ability, indeed the privilege, of communicating with other mammals, and so we are the ones with the most to gain from the status quo staying as it is. But many of the others, the Non-Comms, clearly feel left behind.

They feel excluded, and we need to acknowledge and change that."

"You mean like the elites of olden days. We're all having a great time at this wonderful party. Sharing the world with all the fantastic creatures and they are, um, they are…"

"Outside, looking in through the window," finished George, nodding. "Yes."

"But that's no excuse for the violence, for the hatred, is it?"

"No. There is never a good reason for that amount of hate or premeditated violence." He smiled sadly. "If we are to avoid returning to the dark age of the twenty-first century we really need to look clearly at the past." He paused for a moment before continuing earnestly, "At some point in our pre-Siklus history, it seems that the human population was divided. There were those who, like you and me now, understood that all life is precious. They approached life from the premise that we are all equal. Different, but equal." Flo nodded. "But there were others who didn't. It was that simple. If they considered other forms of life valuable, it was only in monetary, exploitative terms."

"I heard about that. Like the time when a new little frog was discovered. It could put itself into a cryogenic state, apparently. So some people thought, 'Oh, that's so cool, clever frog, let's protect it,' while others tried to work out ways to enable humans do the same thing, and they killed all the frogs in their experiments."

"Hmmm. Yes, I suppose that's as good an example as any. As I was about to say, the purpose of these archives is threefold. The first is to remind us of where we have come from. The second is a warning not to make the same mistakes again. The third is to preserve knowledge, for our own survival in the future."

"But your archive does all that."

"In theory, yes. But at the moment our centre is a bit of a joke and I need your help to improve it; to make it useful and accessible."

"Put like that," she said, smiling broadly at him. "Okay. But I'm not sure I want to do this alone. Seb's studying, Lonce has gone. Atticus is busy - you know he's just discovered that Finch had his pups, so he's got his paws full with them - and you've just said that you can't go."

"I was wondering whether you'd like Torigon to go with you. I know she's still up at Helmsley, but she might be willing. What do you think?"

Flo paused. "I think I couldn't imagine anyone better."

Some months later.

Flo and Seb were both busy over the following weeks. He was adjusting to the routine of the academy and she to the work at the Archive. Her apartment was empty without Lonce. If she was honest, it was unbearable. It was that feeling of loneliness more than anything else which made her accept George's offer, but she still hadn't had the heart to tell Seb. She knew he'd be gutted. But time was running out now and she owed him some warning. One weekend in late summer she invited him for a picnic under the willows on the waterfront.

They'd eaten their fill and now lay half asleep on the grass. The remains of the picnic were spread between them. Even without opening her eyes, she was acutely aware of him sprawled on the grass. She'd miss him. She was only just realising how much. After a lifetime together it was impossible to imagine being apart. She was still only just coming to terms with losing Lonce.

"Seb," she said. Her voice was low, as if being quiet would make the words easier to say. "I have something important to tell you. George wants to send me over to Grand Columbus."

"What?" He sat up, suddenly alert. "Are you going to go?"

"Yes."

"Why? Why would you do that?"

"I can't think why," Flo snapped, sitting up too. "Other than having a life to lead, you know. Oh yes, and I want to. I want to see the Americas."

"But, but, are you going alone?"

"Torigon's going to come. She's arriving next month." Seb looked so devastated she softened her tone. "I'm sorry, Seb. We'll have plenty of time to see each other before I leave. I promise we'll get together lots." He still looked miserable. She tried to lighten the mood. "The only problem is." She paused.

"Yes?"

"We'll be a long time at sea." She didn't get the reaction she'd hoped for. As a mood lightener, it hadn't worked. "You do remember how much I hate sailing, don't you?"

"Hmm. Pukey Flow," he answered finally, but his voice was bitter. "How could I forget?"

"You should be happy for me."

"I just thought we'd do a trip like that together. I mean, us, together. You need looking after. I mean, someone's got to keep you out of trouble."

They were standing now. Close. Staring into each other's eyes. She could see hurt in his, as if she'd betrayed him. Goodness knows what he thought he could see in hers. She hoped determination and strength. But the hurt in his, she couldn't believe she'd caused that.

"You know me better than that, Seb. I'm going. I want to go. But I'll be back. Besides, I doubt you could keep me out of trouble." She smiled at him. "I'm sorry you're not coming. I'll miss you. I love you. But I don't need you to look after me. Your family and George have looked after me ever since I can remember. You've always been there for me, like a brother, a best friend. I've never had a chance to see what I can do on my own. I need to try, at least. It's time I started being independent." She flung her arms around his neck and squeezed him tight, trying to imprint the feeling in her heart for ever. "But that doesn't mean that I'm not going to miss you. It doesn't mean that I'm not scared."

"You love me?"

"Is that all you took from that whole speech?"

"Flo," he said, smiling, as he gently prized her off. "It's all right. I understand. Really I do. I was just shocked. I know you have to go and I'm happy for you. Besides, being scared never stopped you. But don't worry; I'll still be here for you when you get back." And to prove his point he pulled her again towards him and kissed her. As she kissed him back, a whole realm of possibilities opened up before her.

She'd never felt so confused, so broadsided before. She leaned into him, opening up, relaxing into the strength of his body. It really was decision time and suddenly, unexpectedly, she knew what she was going to do.

DISCUSSION QUESTIONS FOR BOOK CLUBS

1. What feelings did the book evoke for you?

- Were you amused, upset, bored, angry, intrigued?
- Did you have to force yourself to get through it or were you unable to put it down?
- Are you glad you read it?

2. How do you feel about how the story was told?

- Did it start too slow or end unresolved?
- Do you wish it had been told from a different perspective?
- Did it jump around too much or hold you in suspense?
- Was it too long or too short? What would you cut or add?

3.What did you think about the main characters & their world?

- Did you like the characters? Were they believable?
- Did you approve of their decisions and behavior?
- Who did you relate to the most/least?
- How well did the author build the world?
- Would you have wanted more description?
- Did it seem believable? Why/why not?

4. Which parts of the book stood out to you?

- Are there any quotes, passages, or scenes you found particularly compelling?
- Were there parts of the book you thought were incredibly unique, out of place, thought-provoking, or disturbing?

5. What themes did you detect in the story?

- What were the main points you think the author was trying to make?
- Did you notice any symbolism?
- Would you describe this story as allegorical?

6. What did you think about the ending?

- Were you satisfied or disappointed with how the story ended?
- Is anything left unresolved or ambiguous?
- How do you picture the characters' lives after the end of the story?

7. What is your impression of the author?

- What do you think about the author's writing style?
- Do you have a sense of the author's personal interests throughout the book? If so, what do you think they are?
- What do you think about the author's storytelling ability?
- Would you read another book by the same author? Why/why not?
- What do you think the author's purpose was in writing this book?

8. What changes/decisions would you hope for if the book were turned into a movie?

- Which sections would you cut?
- Who would you cast to play the main characters?

9. How does this book compare to other books you've read?

- What other books did this remind you of?
- Did you like it more or less than other books in the same genre?
- Is the book different in any way from the books you usually read?
- What do think of the book's cover? How well does it convey what the book is about?

10. How did this book change you?

- Do you have a new perspective as a result of reading this book?
- Did you learn something you didn't know before?
- Has your attitude or behavior changed?
- Did it leave you feeling hopeful or despairing for the future?

Happy Discussions!

ABOUT THE AUTHOR

Rachel Caldecott studied Expressive Arts in Brighton before trying her hand at a variety of jobs. These included working for an independent film production company, a Japanese travel agency and some well known NGOs. She currently lives in Southern France with her husband, their two children and a tribe of rescue cats. When not writing, she helps her husband in his glassblowing business and makes her own handmade jewelry.

Her interests include human and animal rights, the environment and politics. Since 2015 she has been involved in helping refugees and collecting medical donations to send to Syria.

Watching wildlife documentaries and observing her cats inspired her to ask: "What if animals are smarter than we think they are?" And with that one question, this novel was born.

CONNECT TO THE AUTHOR

Thank you for reading *The Panopticon Experiment*. I hope you enjoyed reading it as much as I enjoyed writing it. If so, please take a minute to leave a review. No essay needed, just a few words are fine. Marketing is the hardest part of being an Indie writer. A few kind words would make my day and generate interest in my work, helping me fulfill my dream of becoming a full-time author.

I love hearing from readers, so connect with me at any of the coordinates below:

Also, opt-in to my mailing list and gain exclusive access to a variety of bonus materials.

Email: caldecottrachel60@gmail.com

Wordpress blog is: rachelcaldecottwriter.home.blog

Amazon Author Page: amazon.com/Rachel-Caldecott-Thornton

Made in the USA
San Bernardino,
CA

58571526R00192